The Brandon Book of

Editorial Director of Brandon since its foundation in 1982, Steve MacDonogh is also the founder of Mount Eagle Publications and is a former chairperson of the Irish Writers' Cooperative and former president of Clé, the Irish Book Publishers Association.

THE BRANDON BOOK OF

IRISH SHORT STORIES

Edited by Steve MacDonogh

BRANDON

First published in 1998 by
Brandon
an imprint of Mount Eagle Publications Ltd
Dingle, Co. Kerry, Ireland

ISBN 0 86322 237 4

A CIP catalogue record for this book is available
from the British Library.

Published with the assistance of the
Arts Council/An Chomhairle Ealaíon

Typeset by Koinonia, Manchester
Cover design by the Public Communications Centre, Dublin
Printed by ColourBooks Ltd, Dublin

Contents

Contents

Introduction

IN THIS collection I have sought to represent something of the range and quality of short fiction being written now by Irish writers who have emerged during the last twenty years. I have thus discriminated against longer-established writers, partly because their work is well represented in many other anthologies but principally because I wanted to focus attention on the strength in depth of more recent writing.

Irish writers have over the last hundred years made contributions to world literature out of all proportion to the small size of the country. Whether the new generation of writers is more remarkable than previous generations remains to be seen: mature assessment requires the passage of time. Assertive press releases and the hype surrounding a few advances do not mean that all Irish writers are geniuses. Nevertheless, it is clear that in recent years there has been a certain creative flowering in Ireland which has been reflected in many of the arts and in the entertainment arena.

There is a marked contrast between the gloom of the censorious and penurious 1950s, through which many outstanding writers struggled with demons internal and external, and the self-confident 1970s when young writers emerged who had no time or inclination to contemplate failure. Indeed, we came a long way in just ten years from Frank O'Connor's complaint that in Ireland "The literature of the past is simply ignored; the literature of our own time is either ignored or banned by law." (*The Backward Look*, 1965)

David Marcus oversaw in the '70s a wealth of new short story writing in the *Irish Press* and with Poolbeg Press; the Irish Writers' Co-operative launched new writers; both Irish and British publishers took on and developed writers. Important supporting roles have also been played by magazines, newspapers, radio stations, and the Arts Council. So that now there is a context of achievement and of possibility which is both national and international. Many even of our newest writers have been enthusiastically taken on in translation by European publishers of literary fiction. In the late 90s more young Irish writers than ever seem to be being published more extensively than ever, but what I find most interesting and impressive is not the quantity of writers but the quality and variety of new writing.

Literary editors and journalists find it convenient from time to time to review two or three Irish fiction titles together and to explore the phenomenon of new Irish writing, and this anthology is a similar exercise in packaging, but I discern little of a specific quality of Irishness about new writing from Ireland. Undoubtedly common themes and aspects can be discerned in retrospect from Irish writing of any period. Of one of the writers in this collection it has been said that "Brian Leyden speaks very directly to a culture in transition from pre-modern to post-modern", and something of that phenomenon of transition comes across, I feel, from the collection presented here. The writers are individuals of widely varying backgrounds who respond through different approaches to language to a broad range of different life experiences. They write out of themselves rather than out of any particular sense of Irishness. They write in some instances of a type of city flatland or suburban life which differs little if at all in its essentials between the cities of the more developed countries of Europe. Yet they write also in ways and about circumstances which may strike the reader as unmistakably Irish. They write stories set against the backdrop of multi-cultural California; of rural or small-town Ireland in the present and in the past; of urban working-class and middle-class Ireland; they write of the inner workings of the emotions without the least hint of geographical location.

One specific omission from this collection is of pieces in the Irish language; this is because the book is geared to a broad English-speaking audience; but readers may wish to note that much new Irish-language fiction is being written and published. There are other omissions, many other writers who could have been included, writers I would have liked to have included. But, while it makes no claim to be comprehensive, this collection stands, I think, as an exciting, diverse sample of Irish writing now. How the writers featured do or do not relate to the Irish short story tradition, I leave to others to discern in retrospect. For the moment I am encouraged by their individuality and diversity, qualities I hope readers will relish.

Steve MacDonogh
January 1998

Mary O'Donnell

Twentynine Palms

AFTER HIS big fists smashed the face of a pretty boy outside a gay bar, Bob was sent to the brig. Connie wasn't surprised. Somehow, the remorse that accompanied every hangover didn't ring true. She knew Bob had lied about attending AA meetings. She recognised the effortless innocence, the way he looked her in the eye because he was forcing himself to, because he had trained himself to act honest. Once or twice he made her feel as if she was the one with the problem. In the end, she despised his innocence. No way was she going up the mountains with a lush like him. The fight resolved her dilemma. From what she heard afterwards, the gays weren't having any of it, though by the time the cops arrived it was too late for the guy he'd picked on.

Early in the mornings as she rushed to get to work, thoughts of Bob arose, like shards breaking the surface of something barely calmed. He might, had he wished, have possessed her; not by force, but when they weren't tripping, by sheer contemporary charm, with endless discussions about their 'relationship' and the direction it was heading; in the end though, always getting his own way.

'What the point of a guy like that, eh?' Maria would say, throwing her hands in the air. 'He have nothing, he know nothing. His folks crazy on God. What the point?'

Maria knew all about folks who were crazy on God, about statues and candles, pieces of charred wood, beheaded chickens, their necks drooling sticky blood, crucifixes and ecstatic dances. San Diego verged on being her home. She didn't plan on heading back south.

The God-groupies didn't freak Connie. She'd never known fundamentalism, even in Ireland. Now, she accepted it as a natural part of the exoticism of exile, part of the self-conscious thrill that came each time she experienced otherness, in whatever form.

'You watch him. He get like his Mom and Dad. You wait,' Maria had warned. But Connie picked and mixed her cultures, her religions, her music and her food. Even on her baby-minding money, she loved the place. The heat had made her thin, the dry, relentless breath of desert air had shorn the saddlebags on her hips and the generous heft of her breasts. What remained now was a slight, youthful frame.

There was little time for anything but work. Her habit, confined to weekends, mostly amounted to a few snorts on Sundays. She liked to treat herself, kept some Irish pound notes rolled and ready, just in case.

For three dollars an hour six days a week, every second weekend free, she expended herself on the infant child of a couple who also worked long and irregular hours. Ray was a square-skulled army husband. Shirley, sweet and cutesy, was in charge of human resources at a micro-chip factory. Every Thursday night, she stayed up to bake gingerbread cookies, corn bread and apple pie with cinnamon. On Fridays, Connie sometimes had to do the weekly shopping, but between the coupons and special deals which Shirley and Ray always knew about, it often involved a trip in multiple directions, from Coronado right across to Lemon Grove and on to the Parkway Plaza at El Cajon. Mostly, Shirley organised the shopping trips. With those big Bambi brown eyes, it was hard to imagine her dealing with staff at the factory, never mind sacking anybody.

Once they left the condo, Ray in his brown and silver saloon, Shirley in an older sports model, Connie's day began.

She smoked in the garden and played with the baby, jigging him on her knee to songs from her own childhood, faster and faster until he giggled and clucked with delight. Maria's employers forbade smoking, even in the garden.

'Where a girl supposed to smoke?' Maria would fling her arms in the air. 'Under the sheet in the dark? Huh? In the shower? That suits them of course, these American dope-heads...'

'Maria. Maria,' Connie would say patiently. 'Dopeheads these people are not. Come on, Maria. You've got to improve your English if you want them to take you seriously.'

'I guess,' Maria would sigh.

'So listen to words, Maria. Listen to me.'

'You not perfect. You Irish.'

'But I speak good English and these people – not dopeheads – like the sound of what I say.'

The baby usually woke sometime around mid-morning. Connie would feed and bathe him. She enjoyed his solid, confident weight, the way he would suck her cheeks and chin, ravishing her in his sweet slobber. How bizarre, yet how normal, she thought, to be so clean inside your body that even your saliva was sweet.

Ray and Shirley liked the way she spoke.

'Sure is a million times better than that last Irish girl we had. She was from Cork – right honey?' she called to Ray.

'Kerry, sweetie, Kerry,' Ray intoned from the bedroom.

'No, hon, that was the one before her. Cork, darned sure it was Cork.'

'Ker-ry...' Ray sing-sang in his patient, bossy voice.

Shirley gave a tight smile in Connie's direction. 'Anyway, wherever she was from, we never could tell just what she was sayin'. Her voice went up an' down, all over the place. A real Colleen.' Shirley's smile was affectionate when she looked again at Connie. 'Hell, you're fine.'

Connie started that same day because Shirley thought she should familiarise herself with the baby's health and allergy profile. She listened and nodded continually, wishing Shirley would just shut up. The next morning, she cast her eye along a three-page list of instructions, written in careful, elegant cursive.

Life swung full circle. Things that had once made Connie uncomfortable now guaranteed all-round approval. As a teenager, her northern accent seemed all wrong. There were times and places when the whole family sounded out of place, in restaurants, in certain Dublin shops, even on holidays. Once, when she was thirteen, they spent two weeks in a castle in Wexford where most of the guests were English. The only time she'd felt comfortable was at Ballyhealy beach, when she and her brother Gavin would wait till high tide before diving off a solitary mass of rock.

At dinner every evening, English voices announced an unfamiliar, yet approved of, standard. In comparison, their softer Irish tones seemed obliquely related to the language they shared. On that holiday they became islanders, hobbling after their betters.

One day, as the four of them picnicked at Ballyhealy, two of the guests, a blonde and a dark-haired woman, stopped to chat.

'Splendid day, isn't it?' the blonde one beamed. She was wearing the smallest psychedelic-green bikini Connie had ever seen. Connie wanted to cringe as both her parents, normally competent, able people, pulled themselves together hastily on the sand-covered bedspread they used as a beach blanket. They'd never got around to acquiring a satin-edged tartan Foxford rug, or any of the million and one aids to beach life in a windy climate which the English acquired – the stools, chairs, collapsible tables and windbreaks. The bedspread was torn in places and soiled with paw-marks. A layer of dog-hair was evident from the times when they would throw it along the back seat of the car so as to save the car from the dog's muck.

'Oh, fine day indeed,' her father replied too eagerly.

'We're trying to organise a volley-ball team for this after-noon,' her friend continued, tossing straight black hair over her shoulder, then snapping her finger beneath the bottom of her orange and black polka-dot swimsuit so as to pull it down over a tanned left buttock.

The blonde took up as if on cue. 'Should be a spot of fun. Care to join in?'

'Ah no. No. Thanks all the same. We're –' her mother stammered, lost for words.

'We're not great ones for sport,' her father took over again.

'Oh it's nothing serious. Come on, you two, buck up,' she teased, 'High time you took your noses out of those books!'

The women haw-hawed at her patents' upturned novels, already smeared with Nivea and sand.

'*Do* think about it,' the dark-haired woman urged.

'Well. Sure we'll see,' her mother relented.

'*We'll see?* Splendid!' she said in a high, victorious voice. 'I know that's Gaelic for yes!'

The women waved at them and headed on down the beach at a brisk pace. Gavin and Connie looked at one another as their parents murmured and mumbled, her father briefly imitating the dark-haired woman's voice, her mother falling around the place laughing at his feminised 'Splendid!'.

Connie couldn't remember now how the volley-ball episode resolved itself, recalling instead the feeling of exclusion that dogged her throughout that holiday. They weren't excluded, of course, but for the first time she discovered that the things she took for granted – turns of phrase, her accent – were *alien*. She, her parents, Gavin and all belonging to them, and all the people to whom they weren't related, the citizens of the island of Ireland, were *different* by virtue of the way they used language. To outsiders, they might even seem comical, speaking in a *brogue*.

She thought of her parents that day, at peace with their books, her father dug into the highly-praised *Strumpet City*, a fictionalised account of the last, poverty-stricken years of English rule in Dublin. Her mother, she recalled, had confiscated *Last Exit to Brooklyn* from Gavin, but in the meantime was absorbed by its dense, forbidding print, her face dismal, uttering the odd gasp, the occasional 'Oh my God...'

Years later, the feeling of bewilderment returned when a musician she knew, a native Irish speaker from Kerry, said how he had not known before the age of ten that people didn't speak anything other than Irish, that what he had been reared to was of no importance in the context of world languages. He had wept, he said. No other discovery, neither the challenge of sex, nor the knowledge that Santa Claus did not exist, had the same effect on him.

Connie hadn't wept on that holiday. She'd enjoyed the two weeks, despite being outraged when the owner of the hotel described a local man brought in to the castle one evening to entertain the guests with his stories, as a 'native'.

By the time they returned home, she had decided that nobody would ever think less of her on account of the way she spoke. If people didn't progress beyond judging according to accents and words, she reasoned, then nothing ever changed. Some people were so stupid that they would always need the reassurance of having their own accents echoed back. Those people didn't matter, but if they had power over you? She began to work at her own accent, learnt to inflect her voice, saying 'little' when formerly she would have said 'wee', and 'scold' where once she would have said 'give out'. She stopped saying 'but' at the end of her sentences, a local peculiarity in her county.

Maria, intent on making money in California, possibly even marrying an American, wasn't bothered about her clumsy Spanish patois. Her mouth, throat and tongue seemed to burst with unshapeable words; although her vocabulary grew, with every syllable, her accent remained defiant.

The baby kicked and cooed in his basket. Connie removed her headphones, clicked off her Walkman. '110 and rising,' the weatherwoman had said. The weather was never like that back then. No drama. Nothing to be watched, monitored or slotted, as it was now, into the mythology-kit of the urban pioneer. In Ireland, moisture and the weather were inextricably entwined. Something else from the day at Ballyhealy beach surfaced. Her father, heating water for their picnic on 'the Volcano'. It was a metal contraption, a cylinder within an outer hollow ring. Just as he'd packed the central cylinder with tight balls of newspaper and had set it alight, Gavin had muttered under his breath and nudged Connie.

'It's them.'

Connie tutted. The newspaper began to curl and flame, eventually reddening. Just as the water in the outer ring began to simmer, the Englishwomen stopped again on the way back from their walk along the beach.

'Oh, how wonderful!' the dark one exclaimed, a piece of bleached wood clamped under one arm.

'Soopah, absolutely soopah!' The blonde clapped her hands in delight as the water sang and hissed malevolently in its outer ring, within which the newspaper roared and writhed.

'What a clever idea! Where did you find it, do tell, it's just the sort of thingummy we could use on our moors hikes –'

Connie's mother and father stared at one another, as if puzzled.

'Where did we get it?' her mother said. 'You see, it's always been with us, just one of those things.'

'Second-hand shop?' her father queried.

'After we tied the knot?'

They both nodded.

'There was never anything like it in our family anyhow,' her father said firmly.

'Nor mine. I think we must have picked it up in Flaherty's auction rooms, that's it,' her mother added.

'Isn't it sweet?' the blonde gushed.

They watched in silence, momentarily lost for words as the water suddenly bubbled, boiled, then surged in its container. In the end, Connie's mother gingerly poured the boiling liquid into a teapot, swearing quietly as a drop of water slopped on to her bare foot, her face red beneath the admiring gaze of the two women.

'When you see that Bob again?' Maria enquired late one Friday night as they finished a bottle of red.

'Who knows?' Connie said, emptying her glass.

Maria smiled grimly. 'You meet someone else. *Verdad*?' She settled her hands into her lap, as if awaiting confidences.

'I don't hate him, you know,' she said.

'He too bad for that?'

'I'm indifferent. I've grown indifferent.'

'Those were good times, though,' said Maria, crossing her ankles and stretching back in the leatherette armchair.

She felt too old now for good times like that. What it had amounted to was one long brawl, an endless, laughter-filled crawl from bar to bar to nightclub, then back to the condo, his or hers, his if he was out of his head (he could damage his own place, but she wouldn't let him cross her threshold if he was going to behave like a bear on speed).

'You throw out all that junk last night?'

'You know I did,' Connie replied. Souvenirs from the Bob months: stolen plates, glasses, spoons, even a chipped yellow crutch swiped from a smackhead outside a strip joint. Somehow, it had ended up at the apartment and Bob had forgotten to reclaim the spoils of war.

She couldn't go back to Ireland, not just yet, not without a visa for reentry. Sometimes she wanted to visit her parents. They still asked about Bob, but Connie had heard her mother's sigh of relief when she'd had to explain what the brig was.

The night she met Blue Hawk, he was with a boy of no more than eighteen or nineteen. Blue Hawk was clean, but the boy was stoned. They had a couple of shots together, bourbon for him, Tequila Sunrise for Connie, then listened to a crooning Mexican-Indian singer. The woman swayed behind the mike, her broad hips shifting slowly beneath a close-fitting black satin dress which came to her knees. Her stockings glistened beneath the pink and blue lighting, as she swivelled from foot to foot in pink suede shoes.

'So what kind of place is Twentynine Palms?' Connie asked Blue Hawk.

'High desert. Ain't nothing much up there.'

'What do people do?'

'Do?' He clapped his hands on his knees and thought hard. 'They live there.'

'But what do they do?'

'That depends,' he said doubtfully.

People clapped lazily as the woman finished her act. A young Korean stepped up in her place, smiling as the spot zoomed on his face, eyes bright with undistilled fear. He positioned his instrument, a four-stringed oblong, and began to compete with the absorbed hum of voices.

'Ain't much craftwork up there. That what you mean?'

He knocked back the remainder of his bourbon, then looked at her. 'I suppose you have a dream-catcher.' He smiled. 'All white women seem to have dream-catchers.'

Connie smiled, feeling silly. 'As a matter of fact, I have.'

It hung on the wall over her bed, a circular piece of wood criss-crossed with pieces of gut, surrounding a central hole. The idea was that bad dreams became entangled in the mesh of gut, beyond which they could have no ill-effect on the dreamer, but that good ones slipped osmotically through the hole. Three feathers, white and blue, signified flight.

'Well. No harm in that, I suppose,' Blue Hawk replied, smiling.

The following weekend they drove to Bombay Beach in his pickup. They walked and talked. Around them was desert, pure grey-white wilderness. Whatever parts of herself needed losing, she thought, whatever she was in flight from, could be left in the slackening waste. The desert held her, much in the way the beaches in Ireland had once held her. It was a recognition, the purest moment of perception.

'Strange name for an Irish girl.' Blue Hawk remarked on Saturday evening, as they sat by the lake. The sun dipped low, a thin disc spreading like a shimmering layer of crimson foil on the surface of the water.

'Short for Constance. After a famous revolutionary, a very progressive woman. Constance Markievicz.'

'Never heard of her. But maybe I'll call you Constance. If that's okay.'

'Can I call you Blue?'

Three months later, Blue met her off the bus when she arrived at Twentynine Palms. He grasped both her hands, his look measured as he held her at arm's length, then guided her towards the cream and brown convertible. His hair, she noted, had grown longer. He wore blue jeans, a red shirt and turquoise-beaded suede belt. The journey had been long and tiring. She had barely registered place names. Morongo Valley, Yucca Valley, Joshua Tree. Finally, Twentynine Palms and, beyond it, the Indian Reservation.

'How do you feel about that?' Connie asked when they got to the hut.

'About what?'

'*Indian* Reservation. I mean –' she was hesitant,' – isn't that the wrong word? What about –'

'Oh yea, the PC stuff. Native American? Somehow, Native American Reservation has never sounded right to white folks. They ain't never got around to puttin' it on roadsigns.'

The weekend slipped by. She owned nothing, she knew, absolutely nothing. She was as great or as inconsequential as the sands. The people of the earth owned nothing but owed everything to the Great Mother that gave them life. On Sunday they set out early in the cold dawn air, food and drink for the day strapped to their backs. When the sun rose, the chill gradually melted, and heat filled her. Gradually she brimmed with light and sunshine, until eventually she was scorched and wet, glad of the broad hat she wore and the long-sleeved white dress which covered her body.

'Tell me more.'

'What d'ya want to know?'

'About your people. About the way you live.'

They sat, partly sheltered from the midday glare by the stiff spread of a giant cactus, on a bluff that overlooked the plain. In the near distance, mountains, white and grey, places from which some people never returned, too dehydrated, too lost, or just freaked by a cocktail of acid, poppers and the sun. They saw things, she'd heard that. Connie removed her sandals and rubbed sand across her feet, like a child awaiting a fairy-story. Blue opened a bottle of bourbon and gulped slowly. He breathed out, then held the bottle toward her.

'No. Not during the day,' she replied.

'There y'go now. Damn Injuns just can't keep away from liquor,' he laughed quietly.

'It's not like that. That's not what I meant.'

'What did you mean then, Constance?'

'Ah, it's got more to do with the months when I knew Bob. I told you about him.'

'In the brig. Right.'

'Here.' She took the bottle from him. 'Just to prove myself...'

She didn't even like the stuff. Here she was showing her bona fides to Blue, on a heap of dust in the back of beyond. She swallowed and grimaced, then squinted up at the sun, wondering if she was worthy of her name. It was a bit of a farce, the obsession with naming, one people imposing themselves on another people, another land, parents inspirationally imposing their ideas of honour on newborn babies. The recipient never lived up to the original dream. The native country, the native child, heroes, heroines and politics, crumbling to nothing in the end.

'Don't do that. You'll damage your sight,' Blue said gently, as she squinted at the sun. She was thinking about Bob. It had been all play, no work, or as little as possible. She'd handled her hangovers during the week, after the skites from bar to bar in the company of two Latinos, a Swedish woman and a giant of a man, an art professor from Decorah, Iowa. They put their lives on hold, letting deeper reactions build beneath the surface as they drank and snorted. It was a pressure barely perceptible to Connie. They raised hell at weekends. Shirley had remarked on Connie's pallor one Monday when she arrived for work, her eyes glazed, her body like a live, sparking wire. Sometimes they'd buy enough stuff for a couple of weeks' modest snorting but blow the lot in one weekend at the Swedish woman's apartment on Orange Avenue. They'd hang out of her fourth floor window and howl like monkeys at passers-by, yelling and jibbering to catch the attention of drivers, waving until they were waved to. Sometimes they heated tinned soup, or Connie would microwave a couple of Linda McCartney organic dinners. But the idea of food was mostly a joke: between the arguments about sharing the stuff, whether everybody had enough, between Bob and Connie's rushes, then the long hours of sex, give or take a Black Bomber or two; time flowed away. Sometimes, Bob and the others would shoot up. When they awoke from comatose sleep, they needed an instant upper. Connie wouldn't touch heroin.

In the end, the pressure got too much for Bob. She was glad she hadn't witnessed that crazy, belligerent attack on the gay place. Just as the cops arrived, the Swedish woman told her later, Bob puked all over the place, spattering the police wagon, the police, and himself with a mixture of red wine and tortillas.

'Fool,' she whispered.

'Let him go,' Blue whispered back, taking a quiet gulp of bourbon. He stretched out full in the shade of the cactus, then lit a cigarette, his eyes soft and absent as he watched Connie and the naked sky in turns.

After Bob went to the brig she got drunk, surprised at the extent of her relief. She scarcely remembered that evening with the Swedish woman and the guy from Iowa, but formed the impression that they'd got it together while she was out of her head. Two days later they bailed out of the city, headed up the coast to Santa Barbara.

'Know what, Irishwoman?'

'What, Injun?'

'I think you should stay up here.'

'I can't. I've got to get back to the baby.'

'It's not yours.'

'That's not the point. I have a job.'

'So you have work. Holy-holy-holy!' he laughed. 'There's work up here. Plenty of work.'

'Doing what?'

Blue fell silent. Then he laughed again. 'You could – ' he kept laughing. 'You could always give Irish lessons...' He laughed till he bent double. Eventually, Connie laughed too, although she didn't find the remark all that funny.

'Yeah, maybe we can trade native talents. I teach Irish, your lot give me a load of native craft for export to Europe. Native American dreamcatchers, feathers, amulets, headbands,' she snickered.

'Stop right there, Constance.' Blue held a warning hand in the air.

The comparison had had the desired effect.

'It must have been hard, living up here,' she remarked peaceably.

'Originally. It was not something chosen.'

'But doesn't it kill you? Being reduced to this? A reservation, for God's sake! The worst land on the fucking continent!'

'Yes. No. Deep down it's yes. Day to day less so. Like folks elsewhere, we get on with our lives. And think of your own folks. Back when your Constance was fightin' along with them revolutionaries. Y'all lived on a kind of reservation too, right?'

It was true. Theories went out the window, projections about whither and how a people might realise themselves. The Irish had once been the wogs of Europe, Paddys, Shamrock-heads breeding and in-breeding on the other side of the Irish Sea. She thought of home again. Gavin, a banker with Lloyds, lived in Singapore. But something still worked below the surface of their adult lives, something which created a hunger, in all the heat of memory and pre-birth, for acknowledgement. Sometimes she pitied her parents. They did not value the things she knew, not a glimmer of willingness to lean towards the truth of her unfolding life touched them. That blindness she could scarcely forgive. Despite what they imagined it to be, hers was a life of learning.

As the day cooled, Blue and Connie took photographs of one another. The camera lens became a veil with which each could conceal rising shyness, an anticipation. That evening, she said that she might come back to Twentynine Palms.

'Constance,' he said when, eventually, they lay on the bunk in the hut. She gripped his black hair, pulling him down to her face, staring into the brown wells of his eyes. The skin on his cheekbones was moon-coloured, smooth and supple. He was like a tree, strong, leaf-trembling as he spread himself around her. His love-making was by turns slow, concentrated, then swifter, balancing fire, air, as it hit them in waves. It struck up through her, like lightning dancing in sheets around an isolated object, every so often splitting to the core what had attracted it.

'What you going back up to that dust-bowl for? San Diego a good place!' Maria's voice rose an octave higher when Connie got back to the apartment.

'I am returning to Twentynine Palms,' Connie spoke firmly,

'because up there it feels like home to me. And Blue's up there.'

'You crazy bitch,' she swung up to High C again. 'Like I suppose you need a home! Ireland your home. Now you have a home away from all that rain and all those people who say the Irish only good for drinking, laughing and making babies. You no need a desert home.' Maria poured coffee into a percolator.

'Know something, Maria? You're coming on. You've got a hang of the subliminals.'

'Madre de Dio, sub-leem-in-els? What d'hell you mean?'

'I mean the stuff you've picked up about me without thinking about it. The pictures you've put together in your subconscious mind.'

When the coffee had brewed, the women sat back to watch the night. The windows were wide open. There was no wind. Cicadas croaked and rustled. Connie and Maria sweated gently, sipped from mugs painted with black and gold Native American symbols, crunched at ginger biscuits. Connie held a fly-swat and waved it idly at nothing in particular. As she did so, a small lizard flicked its tail, then glided over the window-ledge, out of sight. Maria kicked off her flip-flops and rubbed oil on her legs.

In the distance, cars cut steadily along the freeway. Connie relaxed, smelt the ocean, the warm earth, Maria's oil. She could just make out the writing on the side of a passing truck. *Kinko's. The Copy Center.*

''S nice here, huh?' Maria whispered.

Connie nodded. Her mind travelled the width of a continent, then the width of an ocean, down the vertical tunnels of the past, back to summer at Ballyhealy beach. She pictured her father and mother, bent over the Volcano, packing a full *Sunday Times*, sports pages and all, into the cylinder before setting it alight in the sand. She remembered the tea, not the American kind – thin, iced tea with no comfort in it – but good strong Irish tea, the kind where you couldn't see the bottom of the cup.

Philip MacCann

A Drive

MY OLD man was polishing the aerial of the Toyota. It was a pale day. Kids were climbing into the waste ground at the top of the road. I found a good place in the boot for my Frisbee. My old man mumbled, 'Dear oh dear.' He made his face go baffled and added, 'A Frisbee.' A black woman with a trolley walked past us. Inside my head I mumbled, 'Fat bastard,' and I went in through the front door to get my Lego robot. My old man had just got the car he had been saving up for, with alloy wheels and all, as soon as my mum had died. I thought it was too sporty-looking. He loved it, and I thought he would go mad taking me on trips, but then he had a stroke. When I came on to the street again with MegaMan, his eyes were rolled upwards and he looked like he was jealous of the black cloud floating above us. He had a cross face like he was going to say it wasn't fair about his stroke or something. It was sad but it was kind of funny with the invalid sticker in the back window and all. Now he was looking right in my eyes. He went, 'Where are you going?' like he was curious.

I had to think for a minute. He leaned on his stick. The footpath was sharpening and blurring. 'On a drive,' I said.

He said, 'Oh?' and lifted his eyebrows. 'Off you go then.'

I clashed the boot closed for him and said, 'What?'

'Bye bye then.' He looked at me. He was waiting for me to walk away. I looked up and down the road. He put the lid on a tin of polish.

I started down the road with my robot. I didn't know where

I was going, because the waste ground was the other way. When I was down the road a bit he called after me, 'Hey!' I looked back. 'What about our drive?' I stood for a few seconds before walking up again. Then I got into the passenger seat and he limped along the side of the car. He mumbled to himself, 'The kitchen sink,' and turned in our garden. It wasn't even a new car, it was second-hand. There was a smell of sweat. The window was stiff to roll down. I knocked the seat back a notch. I could hear kids shouting in the distance. Their voices were kind of muffled and warm. Only me and my friends played on the waste ground. Our area had a lot of black families and my old man said, don't play with those monkeys. But I didn't care.

In a few minutes he came out again. He managed to get into the car. He got his breath. He was in a better mood now. He twiddled the gear stick before trying the engine. It wouldn't start at first, but after a few twists it revved up. He took the car carefully off the kerb and peered up at the sky and went, 'Mm.' I looked out my window. Everything was dull and white at the same time. The car stuttered as it gathered speed. We drove past the big poster of the little kid sucking the big ice lolly. 'Gone to hell,' he mumbled and shook his head. I knew he was going to start on about my playing on the waste ground. 'That ground is a place for queer people,' he said. 'Perverts.'

We passed the demolished shop. Then the car started to judder. There was reggae coming from a bar. I spotted some of my friends in a gang at the corner. Delmar leered at us. My dad opened his collar button. I turned to see them through the back window. Suddenly, the car cut out. 'What in hell's blazes,' he said. I grinned at my friends and throttled my neck in a jokey way. We rolled to a halt. There was a big cardboard box sitting on the road. 'Well, that's nice.' He wound down his window. 'That's those bloody bastard friends of yours. I can't keep my car on the street!' I didn't know what to do. He started laughing. 'If you think I'll be defeated by the likes of that rubbish,' he went on. 'No sir, on no account.' His cheek was twitching.

The next afternoon he worked at the engine. He had pieces of it all over the footpath and the car was cranked up. There was a blotch of oil on his face. My eyes kept avoiding it. 'See those spark plugs?' he said. I said, 'Those?' but I was really watching Delmar up ahead. He had climbed into the skip on our side of the road. He trampolined on all the rubbish. I could see him clearly because the light looked very washed. A skinny kid was with him. 'Never mind them,' said my old man quietly. 'Always keep your spark plugs well filed.' He unscrewed one slowly. He took it out. He began filing the tip, 'That sort of thing shows you know better. That you aren't just a complete yahoo.' The kids started towards us with long slow movements. 'Take it,' said my dad. Delmar was flashing his teeth. 'You do it.'

'What's happening?' asked Delmar with his head lolling on one side.

'Dunno,' I said.

I sneaked a glance at my dad. His hand was going up and down on the plug again.

'You coming down the dump?' Delmar wanted to know. On his T-shirt there was a pop star.

'I can't,' I told him. 'I have to do this.' My old man didn't stop filing. I could hear him breathe.

'Don't worry, mister. We won't get in no trouble.'

'Are you watching me do this?' rasped my dad.

I answered, 'Yes.'

The other two sauntered away. Delmar shouted back, 'Is that your brain you're fixing, mister?' I looked down at the spark plug being filed.

'Is that... filed down?' I said.

He twisted it back into the engine. He straightened up and rested on his stick. His eyes were closed like he was taking a dizzy spell again. He wiped his fingers on a cloth. There was a small bubble between his lips.

A bit later I got away and went after Delmar. At the top of the road I turned in behind the hoarding with the poster of the kid sucking the lolly. I could see the both of them in the distance tugging at a rubber belt or something. The sky came right down on to the ground. When I got closer I hauled up some plasterboard. 'Watch out,' I called and slugged it a small distance into a ditch of brown water in front of me. It splashed softly.

'Oi! That was my head,' his friend called across. 'I'm damaged. I'm making a claim against you!'

We kicked through some rubbish and newspapers. I could hear a tiny ice cream van in my ear. The other kid's name was Ancel. 'What, pencil?' I said.

'Shut up, Fuzzy Balls,' he said. He showed a crescent of teeth.

'Kiss my ass, Dairy Milk.'

'You were born to die. And we were born to kill you.'

We chased through brambles down a wild slope. There was more ground at the bottom which stretched across to the rear of some disused shops.

'Why won't your dad let you play down the dump?' asked Delmar.

'Nutter,' laughed Ancel.

''Cause there are perverts down here,' I told them. We lay on our backs for a while looking up at the sky.

One day my old man was having his dinner in front of the TV in the front room and I was in our hall messing with my cars. You had to keep quiet in our house and walk gently on the carpets and all. We were the only ones in the terrace who owned our own house. He had said, think of a place you want to go, but I just wanted to go down to the waste ground. I was thinking how peaceful and empty it was. Men were loading the skip outside on the road.

He called me in because there was a programme on the

open university. 'Exhibition,' he said. 'Photography. I might
drive you to one. Bank holiday. If you keep your nose clean.' I
sat down on the settee. It showed you photographs in an exhibition and it was quiet like a church. All the people were thin
and starving and there were no clothes on some of them. A
man was talking and going from one room to another. My dad
went, 'Well, well.' He was screwing his face up. You could see
loads of arses in the photographs. 'Dear me, dear me,' he said.
He was shaking his head. It kept showing the arses up close.
He didn't say anything. I was feeling sad and heavy. It showed
you a pair of tits. He wiped his forehead with a handkerchief
and said, 'Is this entertainment? Who do they think wants to
see this on television?' I decided to grin. He knocked the TV off
with his stick. 'It's all buttocks on that programme.' He poured
milk in his tea. 'People without their clothes. On television. Is
that the kind of image you wish to see portrayed?' He looked
at me. His eyes were red and he made them narrow.

'No,' I said.

He took a sip from his tea. 'Buttocks.'

I went out into the front garden and sat on my bike
supported by the hedge. There were loud smashes from the
skip on the street. I wanted to think, but then I heard my old
man open our front door. I didn't look around. He stayed there
getting air. Then he turned around. He said, 'What about
tomorrow then?' We were breathing dust from the skip.

'Okay,' I said.

'A drive?'

He let the words hang in the air. It was my turn to speak but
I didn't know what to say so I mumbled, 'Oh.'

He blinked at me.

'Oh?' I back-pedalled a few times. He looked amazed. 'I
offer to take him on a drive and he says, Oh.' I think there was
blood in his eyes. 'Dear, dear,' he said again with a sigh. He
limped back up to the door shaking his head and mumbling.
'He can forget all about a drive. Oh, he says...' When the door

clicked shut I cycled up to watch the men loading the skip.

The next morning I saw Delmar and Ancel perched on the rim of the skip from our front room. I went out the front door. It was a very quiet day. Everything was wan. There were birds in the air like a flying dotted line. He was sitting on the footpath changing a tyre. I hoped he wasn't going to take me somewhere. His stick was on the road and he was watching me. I started walking towards my friends, 'Hi,' I mumbled as I passed him. When I was a few yards up the road he called after me. 'Tomorrow.' I stopped and turned around. He was getting his breath. 'You, me. A drive.' He tried to say it firmly, and stared hard at me. Then he narrowed his eyes again. 'Unless you have a prior engagement?' I shrugged my shoulders. 'Think on,' he called.

I walked with my friends to the top of the road. There was no air and the day was like whitewash. All the streets were empty because it was a bank holiday. An ice cream man was eating a cone in his van. We nipped in behind the hoarding to the waste ground. We decided to go looking for perverts. We walked across the rubble. I upturned a heavy stone with my heel. Everything was quiet like after a nuclear attack. Ancel said we could find pornography at the back of the shops. I had never had the opportunity to see pornography, but I was interested. I daydreamed about it as we walked along. There were photographs of people naked, but not skinny people. I imagined a mum and dad standing up for a photo with their arms folded and no clothes on. My mum died when I was a tiny baby and I can't remember her.

We climbed down the slope. As we walked across the loose stones there were interesting things to prod at. Ancel picked up a dark half bottle. We idled along the wall of the shops. Delmar stamped on a can. A shadow appeared beneath us and faded away. There was a bit of paper on the ground. It was the corner of a magazine. They ran up to me, but then I dodged them and beat along up the slope. I crouched in the grass and looked at it. It was a bit of a picture of a person. I couldn't guess what part of the body it was because it was so close up. I didn't know if it was pornography or not, but it looked sexual. I leaned on one elbow and rubbed my dick to try to get it hard. I felt like having a piss. I looked up to see where Delmar and Ancel were. Then I saw a man on the slope. All of a sudden, my elbow slipped.

I fell forward on my face. A thistle was beside my cheek. When I looked up the man was passing me and trotting down to the bottom of the slope. He was white with a blotch on his face. My heart was thumping.

Ancel hurried over. I sat up. His words splashed out. 'Is he a pervert?'

'Yeah,' I said. 'He tried to touch me.' Delmar skidded up on his knees. I made out I was laughing but I felt a bit mixed up. 'I told him to fuck off and he legged it.' We watched the man disappear behind the corner of the shops. 'Did you see his red blotch? It was mad, wasn't it?' My voice was a bit dry. 'You should have seen it when I threatened him, it turned as white as that sky.' Ancel dug for a marble sunk in the mud and lobbed it at the shop corner. 'He's a pervert,' I said.

We got to our feet and walked back across the waste ground. 'What'll we do now?' said Delmar. Ancel scooped up a rusty battery. He swung it. A tiny bird flew into the corner of my eye. There wasn't anything to do. I felt a bit sad. I didn't understand how he had a blotch on his face. We walked over the waste ground throwing stones up into the sky for a while.

The car was ready for a drive the next day, but it was a dark day and my old man said he didn't feel well. Neither did I but he decided we would go anyway. I took MegaMan in the car again but he didn't even notice. He flung his stick in the back seat and climbed in the car. 'Alright,' he said and we started off. We drove past the big bill poster and I saw Ancel standing underneath it. A cream ambulance was parked on the road. I was trying to get the seat at the right notch when all of a sudden he beeped his horn. He slowed down. He pulled in outside a newsagent's on the main road. I put the seat back and relaxed.

A woman came up to the window and he wound it down and started chatting to her. Two men walked in front of the car and one touched the bonnet. My dad was talking about the car to the woman. He called it a beauty and said, 'He loves it. He'll tell you.' I had my lips against the window when he poked me. 'Tell her,' he said. I looked at the woman. She looked dreamy. My dad's face was a bit purple. I started to wonder if his dick was sticking up under his jacket. Two men were standing behind her talking. He was going on about the car in a weird way and I was embarrassed. I thought if I had to say anything about the car I could get him back and say the car was crap. 'It just glides over the road,' he was saying. 'He can't get over it.' He looked straight at me and said, 'Tell her. Tell her what a car it is.' I didn't know what to say. I was pissed off. The woman was looking at me.

'Are you not going to tell me?' she asked. She winked at me. She was okay. Just then one of the men behind her turned his head to the side. He had a big blotch on his cheek. He was the pervert from the waste ground.

'Go ahead,' said my old man, 'tell her.'

My heart started thumping. I hoped the pervert wouldn't see me.

'What car?' I mumbled.

The woman glanced at my old man. She gave a laugh. My old man was blinking and smiling. 'That was a good answer, son,' she said. She was jittery.

'Well, now,' said my dad. 'Well, that was unexpected.'

'He's not interested in cars,' said the woman. She was right about that. I wanted to get a look at the pervert. I had a picture of him walking on the slope with a big blotch.

'Him? I don't know what I'll do with that bloody clown. He can hardly change his own knickers.' Then I wished I hadn't said that. I slipped down on my seat to look at the pervert without my old man knowing. The woman chatted on a bit. At last she went away. Then my dad switched the engine off. He pulled his collar open. I was waiting for the pervert to look around so I could see his blotch. My dad looked right at me. His eyes had gone small and beady. He said, 'What car? Just the bloody car that's taking you... out of the slum... you seemed to be suited to.' He took the keys out of the engine. Now the pervert turned away and started walking right in front of the bonnet. But I couldn't get a look at his face because my old man was pointing the keys at me. 'Let me tell you. From now on we will manage independently,' he was saying. 'You can play on the waste ground till your heart's content.' I wasn't listening. I was thinking about the waste ground. I loved it down there. 'You will not enjoy any benefits from me, any drives, information, advice, no sir...' He was still going on. I wished my dad was dead. He made me miss seeing the pervert's blotch. He was biting his lip. He wouldn't drive.

Roddy Doyle

The Lip

H<small>E WAS</small> eating cornflakes when he heard the noise. Actually, it was cornflakes and Weetabix – the Weetabix hidden under the flakes, and a sliced banana for realness. He only had breakfast every other day, always standing up. He still told people he didn't bother with breakfast. Hanging on to his old self. Maybe. His cornflakes. He hated that. *His.* He remembered his mother answering the phone years ago. 'He is, yes. He's watching his Top of the Pops.' He'd never watched it again. He was taking the spoon out of his mouth when he heard the noise. It was a thump sound and it terrified him. He ran. Something about it – fruit hitting a wall. Something had happened. The kids, his wife. The thump, then silence.

They were on their holidays.

He was out of the kitchen when the screaming started. The kids. All of them. Christ christ christ christ. He ran around to the front. It wasn't his house. He didn't have the distances right. He hit the corner but he felt nothing. The car was in the way; he still couldn't see anything. He was still holding his spoon. *His.* Just the screaming. The three girls and his son. All of them. Where the fuck were they? And his wife. His spoon. Christ christ jesus christ. He ran up to the car. He was going to climb over it. He had to get there. He saw now. The girls were standing in a row in order of age, their mouths wide open, all crying. Where was the boy? He went around the car. A scratch on the bonnet. Parked too close to the tree. Where was the boy? He let the spoon drop on to the gravel. Christ christ. The boy was sitting on the gravel, right up against the car. He was crying and dropping pebbles into a red plastic bucket. There was nothing wrong. No blood no flesh. He was dropping pebbles into a bucket. There was nothing wrong there was nothing wrong.

Then he saw his wife. She came from behind the tree.

He was hungry.

She came out from behind the big tree. She was wearing a red and white shirt. He smiled. She'd scared the kids. Playing. Running after them. She did great faces, could change her face completely. She'd scared them, running after them, howling, her arms up in the air. She'd scared them that way. One and then the others had followed. Her face now. She was still playing. He laughed and felt himself getting angry. He was hungry.

Her lip. It was broken in half.

The girls stood in a row and wailed. 'Ma-mee Ma-mee.' The boy dropped stones into his bucket. His wife's top lip was ripped in two. There was a triangle of blood and nothing where the lip was split. The reddest blood he'd ever seen. Drop by black-red drop falling on to her shirt and changing to a lighter shade. 'Ma-mee Ma-mee.' A nicer shade. Her eyes were huge and horrified and dead. He ran to her. So much blood. 'What happened?' So dark. So much of it flowing out of her. 'Ma-mee Ma-mee.' He held her. Avoided the blood. Prick. He held her properly. 'Love?' She looked through him. 'What happened?' She looked at him. She saw him, then nothing. He wasn't there. He meant nothing.

Jesus jesus jesus.

Look at me, look at me.

He turned to the girls. 'What happened?' It was useless; they couldn't talk. They looked at their mammy. They wanted her to see them. They wanted her back. His son. Still plonking stones. 'Stop that, will you.' He looked at his wife. She didn't know he was holding her. 'What happened?'

The blood was almost black. It was full blood. She was starting to shake. Jesus jesus. Something something. 'Sit down, love.' He had to do something. He had to organise. 'Just sit here, love.

Come on'. He had to get her to see him. What had happened?
He looked around. No animals. (There was a farm to the left,
on the other side of the ditch and hedge. They'd seen cows in
there, said hello to them. They'd heard a tractor.) They were
only here a day. He got his leg behind her knees and forced her,
pushed her down on to the grass. He held on to her. Blood on
his jeans. It looked good. Prick prick prick. Now what? He was
hungry. How could he be? All of them into the car. No no;
madness madness. She was shivering now.   A jumper or a
jacket. A phone. Where was there a phone? Where were they?
Jesus, he couldn't remember. Kerry. They were in Kerry. On
their holidays. Lovely. Their first full day. Lovely, lovely. He'd
try again. 'What happened?' And the house wasn't as good as
the picture in the brochure. And the grass was wet. What could
he do? She wasn't there. Her eyes were looking into nothing.
She didn't know she was in pain. He looked at the children.
The boy was emptying the bucket. 'What happened?' He was
crying because the others were crying. 'What happened?' He'd
start filling the bucket again now. He was a single-minded little
fucker. Stop that. He loved that child. He looked from girl to
girl. One, two, three. One of them closed her mouth and
gulped. Poor little thing, she was going to talk. Go on go on.
'What happened, Daddy?' Oh good jesus. 'It's alright, love. It's
alright, it's alright'. He had to do something. He had to act.
There was pain here. He was in charge. This was his family
here. He was hungry. What would happen if he got them all
into the car? Would they let him? Where would he put his
wife? The boot. Prick. What would he do? Would she be able
to sit up? Where was the doctor? Where was the hospital? A
phone. Phone for an ambulance and wait. That was the best.
Bee-baw bee-baw bee-baw. He looked at his wife. The bleeding
had slowed. It seemed to have slowed. The blood on the lip
already looked old. Ready to harden. Jesus jesus, though, she
was really shivering now. Fuck. Her mouth. There were teeth
gone. Gums. 'Hang on.'

He ran.

He was doing something.

Into the house. Straight into the living room, no hall. A pokey little kip. Nothing like the brochure. A jumper, a jacket, a blanket. Where where where? Bee-baw bee-baw. He was saving a life. In command. He was making it up already, the story he'd tell when it was all over. God, he hated himself. He'd always been like that. His Top of the Pops. He had watched it again, after he'd heard his mother. For years afterwards. He'd watched it last Thursday. He couldn't even see a jumper. Christ jesus jesus. Up the stairs. Up the stairs. *Suas an staighre.* He bounced off the wall on the landing. De-den. Starsky and Hutch. The bedroom. The *master* bedroom. A jumper on the bed. One of her own. Jesus he was starving. She'd walked into a branch. She'd run right into it. Chasing the kids. That made sense. The way she'd come out from behind the tree. Strolled out. Was there a branch like that? He didn't know. He had the jumper. Have gun will travel. The window. A shite view of nothing. There was something, though. Down there, in the cottage beside them. Cottage. Neighbours. Like themselves. On holiday. A Volvo outside. He'd heard them last night, one of them trying to play a tin whistle and another one laughing. They were in the kitchen. He could see them. Eating. Not talking. Neighbours. Help. Down the stairs. De-den. Out through the kitchen. Jesus the place was filthy already. They might be German. The neighbours. His cornflakes still on the table. A mouthful. Prick. No spoon. Ha ha. Serves you right. Food at a time like this. Prick. Out the back door. Would he go over to his family first?

No.

He ran.

'This ain't no party – this ain't no disco.' Always the same song in his head when he started running. The neighbours. It wasn't just wet. The grass was soggy. Not in the brochure either. Stop that. It never stops raining here. Stop that now.

'This ain't no fooling around.' Off the grass, on to the gravel. Running on gravel. Crunch crunch and crunch. A man with a mission. A prick. A creep. Focus focus. Focus. Great band. Dutch. Sylvia. Hocus Pocus. Hup-two hup-two. Thijs Van Leer, keyboards and flute. Stop that. His Top of the Pops. His wife for fuck sake, the kids. 'This ain't no Mudd Club.' Concentrate. 'Or C.B.G.B.' Nearly there. Secluded. Brand new. She'd have a scar. Stop. Nearly there. Could see the Volvo. 'I ain't got time for that now.'

He ran.

He was fit. He could go on forever. Adrenalin. He loved that woman. His daughters, his son. He was terrified. Less blood but she'd been shaking. And her eyes. He loved her. He loved it all, husband and father. It suited him. The neighbours. They'd be German. Or French. No problem. No problemo. Or English. Or from the North. My wife's had an accident. So what, fuck off. Stop that. Protestant bastards from Ballymena. Stop that. Nearly there nearly there. He was fit. The Volvo. Christ christ just in time. They were going out. Gotcha. 'Hello.' Hello? 'Sorry to bother you.' Jesus jesus. Your wife your wife. They were looking at him. A man, a woman and a boy. A mentally retarded boy. The face. Could have been any age. 'Do you speak English?' The woman laughed. But they were looking at his face. They could see something. The blood the blood. The man spoke to him. 'What happened?' They were staring at him, even the retarded kid. He wanted to cry. 'I don't know,' he said. 'An accident. I think.' Jesus. There was another one, sitting in the car. A girl. A teenager. A good looking kid. A kid. 'My wife's cut her lip'. Jesus. Cut her lip. Shaving. Shut up. 'It's split'. His hand up to his own lip. Showing them. He still wanted to cry. 'Oh God,' said the woman. English accent. 'In two,' he said. The girl was rolling down the window. Mind your own business. Stop that. 'I don't know how it happened,' he said. Beginning to enjoy himself. Prick. He had them. Hanging on his every word. 'Where?' said the man. Dublin accent. He still wanted to cry. The kid in the car had her hands up to her mouth. Good looking girl. He was covered in blood. His wife's blood. 'Over there,' he said. He could hardly pick the words. He had to pull them out. 'Sorry.' He looked down at himself. His shirt. 'I'll never wear this shirt again.' What did he say that for? It was a tribute. Gobshite. A statement of his love. Gobshite. They were looking at him. 'I couldn't,' he said. The man was trying to get past him. A few years older than him. 'Where are you going?' Not as fit. Tits under his T-shirt. The girl was looking up at them. He grabbed his arm. Why? 'Where are you going?'

'Let go.'

'Where?'

'Let go of me.'

What the fuck was he doing? Your wife, your kids. What was he doing here? The retarded boy was grunting. Your wife your kids. The kid in the car. He let go of her father. 'Sorry. I'm confused.' Jesus.

'Your wife,' said the man.

Phone. Yes. 'She'll need stitches,' he said. Better. A bit of clarity. It was coming back. A scar. Shut up. He didn't mind. Do you see that scar? Shut up. Do you know how she got that scar? Shut up. 'Could you phone for an ambulance? The kids,' he said. 'I can't leave them. They saw it happening.'

'Oh God.'

The woman. I never knew I could run so fast. Shut up. The man to the woman. 'I'll have a look.' The kid looked trapped in the car.

'Are you going on a picnic?' Jesus. Jesus fucking Jesus. Death death death. What was he doing here? I never saw so much blood. Shut up. In my life. Shut up. The man was gone. 'Thanks.' He followed him. He was up ahead. The nerve of him. Shut up. He ran. The man was only walking. A car starting behind him. He looked. One of the other cottages. Just a car starting. He was in trouble here. Big trouble. It was about

to be taken off him. His family, his responsibility. But he was
catching up. He'd get there first. Take over again. Start again.
Would you phone for an ambulance please. Like he should
have said in the first place. Eejit. My wife's had an accident.
'This ain't no party.' Shut up. Catching up. Would you phone
for an ambulance please. Like a good man. Shut up. And take
your Brit wife and sprogs with you while you're at it. Shut
shut. Traitor. Shut shut shut. Jesus. Nearly there. The kids
might be traumatised. Whatever that meant. Some holiday.
Stop. He wanted to cry. He really did. They'd be grand.
Cornettos and McDonalds. T.L.C. No McDonalds around
here. Limerick was the nearest. Would you go to Limerick on
your way back from the phone-box. Shut up. Like a good man.
Shut up. I never wore that shirt again. He was going the wrong
way. The man ahead. He was going to the front door. Ha ha. I
threw it in the bin. I burnt it. I gave it to the Vincent de Paul. I
gave it to the Lynsey De Paul. Top of the Pops.

He ran.

There they were. His family. His wife was standing up. The
girls were sitting down. How long had he been gone? He'd let
them down. No. He was hopeless. No. He'd get there before
the other fucker anyway. Scars were nice. Scars were cool. Each
one told a different story. Shut up. Thank God I was there.
Prick.

She saw him coming. His wife. She moved to him. There
there. He held her. 'It's okay, love.' He held her. 'There's someone coming.' It was good to be back. Real feelings. He
understood again. He looked at the girls. They were calmer.
Tired. They'd be fine. They were lovely. 'Hiya, girls.' A rock.
His wife's head on his shoulder. His hand on her hair. He cried.
'It's okay.' The man was coming. Out the back door. About
time. The girl in the Volvo. Sixteen. Seventeen. It was hard to
tell these days. *These days.* The man was coming. Do you
believe me now? Do you do you do you? The man was coming.
Paddy last. He spoke before the man arrived. 'If you phone for

an ambulance I'll stay here.' Mister Decisive. The man raised a hand; okay. He turned and ran. He tried to run. Fat bastard. It was fine now. He'd let them down. The boy was still putting stones in the bucket. He'd be an engineer. He'd let them down. Yes. All this time. Minutes. He didn't know how long. He'd done nothing. His wife's head on his shoulder. She didn't know that. The oldest girl. He smiled at his oldest girl. 'Put on the kettle for us, love.' She obeyed him. She ran. 'Good girl.' He was in charge. He was saving them. God he loved them. He was happy. I'll never forget it. Shut up. Some way to start your holidays. Shut up.

Ursula De Brún

Signs

'HE MUST be half deaf.' Marie raised herself up on the pillow, fighting a wave of nausea. She could picture him, Seamus, her husband of almost eighteen years, and knew how he would be – legs stretched out in front of him, ankles crossed, arms folded and his attention held by one of those interminable football matches. Half deaf, wholly engrossed. She reached for a shoe, banging the floor as a wild and familiar anger surged through her. The squawking reduced to a murmur. She fell back on the pillow. Message received. Maybe that was how she would break the news to him – via a shoe. I – am – pregnant. Tap. Tap. Tap.

She deeply resented this ability he had to become engrossed: in work, sport, reading, it didn't matter what, while she still couldn't settle her mind long enough to plan an hour of her day. To her it was a sign. Just one more sign to prove that 'Mr Evenkeel', as she had taken to calling him, had forgotten his son. She felt a familiar scream lodge at the back of her throat, but she couldn't let it go since, once started, she knew it would never stop.

She wanted her son back. She wanted one more chance to hold him, to hear him laugh, to have him say 'get real, Mum' when she suggested something he found silly. A friend had hinted to her recently that perhaps it was time to move on. That after a certain number of years, grief could become wallowing, only hurting herself further. This was the same friend who talked with happy exasperation of Junior Certs and student exchanges to Stuttgart. Of how she couldn't keep her son in clothes at the rate he was growing. The same friend whose hallway had a schoolbag smell and clumps of muck where football boots had fallen from hands impatient to grab a snack. Was she wallowing? She didn't care. She'd damn well wallow if she wanted to.

Perspiration slid now from her forehead to her cheeks. She remembered feeling this unwell when she was starting with Gareth. She'd thought then that she had a bug or a touch of food poisoning. She'd been prepared for the worst, but not for being pregnant. She wasn't prepared for it now, either. Food poisoning. How would Seamus take this new bout of 'food poisoning', this 'bug', inside her? Would it please him? Damn right it would.

He had broached the subject of another baby just once. They had gone out for a meal in an effort to put a semblance of normality on their shattered existence. Gareth had been dead then, just over a year.

The wine had mellowed her body, usually so rigid and alert. Seamus had read this as a sign of some sort because he began hesitantly. 'We could... I mean, it's not too late for us...'

She had stiffened then, but he held her hands tightly, gabbling suddenly, in an effort to have his say.

'We could have another baby. We're not too old. Please, Marie, think about it...' She had rushed for the ladies room, vomit rising in her mouth. He had wanted her to replace a 'life for a life' just like that. It was all so simple to him. She had been vicious on the way home. I hope we die, she told him. I hope this car crashes and we die screaming. Seamus remained silent, his eyes focused on the road. She finally slumped against the window, the wipers taking over from where her screaming left off. He never mentioned the subject of a baby again. He slowly became what she now called engrossed, skirting her. They rarely engaged each other except for the odd, desperate bout of lovemaking that started with a careless foot touching a leg that didn't instantly withdraw.

She propped another pillow behind her head; the perspiration had turned cold on her body. Her hand touched her belly.
She could feel no love for this tiny, embryonic life even though,
barely established, it was letting her know that it had become
part of her. Seamus would love it, though. If it turned up with
red and green stripes he'd be as pleased as it was possible to be;
basking in all the congratulations.

She dreaded that word. Congratulations. As soon as she
began to show there would be the 'congratulations', the hugs,
the beaming smiles. They would tell her how happy they were
for her and Seamus. How the two of them deserved the best of
luck, the reason, of course, being discreetly tucked aside. By
universal agreement, they would allow the new baby to replace
Gareth. A focus away from their awkwardness with her grief.
They would stop avoiding her in the street. She would no
longer be 'grief-stricken'. They would presume that it was all
over. Already she hated them.

She reached under the bed, her hand searching out the shoe-
box. At least her doctor had had the grace to be awkward
when he had congratulated her. He was one of those clean cut,
'God's will' types with at least half a dozen kids of his own. She
didn't know why she still went to him except that it was easier
than starting anew with someone else.

And that was it. She was afraid of starting anew, especially
as a mother. She had been no good at it. What good mother
wishes her son's life away? Getting her wish when he was
barely twelve years old? She turned on the bedside lamp and
lifted the lid of the box. There it was, a boy's life, captured on
polaroid, preserved in a shoe box.

Of course, no pictures of him in the womb when she had
first begun to resent him, squealing in horror at the purple
streaks that crossed her belly. Seamus had found her sitting on
the lid of the toilet, crying.

'But aren't you supposed to look like that?' he had asked,
without much conviction.

She pulled out a photograph. Her in the old pink armchair breastfeeding Gareth, her neighbour of the time beaming in the background. She had been so angry at Seamus for taking that picture.

'But you must have one,' the earth mother had cooed. 'I have one with all of mine.' She hadn't doubted it. The woman had been so sickeningly enthusiastic about motherhood; proud of the fact that she was still breastfeeding her vegetarian two year old. Marie had looked down at Gareth, latched piranha-like to her sore nipple, and dreaded the thought of him ever having teeth. A few weeks later she had stopped breastfeeding, much to the distress of her neighbour.

'He'll suffer in later life,' she had warned.

Well he didn't, she thought, shoving the box back under the bed, he didn't get the chance.

She could hear Seamus now banging dishes down in the kitchen. The smell of rashers made her realise just how little she had eaten since the morning. Seamus had brought her a mug of tea earlier but she had let it go cold, and now the smell of it on the bedside locker made her feel ill again. With a sigh, she padded to the bathroom.

'I heard you getting sick.'

He was on the landing when she came out.

'It was nothing.' She watched uncertainty flicker over his face before he asked her if he could get her anything. She shook her head. As he headed down the stairs she stared at his retreating back, shocked at how collapsed his body seemed. When had he stopped being tall and broad-shouldered? She had married him, if she was honest, because she felt he would take care of her. But it hadn't worked out like that; he never quite knew what she needed. She pulled a towel from the hot press. She would have to go downstairs and talk to him. He had a right to know how things stood.

He was halfway through his tea by the time she had showered and dressed. She quickly looked away from the remains of a runny egg. He was predictable in all ways, right down to the way he liked his eggs; no changes allowed. He poured her a cup of tea.

'If it's gone cold, I'll make more.'

It had, but she told him it was fine. She watched him butter a slice of bread, cut it in half, fold over a piece and bite into it. She'd been watching him do this for almost eighteen years. He was a man of moderation, her husband. Steady. The most fervent accolade he ever received was steady. She let out a sigh. He looked up and held her gaze.

'I know about the baby,' he said.

She banged the table. 'That bloody doctor had no right.'

He grabbed her fist. 'It wasn't the doctor,' he said, quietly, 'I guessed.'

'How?'

'I'm not stupid, Marie. I can read the signs.'

She felt an hysterical giggle bubble up from deep inside her. Seamus read signs. Her signs. The man on the steady track had been alert after all.

'Why didn't you say anything?' she asked him.

He stared down at the hand that gripped hers. 'I didn't know if you wanted it. I thought it was better to leave it with you.'

'For how long?'

He cleared his throat. 'Until you made your decision.'

She was winded. What did he think she would do? Get rid of it? She stared at his bent head, digesting the fact that he would have let her if she'd wanted to.

'I never thought about... you know...,' she said finally.

He looked up then. 'I'm glad.' And she could see that his eyes were bright with unshed tears.

'Seamus,' she said quietly, 'I'm so sorry for the way I've been. There are women who shouldn't have babies, although they do, and I'm one of them.'

'That's not true,' he said, 'you were a great mother.'

She tried to protest, but his words of encouragement and

enthusiasm washed over her while she struggled again and again to surface to the truth. How she was always hurrying Gareth as a toddler, even when there was plenty of time for a stroll. How, when he played with water at the sink, she was oblivious to his squeals of pleasure because all she could think about was where the hell the water was seeping. How many times had she asked herself what made her rush through her son's life using up twelve years waiting for a time to herself? If she couldn't answer the question, then she was sure that the problem still remained, a sleeping monster ready to surge upwards and take her over again at the very next chance.

Seamus pressed a tea cloth into her hands and she wiped her eyes, aware of his stricken look.

'Don't you see,' she said, 'I'm scared.'

'Then that makes two of us.' He gave her a half-hearted smile. 'I've lost my confidence in being a dad.'

She was surprised. 'But you were a good father. Gareth adored you.'

'Good fathers don't ignore vital signs.'

She leaned towards him. 'Seamus, even the doctors got it wrong. You couldn't have known.'

'You would have.'

'I wouldn't. Besides, I wasn't there, was I? I was off with the girls.' She stood up and got some kitchen paper. 'There's something lacking in me, Seamus,' she said, blowing her nose.

'There's nothing lacking in you,' he said.

He stood up to clear the table. She watched him slowly sweep crumbs into his hand. Neatly stack his dishes in the sink. This was the side of him she knew best. He had a method for all he did, a slow, steady method. Just what they would both need in the months and then the years ahead. She took a cloth and began to dry the dishes he was washing. They stood side by side. Something told her that this was her new reality. This, and a small swelling covered now by her husband's wet and trembling hand.

Patrick Quigley

The Girl in the Yellow Dress

THE GIRL in the yellow dress and red beret arrived in Dublin's main bus station, Busáras, on a windy March afternoon. She looked around the circular waiting room at the weary travellers and patient homeless on the benches. Always the same kind of crowd even if the faces were different. The same slow sweeper guiding a long brush with a flat head around the feet and bags on the tiled floor.

She appeared on a traffic island where the roads wind around the glass and concrete island of the station. With a small brown bag clutched to her side, she stood among the streaming traffic as if taken root in the concrete. Other people joined her on the strip of concrete, downstream from a set of forlorn pedestrian signals, from which they began to play Russian roulette with the traffic. She chewed on the remains of an apple and looked across car roofs at a bronze sculpture behind the railings of the Custom House. A tall naked woman confronted the March sunlight, holding a long downward sword in one hand, comforting a grasping figure with the other.

The girl stood with her bag in her arm among the waves of metal pouring around her. Her yellow reflection flowed past her on the sides of cars and vans. On the oncoming vehicles her dress grew from a yellow clot on the side panels, unfurling into a rippling flag, unreeling into long webs as the traffic sped away.

She wandered the streets in a zigzag pattern, stopping to look at three sculpted heads in Abbey Street. Set on a corner of the footpath, the smoothly polished heads seemed to be engaged in a silent dialogue with each other. The girl stood among them and looked into their faces as the busy crowds went past without a glance. On the high pediment of a cathedral, stone saints blessed the passers-by, the fingers eroded from ancient hands. She came to O'Connell Street and walked beneath the row of official statuary on the central island. Upraised arms and stern faces were still visible between the unleafed branches of the plane trees. In the centre of the street she sat on the granite plinth around the Anna Livia fountain. She took off her sandals and let her feet cool in the water among the floating hamburger cartons and empty chip bags. The water gushed from a hole behind the bronze-green head of the reclining river goddess, splashing like tears from the eye ducts, forming rivulets down her neck and chest.

This is the way she went through the city, wandering from one street to the next, passing up one street and down another almost parallel to it, diverging from busy thoroughfares into narrow alleyways inhabited by smouldering mattresses, abandoned sacks of rubbish, bicycle frames stripped of wheels, brakes and handlebars. Pigeons sorted among the gutters, glancing sideways at her bare heels in high strapped sandals. It took her hours to travel to her destination by her peripatetic route to Glasnevin. In Sherrard Street she stopped before a tableau sealed in a glass alcove beside the door of a two-storey house. Two plaster figures were painted in simple bright colours. A tall white missionary in cassock and light brown beard poured water on the head of a crouching black man. The convert kissed the stole at the missionary's waist. Here her pale eyes drank in the details and she pressed her hand to the cool glass, her lips moving silently.

'It's a bit dark, but it's cosy.' Mrs Delaney poked at a piece of loose material on an armchair. It ripped in her fingers and she tucked the torn strip into a hole. The girl in the yellow dress hardly looked around the flat, paid no attention to the damp smell exhaled by the empty cupboards, the stains on the ancient wallpaper, the furred remains stuck to the plate on the cooker. There was a window sealed up with layers of paint, insulated with cobwebs shaking from the movements of disturbed spiders.

'It's fine.'

'Forty pounds a week. Two weeks in advance. Take it or leave it. I have other offers.'

Mrs Delaney drew in her breath, expecting a fight that didn't come. The girl emptied her purse on the table, sorted the coins from the notes. She put the notes into the hollow of the landlady's plump hand.

'This is all I have.'

'That's not one week.' Mrs Delaney glared at her. The girl shrugged, the bones of her shoulder blades moving beneath the thin material. Hard to tell her age. The look of a person who had never grown on her smooth skin. The skin white, but a hint of strange food, foreign places in the bone structure.

'All I have...'

'You can have it. I'm not able for these stairs. Not at my age.'

She paused at the door. The girl was still standing at the table.

'I forgot to ask your name.'

'Just Lina. You'd forget the rest.'

Mrs Delaney grunted.

'Our names are strange to your ears.'

'Have you got work or anything?'

'Oh yes.' The thin face folded into a smile. 'Much work to do. So much to see. Thanks very much.' She folded her arms and looked down, rolling a piece of grit with the heel of her sandal.

'I don't want any funny business, that's all. This is a respectable house.'

'Yes.' When the door closed the girl crossed to the dusty mantelpiece above the fireplace filled with crumpled papers. A Child of Prague statue held up a hand in blessing inside a cracked glass canopy. She smiled at the small figure in its heavy robes, a tiny red heart on its chest, holding up a globe with a cross on top. 'A respectable house.'

Mrs Delaney crept down the stairs into her room on the ground floor. Her slippers slid across the track worn in the carpet to the table beside the television. She held the porcelain dog under her elbow as she removed the lampshade from around its head. The brown and white mountain dog held a lit bulb in a black socket in its mouth. She took an eyepiece from her pocket and screwed it into position over her right eye. The metal strip on the notes stood out starkly against the bulb. She put back the lampshade on the dog's head and slipped the notes into an opening in his stomach. A frayed cat crept around the carpet, pulling at cords as it whimpered for its breakfast.

'Not yet, Sam. You're always hungry.'

The old woman sat on her chair and listened for the pulse and heartbeat of the house – doors closing, water running through pipes, a drip of water on tin somewhere on the third floor. Sam crawled into her lap, looked pitifully into her face. She rubbed the cat's forehead.

'I doubt, Sam, if that one is all there.'

When the door closed Lina slipped off her sandals. She lay on the bed while tormented springs groaned beneath her. Her eyes closed before her head touched the stale bed cover. The newsreel of the paralysed city ran through her mind. The white sky pouring in from the high uncurtained window; a breeze blowing through the bullet holes in the glass. She lay against the wall listening to the mortar crumble with each sniper shot, hour after hour.

Despite Mrs Delaney's efforts she saw little of her new lodger. A week passed and there was hardly a sound from the flat. No music or voices; no banging doors or presses – not even a scrape of metal on plates. The girl didn't leave the house between eight and nine in the mornings. Then the house shook with banging doors, flushing toilets, the sound of things falling on the delicate floorboards. After nine silence settled on the house but for the complaining of arthritic boards that cracked and groaned all day long. The new girl slipped out sometime during the morning when Mrs Delaney's attention was distracted by the phone-in radio programmes.

'No, Mrs D, I only met her in the hall once.' Mairead was usually a good source of information. A red-faced girl from Meath who worked in the Civil Service and knew everybody in the house without making any effort at all. In Mrs Delaney's experience it was very hard to get to know people and the harder you tried the more they drew into their private shell.

'She might be a bit lost.' Mrs Delaney shook her head. 'New to the city like. I know what it was like when I came up to skivvy for a family in Rathmines forty years ago.'

Mairead excused herself. She had heard Mrs Delaney's story many times over.

Mairead made a point of asking how the girl was as she passed in a flash of yellow, dazzling against the dark limbo of the wallpaper.

'If ever you need anything...'

'Nothing,' the girl said, the word a shining bubble drifting on the air behind her. 'I need nothing.'

Lina crossed and recrossed the city. In St Stephen's Green she spent a long time before the Three Fates near the gate at Leeson Street. The three women held the thread of life between them, one unwinding from a spool, the other stretching it with her hands while the third held a scissors to cut. Beneath the evergreen oaks she discovered Moore's bronze of the poet, Yeats – a flame in dark green bronze without face, legs or arms that seemed to breathe with inhuman power. In the secluded garden behind Earlsfort Terrace she came across a sad family of concrete figures before the stones of a dried-up fountain. A century of Irish weather had washed off the noses and ears, pulled off fingers and hands. Red oxide leaked from rusting metal supports like the blood from internal wounds.

'She keeps odd hours.' Mairead stroked the cat as it passed from lap to chair to table and back again. She pushed the head with the begging eyes gently away. Mrs Delaney sucked in her lips.

'Any men?'

'I don't spy on her.'

'I'm just concerned about her. She owes me rent. There's not a sound when I go up. I'd put her out, but... ' she eyed Mairead, 'she might need a social worker. I don't want anything to happen to her in the house. There'd be reporters with microphones and things all over the place. I could be on the radio.'

'I'll have a wee word with her.'

But there was no answer when Mairead went up the stairs and knocked at the thin door. Just the mutter of evening traffic out on the road and her own heartbeat pounding in her blood. It was at the change from winter to summer time, when the hour of the clock goes forward and the spring evenings are suddenly flooded with light. She loved to go out and look into the gardens at the daffodils, crocuses and narcissi that burst out of the damp and surprised earth. Cherry blossom lay in drifts on the edge of footpaths, in the angles by garden walls. She was crossing the road by the Botanic Gardens when she saw the yellow dress moving ahead of her. Mairead followed the girl into the gardens and down the hill to the rose garden. She stopped before a marble statue of a man in long robes secluded among the bushes in a corner beside the river Tolka. Mairead coughed as she came up the path. She commented on the beauty of the evening and stopped. Lina smiled at the statue and turned to her: 'It's Socrates. Imagine finding him here.'

'Was he one of the Romans?'

'Greek. One of the great philosophers.' Lina's eyes shone. 'He taught how we should question everything.'

'No wonder they didn't teach us about him. I never passed no remarks on him. Just the man with no toes.'

Lina caressed the stumps where the marble had broken off. To Mairead the girl was as still as a statue herself, her face the texture of marble, the breath hardly disturbing her body.

'He has such life, such intensity in him,' the girl said.

'Yes. I suppose he has. When you look at him like that.'

As Lina was out for a walk in the mildness of the evening, Mairead found herself walking towards the city with her.

'I love to walk the city,' the girl said.

'Isn't it dangerous?'

'I don't mind. If people think you're harmless, they leave you alone.'

'I'm not sure about that.'

But still she walked with her, the pair of them talking in turn. They walked around the dense streets at the core of the city.

'You have an unusual accent,' Mairead said.

'I thought it was ordinary.'

'That's just it. You could be from anywhere.'

Lina just smiled, made a remark about a weathered stone face on a church porch. They climbed stone steps beneath the bronze statues of the Children of Lir reflected in an oval pool. Four huge swans struggled to launch themselves into the chill air, sprouting from the shoulders of falling human shapes. Mairead shivered, but Lina seemed oblivious to cold in her bright dress, her thin arms sticking out of the short sleeves.

They went down a street of shuttered shops to a group of serpents on a granite base with women's heads staring at the traffic on Summerhill. Someone had painted white helmets with chin and nose pieces on the heads. Near by, Charles Stuart Parnell stood erect in double overcoat at the base of a marble obelisk, one dark arm pointing into the clouds of sunset.

Behind the glass window of the General Post Office a raven perched on the shoulder of the dying warrior, Cú Chulainn. Mairead noticed that Lina stared intently at the statues, her gaze seeming to look beyond the faces of stone and metal. They stopped beneath the monument to Daniel O'Connell where the Liberator stood with his head covered in bird slime above a great drum surrounded by nineteenth century people in rich clothes. Lina stared not at the patriot or the burghers, but at a wolfhound looking up into the thoughtful face of a huge winged angel.

Mairead's feet ached from the miles of hard pavement. They sat on a bench in Liffey Street beside two bronze female shoppers with shoulders stooped, shopping bags stuck to the concrete paving slabs. Lina leaned against the round shoulder of the nearest figure. Her dress was an orange shade of yellow in the underwater light from the street lamps. It was a night for late shopping and people passed through the narrow street to and from the Halfpenny Bridge that curved above the Liffey. An empty bottle rolled between their feet.

'When I look at people on the streets I see a blur,' Lina said. 'They move too fast to get a fix on them. Even when they slow down they're still jumpy, unsettled, always thinking, wanting something...'

Mairead watched the pedestrians piling up at the bridge, some of them dashing before oncoming traffic to cross into Liffey Street. They rushed up the street, twisting to go around the seated figures. She noticed the men scanning them as they passed, watching the road, the traffic, the shop windows, all at the same time.

'Do you prefer statues to people?'

'Statues are alive too, but in a different way.' She touched the bronze face of the middle-aged shopper, strangely life-like, as though the breathing person had stepped out and left a shell behind. Mairead tapped the head with her hand, heard the echo of skin against hollow metal.

'There's nothing there.'

Lina gave her a pitying look: 'They have an inner stillness.' Lina looked out across at the blue spotlights on the curved metalwork of the Halfpenny Bridge.

'The city I come from was pulled apart in a terrible war. All the day we had to stay in our apartments and listen to the bombs and bullets falling, killing, exploding.'

'I think I saw a documentary...'

'So many people were killed.' She pressed her cheek against the bronze face. 'You had to make yourself numb. Like a statue.'

'But you survived.'

'Yes,' she smiled bitterly. 'The soldiers stopped me as I tried to get out. I was taken to a camp..., but I survived.'

'And now you're here.'

'I just go to places.' She sat up straight, her hands on the bench. 'I stay a little while and then I go.'

Mairead yawned. A cold wind gathered on the Liffey and blew into the street. Her legs nearly crumpled when she stood up.

'We'd better take the bus home. I'm cold and tired.'

'You go. I don't have money.'

They sat upstairs on the bus, rocking along the patched-up streets. Mairead was horrified to discover that Lina lived on over-ripe fruit left by the street traders in Moore Street.

'That's awful. You should go to the Social Welfare.'

The girl looked out at the lights swirling in the glass, at the buildings surging towards them, receding as the driver changed course with a turn of his wheel. Her white knuckles gripped the aluminium seat rim.

'All those questions. They try and turn your life into a set of questions and boxes.' A shiver ran up through her body, wrinkling the skin on her forehead. 'I hate forms and questions.'

'But you'll starve.'

'I won't starve. I'll get money soon.'

One breezy Sunday afternoon she went to look at a statue of Our Lady Queen of Peace high on a dashed grey wall above a busy road sloping towards the river. She climbed on to the plinth and imitated the pose with the hands held at the side, palms outwards. The wind carried insect voices across the buildings to her. She looked across the road at a group of people kneeling on a triangle of grass between traffic lights and a street of houses. Their white heads were bowed, hands working the beads in their fingers.

Lina lay in the darkness watching the statue move, unsure if she was dreaming or remembering. A man with granite-grey skin and hair winked at her, his frock coat and waistcoat covered in quarry dust. Classical music played from a machine at his pedestal and he moved his hands stiffly in the air. He cocked his head and listened. As the violins surged he placed his hand across his heart, holding down his head. Her eyes filled with tears and she cried for the man-statue, the living-dead man with his stiff movements. An admiring crowd stood on the pavement outside the Frankfurt Messeturm. In the background a towering black figure let a hammer fall on an anvil, slowly lifted the hammer again. In Berlin a woman with blue skin danced in the Tiergarten. She wore a long pink dress, her breasts bare in the sunshine in the style of ancient Crete. In Heidelberg a Palatine prince in flowing wig and gold-rimmed coat moved slowly with a cane, children playing about his legs. He poked at a child with the cane. A land of moving statues.

Mairead walked through Grafton Street on her way home from the office on St Stephen's Green. The street was full of tourists, standing around with lost expressions, consulting maps and guide books, searching for something to look at, amazed that nothing had been prepared for their entertainment. Five o'clock and the street blocked with crowds gathered around buskers. Flower sellers spread buckets of tulips and carnations on the pavement at the junction with Harry Street. A Japanese man stood videotaping a pavement artist near

Duke Street. The yellow dress looked familiar on the figure with swan-white face and hair sitting on the pavement. Rock music blasted out from the open front of a nearby music shop. A procession of expressions passed across the white face as the music played – love, sadness, joy, horror. A tiny bowl rested before her and she gracefully nodded her head as small coins were placed there.

'Lina,' she called. 'Are you begging?'

The chalk face slowly opened in a smile.

'Mairead. See how I have learned?'

The young man stumbled against the door frame.

'All those stairs.' Her dress seemed to glow in the shadows as she pushed in the door.

'You have to be quiet,' she said. 'They're all asleep.'

'Ah...'

She left the light button untouched. Instead she lit a candle, placing it on the table. He sat on the only chair and looked up at her.

'The smell is dreadful.'

She shrugged.

'It's quiet. Private.'

He looked around at the bed, the street map pinned to the wall. Blue lines all over the streets and roads. He went across to look. Hard to make much out in the bad light. She had marked places around the city centre with blue circles, indecipherable notes scribbled across any blank spaces. Drawings of stick people around the margins. She took a stick of celery from the table and watched him.

'What's all this?'

'Those are places I like to visit.'

'The city is a dangerous place,' he said. 'You should stay off the streets.'

Her jaws crunched on the celery. Her eyes seemed to shine with a predatory light. He took off his leather jacket and put it on the back of the chair. He watched for a reaction as he pulled on a latex glove. From an inside pocket in the jacket he took a revolver and cradled it on the palm of his hand.

'Ever see one of these?'

She shook her head as she bit another chunk off the celery.

'The city is riddled with drug addicts. We're going to clean the dealers and criminals off the streets.' He loosened his tie. 'Do you have a drink by any chance?'

'Water.'

'Not what I need.' He turned the gun in his hand, aimed at the cooker. She giggled. It was the first time since he met her wandering by the canal he'd seen her laugh. He put the gun away and packed the glove in his pocket. The bareness of the room made him uncertain. He stood up and moved towards her: 'I'd better go now.'

It annoyed him the way she just lay on the bed. Every time he moved the springs groaned as though some damned soul was embedded in the stuffing, tormented with the weight.

'Just lie with me,' she said.

He gave up the attempt to coax a response from her breasts and lay with his hand against her bare thigh.

'Hold me a little while.'

'You're a weird girl.'

One night she let Mairead persuade her to go to the cinema. She gaped at the rows of seats, the high lamps painted to look like stars on the black ceiling. But when the film started she took fright at the massive screen. Faces of the actors were huge as the sides of skyscrapers above the audience. She looked carefully and she saw the faces were heavily lacquered in make-up with facial hair, spots and blemishes removed. They were all gigantic masks floating in space before her. She looked away towards the audience, their small white faces pointing at the glowing screen, their thoughts lost in the giant dream unfolding before them. She turned to look at the people in the rows around her, studying the shapes of their bodies when they were least aware of them.

Whenever she encountered a new statue she would study it until she felt a space open within her. An emptiness that matched the core of the statue. In her dreams she revolved around this free space. In her performances she tried to achieve the stillness and peace of a figure of stone and metal. She noticed people who would stand watching her for hours, staying behind in alcoves and against shop doorways, as if trying to absorb some of her stillness to bring away with them.

The crowds got bigger on the streets as the paving stones grew warmer. She found it harder to concentrate with the growth in noise, the pressure of so many mouths breathing so close to her. A group of street children discerned that she had no protector and demanded a share of the takings. When she shrugged at their threats they sent the youngest to stick pins in her arms and thighs as she performed. The audience stood by with immobile faces as the pins went in.

She was still wearing a yellow dress, her bag beside her, when she came to say goodbye. She wouldn't sit down, preferred to stand in the open door. She took up one leg by the ankle and held it, balanced on one leg, the way a child would.

'Where will you go?' Mairead asked.

'Further west. Too many people here.'

'What will you do?'

'I'll always find something.'

'You're not easy to know,' Mairead said. 'I'm supposed to be a people person. They've moved me into Personnel at work. But I'm up against a brick wall with you. Why?'

Lina smiled into the distance and moved her head from side to side.

'I've tried, you know. Always tried, but people are hard to connect with. I get on better with trees, lampposts, statues. They have such stories in them.'

Mairead never realised she would miss Lina so much. She walked up and down Grafton Street hoping for a sighting of the yellow dress. Several times her heart began to pound as she moved in on a woman in yellow, slowly recognising her mistake as she came closer. Other performers, other tourists stood where she had been. She walked up Parnell Square, recalling the association in the places she passed, linking images of Lina with the statues as she passed. She went into the Garden of Remembrance and ran her fingers in the watery reflections of the Children of Lir. She looked up the steps at the four bronze husks falling, the swans unfolding huge wings, reaching for the twilight sky. Mairead walked up the steps and stood beneath Fionnuala, the one sister with her swaying body. She looked up at the huge metal face, falling hair, the swan rising from her back.

'I wish you a happy landing,' she said, 'wherever you go.'

Sara Berkeley

To Prevent Rust, Weeping and Bleeding

> Estragon: *What is it?*
> Vladimir: *I don't know. A willow.*
> Estragon: *Where are the leaves?*
> Vladimir: *It must be dead.*
> Estragon: *No more weeping.*

SHE HAD a metal head. It had begun to rust in places. Sometimes she felt old.

*   *   *

Set deep in the head were two eyes. Through these eyes, she looked at the world. How could she be sure that what she saw was what was really there?

*   *   *

She met a man. At first she fought from a great distance against the idea of him. After a short time she realised that the way she felt about this man was beyond romance; that it was ludicrous to pretend she wanted to be anywhere but with him. She discovered how to be alone with him. She learned from him. Together, they began to tease out what love meant to them. It seemed they had all the time in the world.

Inside her, placed obliquely between the lungs and enclosed in the membranous cavity of the pericardium, was a heart. Although she had never seen it, she could feel it beat and she believed it was there, resting on the diaphragm, weighing between eight and ten ounces, about one one-hundred-and-fiftieth of her total body weight. The division of her heart into four cavities was indicated by grooves on its surface. That the upper cavities had a separate name from the lower cavities she considered typical of the capaciousness of human civilisation.

*   *   *

After a while, it became clear to her that the man saw other women. She knew that this simple fact was part of something larger that she did not understand. For the first time, she looked into the future without fear. Inside her metal head, the future took the form of a long, straight road that would lead her through a landscape of great beauty and harshness, beyond the distant mountains, into the boundless unknown. One night, he told her about the other women. He said he wanted to stop, to be with only her. He said he thought about it all the time. They agreed it need not undermine what they were building. She said he could keep doing it or he could stop, she would love him anyway. He said he'd stop.

*   *   *

The right half of her heart contained blood, also called impure. Her arteries, aside from the pulmonary, contained blood that was pure. In their course throughout her body, the arteries underwent enormous ramification, echoing out to minute arterioles, which in their turn squirmed and microscopically split into a dense mesh of capillaries. It surprised her that the blood would bother to find its way through this maze. Sometimes she wished it would skimp a little, leave her without feeling for a while.

One bright day they married. The night before, she lay alone in a big house on the coast. The only sound was the sea pounding outside and the thin scratch of her pen. The dress was downstairs, in a dark place, waiting; the pieces of the puzzle were all in place. Salt tears ran down her metal cheeks. She felt at the same time like a grown woman and a very young girl; she could feel all the girls and women she had ever been connect, associate, unite, amalgamate, fuse. In uncertain command of her myriad parts and personalities, she felt, for the first time, whole. Afterwards, looking at the photographs, she saw them, bride and groom, lit with a radiance that came out of nowhere, unbidden, undisguised. They honeymooned in a hot place, an island. He didn't look at the other women in their hotel, the slender women on the beaches in their high-sided bikinis. He looked only at her, sat across from her at dinner each night, watching her with love and tenderness. After they made love in the late afternoons, he rolled back, exhausted, smoked a cigarette, far away. She realised it could ruin them, his passion, if they weren't careful, and that in this case, being careful included being honest. Her failure of courage kept her silent. This was not how it would always be. 'We are four days into marriage,' she wrote, 'and the honeymoon is pretty much completely serene and untroubled. I want no danger at the moment. Trouble and challenge to our happiness can come later; that's alright, I expect it. But not now.'

*   *   *

Under ordinary circumstances, the positions of the upper and lower eyelids meant that about the lower three-fourths of her cornea was exposed. On the margins of the lids were two small openings, the start of the lachrymal canals. In their natural condition, the lids were maintained in their position, touching the conjuctiva of the eyeball, by a muscle that allowed the tears running over the surface to find their way easily into the lachrymal canals. Normally, tears from the lachrymal gland washed gently across her eyes, into the canals, and along the nasal duct into the cavity of her nose. Occasionally, there were too many of them to find their way. This was the case some summer nights, driving home through the haze of evening sun, telling herself in a voice as neutral as she could keep it the stories of the other women. Her lachrymal gland, lodged in a depression on the inner side of her frontal bone, about the size and shape of an almond, worked overtime. Tears welled inside the lower lid, spilled over, coursed down the metal cheeks, dripped off the chin and soaked into her shirt just above the second rib. Her throat ached. Soon, she knew, the soft, ferro-magnetic constituent of her genetic makeup would react with the tears and oxidise to rust. Odd how the red-brown coating, commonly seen as a corrosion or degradation of what was pure, was also used by jewellers as a polishing agent. Jeweller's rouge. Watch and clockmakers in the previous century used a rouge leather to touch up highly polished surfaces until they could see their faces in them. Glancing in the rear-view mirror, she saw her eyes were red and swollen. Twelve miles from home: if she stopped crying now she'd look okay when she got there.

*   *   *

Six months married, she wrote him a letter early one Sunday after a sleepless night. She told him again what Jerry Garcia's wife said in another context to her husband a year before he died: you can choose to do it for the rest of your life and I'll love you anyway. She told him she was scared and why. They were ugly facts that he had scarcely bothered to hide from her. Days when he couldn't be found. Nights he stayed away. Restaurant receipts on the kitchen counter. She held her courage like a rod with a big fish biting. Over the bay where they lived, helicopters dipped giant buckets in the water, then lifted them, dripping gallons, up over the ridge to where a wildfire blazed. They spent two days marooned in their hillside home, bags packed, ready to flee. He held her close to him, told her it was all over, all the playing around. He cried and said if she'd take him, he would stay with her forever. By midnight the following Saturday the fire was contained. They unpacked. Nothing had changed. But he was a kind man. 'Honestly,' she told herself driving home, 'he doesn't want to hurt me. He doesn't know himself why he does it. Women just drive him mad. And he's good to me. Never angry, never in the remotest sense abusive, verbally or physically. Believe me – I don't know that I'd stay if he were violent. But he's exuberant, a happy man. Who can say that about their beloved? He has ideas, he trips over himself explaining them, he speaks animatedly, his brain teems. He's fun.' She stopped then, and thought for a while. Deep in the pulmonary artery, ventricular diastole interrupted the course of the blood, expanding the semilunar valves, checking the flow. Then the blood continued its regurgitation toward the heart. She swallowed. 'There are two of him,' she told thin air. 'I married them both. I love them both.'

*   *   *

Heartache. Was there any reason why pain should reside in the heart? In order to examine the interior of the organ, the origin of her life, her vital energy, her heartsblood, she would, she learned, have to make an incision on the posterior surface of the left auricle from the pulmonary veins on one side to those on the other. The incision would need to be made a little way into the vessels. Then a second incision from the middle of the first, down to the appendix. And there it was. Quite unimpressive really, a hollow fist of muscle, pulsing in the electric light. It looked perfectly healthy to her untrained eye. No sign of inflammation, no obvious interruptions in the steady pumping motion, no cause for alarm. Puzzling, then, the common belief that grief was palpable, a pain of the heart. 'Not that I'm grieving,' she told herself. 'It's not that bad. It could be a lot worse.' Aligning the fleshy edges of the incisions she'd made, she held them neatly closed until the bleeding stopped.

*   *   *

He held her in his arms. She kissed his neck. 'I love your neck,' she said, her voice muffled by the collar of his shirt, 'the way it joins your head to the rest of you.' She surfaced, whispered close into his ear, 'That's in case you couldn't remember what your neck was for.' He smiled. 'I came up to tell you I really love you tonight,' he said.

*   *   *

His leathery hands worked gently. A slow, circular motion, more caress than scour. She thought of him as a jeweller, cleaning old clock faces and coins, polishing the metal till it sang. Beneath his hands, the rust fell away in a fine reddish-brown powder. She smiled, thinking of how he slept in the mornings with the cat in his arms. 'I don't want to hurt you,' he said, his hands working over the contours of her high cheekbones. 'You're not,' she said. When he was done, he stepped back, admiring her. She felt radiant.

*   *   *

'I wouldn't say "Till death do us part," a friend told her, 'because I didn't know what might happen, how I might change. I know I'm not the woman I was ten years ago. I'm not the woman he married.' They agreed that marriage was a constant struggle, a series of compromises, a blend of pain and joy. She thought of the vows she had made with him, and of her belief that she would want to love him no matter how he grew, or what he changed into. She thought about the core of him, the marrow of the man she loved. She wanted love without conditions, without rules.

*　　*　　*

'I don't know what to do,' she told him. 'You're doing everything right,' he said. 'I want to know if you have a plan,' she said. 'I want to stop seeing other women,' he said. 'That's not having a plan,' she said. 'Because nothing's changing, you know?' He said he knew. He looked at her helplessly. He wanted to do it, he said, he wanted to try. It was time, he knew that.

*　　*　　*

'The swing between anger and love is a natural one,' she wrote. 'I know, because I pushed off with my own two feet. Is it a big thing or a small thing?' she wrote. 'I don't know anymore, it changes shape so skilfully and so often. And come to think of it, this feels more like washing than weeping.'

Jennifer C Cornell

Wax

BARRY SINCLAIRE could hypnotise anyone, and he didn't need crystals, or a gold watch and chain. He'd been a child in Draperstown when a travelling showman so entranced a local woman that she sat on display in a shop window for fifty-two hours, before Barry stepped forward and broke the spell. At seventeen he'd cured a woman with a riot of symptoms who had labelled the painful parts of her body with the names of the medical men and women who had treated her previously, without success. His most famous case was that of a man who'd not crossed a road in sixty-four years; even a few of the English papers had printed a photo of the man and Barry, walking together through an open field.

Signs led us through the hotel lobby and up the stairs to the second floor till we reached a long table flanked by easels displaying posters of Barry. Behind the table sat two girls with clipboards. Symptoms? one of them asked my father, while the other one counted our money and recorded the sum before pulling two tickets from the deck in her hand. My father described how he had trouble sleeping, how he'd tried requesting additional hours in the hope that exhaustion would help him rest undisturbed, but with orders way down and nothing new coming in, he'd been cut back to three days a week instead. At home he'd start books he wouldn't finish and cook us large meals he barely touched. There was more to it, too, that he didn't tell her. Though by now I'd begun to accept that apart from keeping a blanket ready there was little I could do, the first time it happened I panicked: I snapped my fingers and waved my hands, called his name loudly, even shook his arm, though the doctor I'd rung had advised against it, but he hadn't noticed. For over an hour we'd stood together in the open doorway, until my father turned without warning and went back up to bed of his own accord.

Stress, maybe? the first girl offered, consulting a list of available options.

You tell me, my father answered. The girl stopped her pencil just short of the page and eyed him without humour. Aye, alright, he added dryly. That'll do.

We were put into groups according to malady. There were seven each of smokers and addicts, nine overeaters and six who drank too much. Those with arthritis went in early while a party of people suffering from migraine who'd been held up at roadblocks outside Cultra were still checking in with the cloakroom attendant in the lobby downstairs. Bed-wetters and nail-biters went in with their parents just as the pregnant women came out, talking of buckets of cold and hot water, induced anaesthesia, and quick, painless birth. The one individual with constipation emerged with a look of relief on his face. In fact, only those troubled by low self-esteem or a lack of self-confidence reappeared looking much the same as before.

One of the men in our group had a dog with him the size of a hen. When they called us in finally the dog hurried after, but the man at the entrance collecting tickets halted the queue and reached back to seize the other man's sleeve.

Hold on, mate, he said. You can't bring him in there.

The other man shrugged. What can I do? He won't leave me alone. I put up fences and he digs out under them. He jumps out the windows if he's locked in the house. He's like bloody Houdini. I've tried to get rid of him, but he won't stay away.

I don't make the rules, the ticket man told him. But he's not gettin' in.

Again the man shrugged. I've given up, he answered. If you think you can stop him, go right ahead.

Just grab'm for us, will youse? said the ticket man wearily, so the man caught the dog by its scruff and handed it over. Someone else fetched a bin and between the three of them they got the dog underneath it. He'll be alright, the ticket man told me crossly as we filed past him, though I hadn't protested. You got a problem with it, ring the RSPCA.

Though he'd led the way into the auditorium, my father left the choice of seating to me. From what was left I selected a place near the front, well away from the exits, but still I disliked the distance between us enforced by the wide, outstretched arms of our chairs, so I got up from mine and stood next to my father's.

Now don't start, luv, he said. Go on, sit down. I'm here, amn't I? I won't run away.

I knew he wouldn't. He was a man who honoured commitments, and I'd made him promise he'd attend in good faith. All the same, it hadn't been easy. If his condition was worsening, as everyone said, it was largely because he'd relinquished concern for it and no longer bothered to fill prescriptions or show up when scheduled for further tests. At my insistence he had seen a specialist, but two days later he was halfway to Poleglass in his nightshirt and slippers, with no explanation whatsoever to offer the occupants of the RUC landrover which had been his escort for nearly a mile. They brought him home discreetly enough, but still the curious had come to their windows and rumours began that the two were related, my mother's absence and his arrest. Only then would he look at the clippings I'd saved, praising Barry. Why not, eh? he'd said, after weeks of resistance. There's no reason not to. It can't do any harm.

What time d'you have, luv? my father asked the woman beside him. When she told him he grunted and turned away.

He's worth the wait, the woman assured him. I've come eight times now and I always enjoy it.

My father cast me a look of gloomy triumph, as if he'd just

won a point that no longer mattered. Where have you brought me, wee girl, he muttered. Eight times, for God's sake, and he's not cured her yet?

Yet when Barry did step from behind the curtain on to the stage, my father sat up and straightened himself like a schoolboy. To save time he'd lost in earlier sessions, Barry dispensed with his introduction and instead moved at once to what he predicted were our most likely fears: that he would abuse his power over us to entertain others, and that in the end, hypnosis would prove an ineffectual cure. While it was true, he admitted, that the treatment could work only if we did not resist it, even so he could make us do nothing that would cause us embarrassment, or was opposed in any way to our moral sense – nothing, in short, that we'd not freely agree to when conscious and in full control. The ordeal would be painless, he promised, and there was no chance that having gone under we would not wake up. The rest was a question of self-empowerment, and our own willingness to abandon ideas that had no foundation, no matter how fiercely we might believe them.

Are youse ready? he asked with sudden energy, and the whole room nodded. When he gave the signal we placed our right elbows on the arms of our chairs and, as instructed, thought about things that weren't in the room while he spoke quietly to our open palms – Fingers, rise up now, he was saying. Muscles, contract – until I saw arms everywhere lift off their cushions, and thought about Gulliver waking from slumber, how even the locks of his hair were secured. Once, as part of a cross-community venture, I'd attended a service at which Catholics and Protestants had gathered together to share their experience of a common God. When they bent their heads to enter a prayer, I too closed my eyes and folded my hands and opened my heart to the same Holy Spirit I could sense communing with the others there, but still I remained outside the experience, alone among the genuine many with a faith in each other and in Heaven as palpable as steam. Now the same failure opened my eyes to the faces around me, expecting to see that private conviction from which I'd always been shut out before. Instead, their expressions were as I knew mine had been, pinched with the effort of concentration, distracted by appetite, incomplete conversations, worrisome footsteps in the room overhead – the difference being, however, that unlike me, they weren't giving in. The previous year I'd had a teacher who had read aloud from Virgil's *Aeneid* while a bat induced chaos all over the room. Its evasive arcs and sudden diagonals had produced such hysteria that another instructor from the class-room next-door had stepped in finally to protest the noise, and even then he'd kept on reading. Only when the caretaker arrived with a broom and murdered the beast did his eyes leave the page. He closed the book then, collected his things from the desk in front of him, went straight to the headmaster's office, but he did not resign, and the next day was back as if nothing had happened. Jobs are scarce, luv, my father said when I told him the story. The way things are these days, if you give one up you'll not find another. I had no sympathy then for that explanation, siding instead with my mother's argument that the meagre security of the familiar should not be the reason we stay in a place where we're no longer happy. But later, after she'd left us, and the drawers in the kitchen filled up with boxes with a single match in them and the cupboards grew cluttered with weightless tins that rattled when shaken, for he would not use the last of anything, and he would not let anyone throw them out – after weeks during which he boiled no water so as not to empty the kettle she'd filled, I began to think it might be more admirable to take on discontent, however sure a contender, if that were the only way left to shield another, to protect them from its hammering blows.

When I looked to Barry for the guidance he'd promised, I couldn't find him; at first I didn't realise that he'd left the room. Sounding so much like the man himself that no one had noticed he'd made the switch, a tape of his voice was slowly winding from one spool to the other in full view of those whose eyes fluttered gently behind their closed lids, their uplifted faces, even my father's, oblivious and serene.

I stood up myself then. I'd just pulled the door shut on the people behind me when I saw Barry step out of a lift across the hall.

Hullo, he said. What're you out here for?

I shook my head dumbly. I had expected him to be apologetic, a little embarrassed, to offer some explanation, at least, as to where he'd been, but instead his expression was that of a man called away from enjoying a short-lived pleasure to attend to some inconsequential matter which anyone else could have handled just as well.

Who is it you're with? The big fella, isn't it? Is that your daddy?

I nodded. We looked at each other in silence for a moment, then he thrust his hand in his pocket and rattled his change.

I'm not a magician, he said, as if refuting an accusation. There's only so much a person can do.

I didn't deny it. I'd tried everything with my father and it had made no difference.

How old are you? he demanded abruptly, then complained, when I told him, that I didn't look twelve. I began to explain I was tall for my age when he said just as suddenly, Give us your hand – and keep those eyes closed, too, till I tell you to open them. An awkward movement tugged me towards him and again I heard the tinkle of coins. I'm going to give you a penny, he continued, adjusting his grip, and I want you to close your fist over it; tight, now; that's it. Now don't let go of it till I give you the signal.

I felt the hot press of that coin, could feel its two faces imprinting my skin, and thought again of the opportunities I'd wasted, knowing at once I'd miss this one, too. On a school trip to Paris with Protestant children, I'd seen an American carve her name into the Arc de Triomphe. She'd been with two

others who'd watched her do it and held her things for her
while she gouged at the stone. I'd wanted at least to register
protest, but a boy I fancied had threatened to leave me, to
pretend not to know me if I made a scene. I'd done nothing
either the time I'd been a witness in the company of others
headed up Botanic Avenue towards University Street – middle-
aged men in professional attire, bakery girls in their pinnies
and caps, a gaggle of students whose jackets and cardigans, too
warm for the season, had been tied round their waists, and a
boy with long hair directly in front of me, a large, lazy dog on
a lead by his side — all ambling past a man who wore boots
that had seen lots of action, lounging with three others like him
on the broken front step of a derelict house. He'd pushed off
from the wall with the unhurried thrust of a swimmer reversing, and then kicked the boy's dog so hard its ribs cracked. The
boy clutched the lead close to the collar, crossed the street at a
trot and hurried back towards Donegal Pass while the animal
screamed, and I kept on walking, we all kept on walking, past
the uniformed guard at the gate to the Gardens, past the RUC
vehicle parked just inside, and there was no reason for it, we
would have risked nothing, no one need ever have known we'd
informed.

You can open your eyes now, Barry said finally, then he
placed his hands on my shoulders as I stood in front of him,
blocking the way, and not ungently moved me aside. Keep the
penny, he added lightly – a wee souvenir, so you don't forget
me. Of course, if you don't want to keep it, you could give it
back.

My eyes fell to my palm and its contents, still tightly
scrolled, but like other watched things it remained unrespon-
sive, though I used all my strength to will its release. Yours it is,
then, Barry said. As he slipped back into the room behind me,
I heard the door just brush the carpet, twice, like a breath.
Across the hallway a lift split open and a cleaner appeared,
wheeling a barrow whose stock of towels wobbed deliciously,

the mischievous spring of the laundered fabric barely contain-
able under her hand. Won't be long now, luv, she called when
she saw me. They'll be comin out t' there any minute, you'll see.

There was a boy beside him when my father emerged. His
arms were thin above the elbow, and his cheeks and chin
looked unused to razors.

You'll do it, then? he was saying. You promise?

Right away, my father answered.

Thanks a lot, the boy said earnestly, and gave my father a set
of keys. We crossed the courtyard together to the security gates
and stepped out on to the street, where taxis had queued to
collect the departing. The boy looked both ways as though
expecting an ambush, then took off at a run away from the town.

What did he want? I asked my father.

Just a wee favour, luv. He doesn't have time to do it himself.

The boy was a joyrider who'd ignored several warnings.
When he was finally forced out of Twinbrook, he'd had every
intention of keeping the promise extracted from him to give up
the habit and settle down, but after three months the boredom
had gotten to him. He'd stolen a Jetta and driven clear to
Lough Swilly, where, on an impulse, he drove the car in. He
slammed his foot down as it entered the water and hung on to
the wheel, casting a broad plume of surf in his wake like a
cheer. He'd done the same with a Clio, an Audi, a couple of
Escorts, amused, for a while, by feigning sympathy when the
thefts were discussed the following day. This time, however,
he'd heard they were on to him. A friend of his mother's,
whose own son had been kneecapped, had told her this time
they'd shoot him dead, but still his mother had gone to appeal.
Because of her he'd been granted twenty-four hours to get out
of the country. He was catching the ferry to Scotland that night.

But what's he want you for?

He keeps bees, my father explained, as if the incredibility of
it still made some part of him widen with awe. He's got a hive
on the roof of Unity Flats.

I'd walked through there once, out of necessity, detoured by partitions the police had erected to block out the sight of a Loyalist protest marching down from the Shankill to the City Hall. Processions were coming from many directions, and there had been fearful talk of the consequences if those with opposing aspirations were to spot each other along the way. Inside the complex the concrete facades had towered above me and I'd had the impression of walls caving in. The Executive was tearing it down now, however, and erecting two- and three-bedroom houses in its place; only a few of the original buildings were still inhabited. Most of the curtains had been pulled from their windows, the naked panes torn by objects that left neat holes upon entry, as if the glass had been soft and silent when it broke. Disused balconies on the lower floors were filling with rubbish from passing pedestrians, and the stairwells had the fugitive look of abandoned campsites. Even the murals were outdated now and beginning to fade.

On the roof of the building the boy had specified sat the hive, raised on cinder blocks and facing south, near a faucet that swelled and dripped and a shed containing the boy's tools and brushes. On a nail by the shed hung a muslin jumpsuit which my father ignored. He'd been stung so often he could approach any colony, managed or wild, without protection, even open a hive ungloved and bare-chested while their bright, humming bodies settled on his. I hadn't his courage. An acquaintance of his, having heard of his talent, asked him once to dispose of a nest he'd found in a tree on his property, from which large numbers of bees set out each day to enter the house through a drainpipe or flue. When I joined my father on that inspection I insisted the insects be well sedated before I drew close. Now, squatting comfortably to one side of the hive, he called me over.

It's alright, he insisted when I shook my head. C'mere till you see.

The boy had told him the queen might be failing and he suspected the colony was preparing to swarm. I watched from a distance as they whirred and huddled, trying to summon what I knew about bees – that through an intricate, mathematical language they communicate distance and direction, and yet are myopic, confused by the movement of branches and leaves; that the queen bee, once mated, returns to the hive and never leaves it; that some fifty thousand of her children, working together, perform the life functions of a single being, the survival of each depending on all. My father and I had begun reading books about their behaviour during the twenty-eight months he worked for a farmer transporting honey and beeswax candles to health food groceries throughout the North. The farmer, whose business was small but successful, had approved of my father's undesigning enthusiasm and enlisted his help in the run-up to harvest. But then the man's son was murdered in Derry and he sold the business. He sold his house, too, and moved to New Zealand, and my father, who could not afford to buy it from him, was forced to give up the van he'd been driving and find work in a factory, away from bees.

With no trees near by for the swarm to land on, the boy had provided a short wooden scaffold in a bucket of sand. A few scouts moved busily along its crossed beams, relaying their signal to the rest of the colony; already a slender column had struck out from the hive. Leave her, my father said when one of their number stopped on my sleeve and argued furiously with the threads that delayed her before flying on. Of the short films on nature we'd been shown in school recently, the best was a slow-motion sequence which revealed the demanding contortions that various species of flight involve. Observing the thickening spout of bodies in motion and wondering how such complex choreographies failed to collide, I almost forgot the unyielding knob of my fist and the coin inside it, out of sight beneath my arm.

You tired, luv? my father asked softly. C'mon lean against me. Close your eyes. I'd've been sleeping myself, to tell you the truth, he continued, but that wee lad was a bundle of nerves.

You should've seen it. I reckoned if I didn't talk to him he was going to explode.

What is going to happen to him?

He'll come back, my father said simply, then shook his head. Maybe he won't. God knows I've been wrong before.

It's alright, luv, he said finally. It's not been a bad day. You missed a good story, but.

What story?

The one Barry told us, when he came back in. D'you want to hear it?

I lay back in his arms as he spoke of a woman, blind from birth, whose sight returned soon after she married. When her husband claimed he could draw illness out of the sick like a splinter, the most distinguished of the world's physicians assembled to see him proven a fake. And indeed he was discredited, his entire practice collapsed in disgrace, people who'd spent large sums of money to receive the treatment lamented the ease with which they'd been duped – until one of his most tenacious supporters stepped to the front of the amphitheatre and put this question to the crowd: if a man had no better weapon against pain and despair than the medicine of his imagination, would he not still have a marvellous thing? The speaker was heckled, expelled from the professional bodies to which he belonged, later he even broke with his mentor, but no amount of medical evidence could disprove the fact that that woman could see.

At length the flow from the hive abated, and my father released me for a closer look. As the spherical mass at the knot of the cross, shimmering delicately, took to the air, I thought of the perfect rows of hexagonal entries they'd left behind and would build again when they resettled: how good it would be, surrounded by sisters, deep in a place where I fit precisely, where all would defend me if I were threatened, where everything I touched was a part of myself. Then the queen fell like soot at my father's feet and he knelt with a cry that turned me towards him.

The handful of cohorts that had fallen with her clung to his fingers when he picked her up. He stepped back with his arm upraised and the swarm surged after him like a crowd of revellers reentering a world where the time is significant to see the last bus of the evening about to depart. When they were first married, a friend of my parents acquired a second-hand home movie recorder, which he brought round one evening to ask them to help him test it out. In that brief film they clasp each other round the waist and shoulders and beam at the camera, their faces pressed close. At the time the house they lived in was empty of furniture apart from a kitchen table and their bed upstairs; in such a space they could waltz or fandango with nothing to hinder them, no obstacle to negotiate or avoid. Now my father moved with the same clean momentum, dipping and spinning, leading the swarm. With the queen imprisoned between his hands, wherever he went he could make them follow.

C'mon, wee woman! he called to me finally, while they churned and swirled round him like a liquid stirred. C'mon, he said. You have a go.

I gave him my wrists and he uncurled my fingers, cupped my hands for me and eased the queen in. I could feel her exploring the crevices there with slow curiosity before the others found her, before my arms were immersed in velvet and cellophane except for the place just above my right elbow where I could still feel my father's sure grip, steering me gently. When we arrived at the far edge of the roof, I turned my palms over so they faced the ground, so that anything left there would surely fall out, and then marked their progress until my father, still taller than I then, and with better vision, told me finally that they'd disappeared.

Aidan Mathews

Charlie Chaplin's Wishbone

IF THERE was any more blasphemy with the skeletons, Charlie Chaplin was over and out.

'I make no bones about it,' my father said. 'Earth calling Timothy. Do you read me?' And he rubbed some aftershave on his tie-pin and his cuff-links because his skin was allergic.

'I do,' I said. 'Loud and clear.'

'Didn't hear,' he said. 'What was that?' And he dabbed a sting of the stuff on my forehead for fun as if it was a baptism.

'Roger,' I said.

Down in the hotel lobby the gong was sounding for dinner. The same waiter rang it like the Angelus each evening so that, twice already in the first week of our stay, clerics had had to stand at reception pretending to pray for the hour of their death while they waited for room-keys.

'They should seal that cemetery good and proper,' my mother said. 'The sand runs off it like an hourglass. Someone will meet their maker there. When we passed it that time, I saw something that wasn't human, even if it was a mortal remain.'

I was thinking what I could do with the pelvis in the tallboy of my bedroom. There were pellets of a foot in my leaky snorkel, though you would need to be an archaeologist with an eyebrow pencil to tell it apart from barbecue cinders. But the pelvis had a way of puzzling you until you felt along the bones behind your belt and pulled up your shirt to be sure.

'Ezekiel,' said my father. 'Where's Ezekiel?'

'That's a Gideon Bible,' my mother said. 'The Gideon Bible is only the bare essentials. When you stay in hotels, you don't want to be reading about Abimbimoloch and what locusts you can eat with broccoli. So Gideon put in the parts you'd like to read when you feel more spiritual or maybe suicidal.'

Actually the pelvis was like a wishbone: something you would hold in your hands by its light, strong right angles while you thought of what you wanted most in the world. If I left it where it was stowed, the chambermaid would faint and the smithereens of her wire-glasses would bed in the brown of her eye for ever after. There could be no ophthalmologists in Kerry, unless perhaps one was staying in the hotel for the fishing and the golf; but he would not want a public patient to be persecuting him at the dinner table. So her gaze would follow me all my life without blinking. And who would marry her? Her eggs would go off inside her, with the calendar dates stamped on them. Yet she would know the names of my children and when they were collected from Montessori.

'Ezekiel,' said my father, 'had a vision. What he saw was all of the bones of all of the skeletons in the world rising up together at the end of time. All the bits fitting. The skull knitting with the spine and the collarbone with the ribs. Etcetera, etcetera. Obviously, I don't know every bone in the body, but the point is, they're human beings, and they don't want to find that their femurs have gone for a stroll in the meantime.'

'I put the femur back. It was the right grave.'

'You think it was the right grave. What does the femur think?'

'It was the right graveyard,' my mother said. 'It doesn't have far to walk.'

She had taken off her safari top to put on the ivory blouse. The tan stopped halfway up her shoulder below the vaccination mark. When she stretched her arms to smell the stubble under them, her breastbone stiffened like a starfish. So I took off my shirt and my togs and left on only the waterproof plastic sandals I could walk in and out of the ocean in. She kneeled down in front of me and began to press the ticks out of my skin, one after another, with her pink pincers.

'If I told Charlie Chaplin you'd been fool-acting with people's remains, do you think he'd let you wear his bowler? Do you think he'd let you squirt his buttonhole carnation?'

My father's socks had stencilled the white flesh of his foot. It was like the stump of a war wound, all streaked with lemon soot.

'And the Watts,' he said. 'What would the Watts say? He may have bombed the Ruhr in his day but it still brings tears to his eyes to think of it. Charcoal of orphans. Whole basilicas of cartilage. I saw him in the bar the other night. His eyes filled up. He was only pretending about the smog in the snug. He was thinking about fire-storms.'

'Hold still,' my mother said. 'Here be monsters.' She was pressing a blood-drop from the crease of my navel, the tiny carcass of a creature that the Hollywood Jews might magnify in their movies about the Stone-age and the Stone-age inhumans running away in their bearskins through the trampled jungles of Liverpool. It stuck to her nail like a bogie and she shook it into the bin among the stones of the peaches.

'Ezekiel,' said my father. 'I wonder would the Watts know Ezekiel.'

What I would do was this: I would wrap the pelvis up in my beach-towel after dinner, slip out the back of the hotel where the croquet had been played before they lost both of the mallets, and walk down in a sort of a stroll as far as the jetty. With a good run and a high swing, I could fling it a hundred yards at least. If they fished it in afterwards, they could call the police; they could call Interpol; they could call the palaeontologists in the National Museum. Salt or fresh, all water washes off fingerprints.

'The Watts? The Watts are Catholics,' my mother said. 'I heard her cursing her zip like I don't know what.'

My father peeled a ribbed white sock over the blades of his toes. It was a moment he hated because it reminded him that he would be tagged after the heart attack, with two L's in his name instead of just one. Even his baptismal certificate was a dog's dinner.

'And there I was treating them like royalty,' he said. 'I'd have sworn on the Bible they were Protestant.'

I wanted to meet Charlie Chaplin more than anything in my life. I would have given two grandparents to touch him in a crowd, and a complete skeleton from the graveyard on the peninsula to have a photograph of the two of us that would cause everyone I knew to feel unhappy and excluded for a long time after they had handed it back to me.

My mother held my genitals in the palm of her hand and studied them. She blew on them gently from in between her lipstick. Tiny nicks all over me were fading to fleshtones: on my shoulderbone, my breastbone, the pleat of my knee.

'Hold on,' she said. 'This will hurt.'

*   *   *

Round and round the washing-line they ran, the fatso with the handlebar moustaches and the ringleted girlfriend. The bowler hat was bobbing up and down in the empty waterbarrel but the bully never noticed. He went on beating his sweetheart like a carpet, raising dustclouds on her back and the small of her back and on her ribboned bustle; and when the broom broke he took off his belt and thrashed her front and rear while his moleskin trousers puddled at his hobnailed boots.

It was the funniest thing you ever saw.

'Settle down now,' said the man in the chef's apron who was standing behind the projector where the hotel manager had sprayed eau-de-toilette like a housepainter's blow-torch to soften the smell of keg-metal and dehydrated vomit in the games-room. But the old gilly beside him had his face lifted to the screen as if he was reading the lips.

'You heard me,' said the projectionist. 'Loud and clear.'

All the children were shrieking and making rabbit ears at

the scowls of thugs on the starched screen, and two of the boys
were standing on the billiard table with the cues in their hands
like hunting spears; and a girl at the upright piano was
pretending to play the silent movie score, spiking the keys with
her stiff, straight fingers and her flopped, golliwog head in its
sawtooth hairband while Charlie Chaplin rammed a plank
from the picket fence into the shaven crown of the walrus
would-be killer and then set fire to his feet. The desperado
went headfirst into the dry waterbarrel with his hooves in
flames like rockets.

'Last warning,' the projectionist said, and his shirt-cuff
shadowed the lens so you could see the tramp's arm brandishing
paper chrysanthemums but not the bowler that he pressed to
his waist-coat buttons or the way he would genuflect while the
woman held his cigarette-finger to her lips like a mouth-organ.

'What they need is tuberculosis,' the projectionist said.
'They need tuberculosis and newspaper in their shoes. They all
smell like fucking Americans.'

But there were no bones broken. Charlie had linked the lady
and they were walking off into the painted mountains while the
bully's longjohns pedalled at the brim of the barrel. The shadow
of those swallowtails stretched out of the picture onto the bump
of the boom and shot across the parquet to the empty waders
under the empty oilskins on the pegs beneath the empty hats.

'Not when you hold them over the side so they can shit in a
downpour,' said the old gilly. 'They don't smell like Americans
then, Skipper.'

Over the porthole door the Exit light was hissing, and the
smells of the soggy beauty-board and the waxed foot-rests at the
overflow bar-counter made the white joined writing on the screen
flicker and fade like the quick-dry copperplate of trick-shop
ink as the cricket skips of the reel stopped short in a last hiccup.

'Is there Laurel and Hardy?' said the boy on the billiard
table. 'Please, is there?' He was the one who had filled a tupperware to the top with sea-water and left it beside his bed to

watch it swell and spill over when the moon came out. But he had no stomach for the crab massacre. The graves in the sand were beyond him.

'You're Laurel and Hardy,' said the projectionist. 'And the Three Stooges.'

You could say it to the tramp. Nothing on earth would bowl him over; or, if it did, he would spring up again like a helium dummy, dust his calves, tweak his 'tache, and waddle into the world. The Pope had watched him in his private cinema, sitting each evening with his Prime Minister and the Vatican gardeners over the mass-graves of their cigarette ashtrays; and Adolf Hitler had studied the shorts on a crank-shaft splice-machine, winding the frames backwards and forwards, spooling and respooling, letting the poor man drop from the cliff-face sheer to the squid and then, just as the breakers jockeyed for his ankles, winching him up again like it was an airlift, like it was Ascension Thursday, raising the dead, reversing disaster, at the very moment that Mr Watt was flushing his cargo from the bomb-bay of a Lancaster bomber over a brand-new German city that looked like the ruins of the Colosseum. So you could say it straight out without preliminaries, without pussyfooting: I took a pelvis from a hole in a sandy graveyard where the wind has been nibbling away for ages now at a lot of shallow graves. I found myself a skull and hands too, ribs galore, and other flinty bits I know where to put by feeling myself. But what do I do with them now?

And he would tip his bowler and tap it shut on his head and trot like a convict in leg-chains into the brown dustcloud behind the violins.

'What do you think of the bikinis?' said the projectionist.

'Ho ho,' the gilly said. 'What do I not think is the question.'

'You should mend your nets at the shore,' the projectionist said, 'and you'd get a real Come, Follow Me.'

'I saw a bellybutton that went out instead of in,' the gilly said. 'I never saw a bellybutton that did that. I thought, would her father have cut the cord, or maybe the mother, and not a proper doctor?'

'Bellybuttons,' the projectionist said. 'I was thinking zips and not buttons. I was thinking how it would look when the sun tanned every part of you the colour of crackling except the covered-up pieces.'

'Step into the shower with me,' said the gilly. 'My face and hands are the colour of creosote and the rest of me is as white as soda-bread. The nurses had a great laugh in the hospital the time I passed my kidney stones.'

'White meat and brown meat,' the projectionist said. 'Even in the dark, you'd know where to go. The white parts would be shining at you like as if they were road-markings.'

'Now, now, Skipper,' said the gilly. 'You're only making it harder for yourself.'

The lights came on then and surrounded us on all sides. In the shadowless glare under a tasselled shade, I could see for a second the spread bones of my hand.

*   *   *

There was silver on the cobblestones in the hotel bar where the day's salmon had been laid out and weighed. My dad was upset in himself over his suede golf-shoes with the little flakes of phosphor where the laces trailed; but my mother said she would go on her hands and knees to strip the fish-scales.

'You're not at home now,' he said to her. 'You're in a four-star hotel. I'll leave them outside the door tonight.'

'I leave mine out to be cleaned,' the Frenchman with the crewcut said. 'But I clean them a bit first. I had my feet washed at an Easter ceremony when I was small and my father was away on business, so I am conscious of how unpleasant they are.'

'Be warned. Beware. The girl put polish on a suede shoe last year,' said Mr Watt. 'Or the year before. I couldn't get through to her. You know the kind that breathe through their mouth.'

But Mrs Watt leaned over to me and her breath smelled of fruit cocktail.

'My grandmother was a saint, ' she said, 'and she breathed through her mouth. Her name was Saint Ellen Corrigan. She is the patron saint of grandchildren.'

'She may breathe through her mouth,' my father said, 'but she earns over two pounds a week at the high season.'

'Thirty shillings,' said Mr Watt. 'That's what I took home at the time. There was an extra five bob because, frankly, you were as good as gone in the rear ball-turrets. As a navigator, you'd be burning up the brain cells, but you stood a better chance of another night in the haystack. Present company excluded. Gunners were goners. Ergo the additional two half-crowns weekly. Blood money. Plus it passed to your lawful wedded in the sad event. As part of your pension. Not that Penny was born then. No, she was born long before.'

'I was born yesterday,' she said.

'I jest,' Mr Watt said. 'She was a twinkle in the eyes of the blessed Trinity.'

'And my best friend was a saint,' said Mrs Watt into my ear. 'Her name was Elizabeth. She was named after another Elizabeth who was named after another one. That is how things go on and on, by going back and back to begin with. My Elizabeth is Saint Elizabeth Robertson. She died of a stain on her skin that I used to wonder about when we played tennis. One of her boyfriends flicked it once with the end of a pencil, and the flap was sore for a week. He kneeled at the funeral service, too, and he was a Quaker.'

'Why was she a saint?' I said.

'I feel it in my bones, funny fellow,' said Mrs Watt. 'Anyone who can dissect a cadaver while she's dying of cancer is a human being; and anyone who is a human being is a holy person.'

'Where was I?' said Mr Watt; but nobody knew. And his wife touched my cheek with her hand, but it was as cold as a corpse from the ice in her gin and tonic. My father was waiting with his story of how he had helped the Benedictines in the prisoner-of-war camp to make wine in exchange for their tobacco ration and how he had memorised the whole of the Psalms before smoking them, page by flimsy page, but the right opportunity had not arisen yet, and he was getting more upset in himself. The Frenchman had sneaked in out of the blue without so much as a by-your-leave.

'Our fathers died in the First World War,' he said, 'and their sons were defeated and interned in the Second World War. That is the history of France in the twentieth century up to the present moment.'

'From the Belle Epoque to La Bardot,' said my father, raising his glass, and my mother was very pleased that he had had the presence of mind to invent this sentence. I knew from the way she swept her breast for breadcrumbs.

'Now you can see why Indo-China was a fracture, and why Algeria has been a compound fracture. It isn't simply that we've lost battles and wars. We have lost face.Unless and until we kill a great many people, we cannot go to bed with our own wives and daughters. Amen.'

'Amen,' said my father because he could not think of the French equivalent. 'But remember Big Ears at ten to twelve,' and he tilted his glass in my direction.

'It's all a question of point of view,' said Mr Watt who was not exactly bearhugging the Frenchman, 'or, if you want to put it in intellectual terms, it's all to do with relativity. Things are relative.'

'The Benedictines used to say,' my father said, 'that the view from forty is the closest we come to wisdom. Babies growing up, parents growing down. Goo-goo and ga-ga. Yourself in the middle, muddled, putting a bit of flesh on the old bones. The port and starboard of human life. Of course, forty in Hebrew doesn't mean forty at all. It means: a very considerable time.'

Mr Watt thought about this for a moment before he continued with what he had been saying.

'Take a man – no name, rank or serial number necessary – who's dropping propaganda leaflets over Düsseldorf in the ember months of 1939. He's been cutting parcel-string with a Swiss penknife over the bomb-bay, and what happens?'

'He falls out,' I said.

'He starts to read the leaflet,' said Mrs Watt.

'I give up,' said my father.

'He realises the leaflets are in French and not in German,' said the Frenchman with the crewcut.

'He drops the bale without slicing the string,' said Mr Watt. 'He hopes it will hit a Nazi on the helmet and smash every bone in his body, from his parting to his pelvis and on down to his piggie toes.'

'Did it?' I said. Because I would listen to my father but this was better than shingles in occupied Singapore.

'God knows,' said Mr Watt, 'but the man who dropped the bale was courtmartialled for endangering civilian life.'

'Was he shot?' I said.

'No,' he said.'He went on to serve for the duration. And the next time he saw Düsseldorf he dropped three hundred tons of high explosives on the residential centre of the city. He started a fire-storm which had all the colours of a Rembrandt in it. They gave him a medal for that.'

'Saints,' said Mrs Watt. 'Each and every one of them was a saint. Grandparents and schoolchildren. Their bones should be relics. Their city is a reliquary.'

'Do you know Ezekiel?' my father said to her. 'The skeleton section? "Then I saw bones in a desolate this or that"?'

'"My flesh faileth, my bones melteth away"', said Mrs Watt. Her pineapple breath ruffled my sunburn. I blew bubbles like frogspawn in the bottom of my Coke bottle.

'No, that's not it,' my father said. 'There weren't so many eths. I'd remember.'

'This boy's anatomy,' said the Frenchman, feeling my vertebrae, 'is the skeleton key to our civilisation. It is much more radioactive than ours because he was born after, and not before, the atomic bomb; a bomb which lit up and laid bare the calcium phosphate structures of the scientists in the desert like the apocalypse of the Last Judgement.'

'Actually,' said Mr Watt, 'I daresay that at the Last Judgement, when the graves open and give up their dead, we'll all sit down together, the bombers and the bombed, and have a few drinks, and not go on about things.'

The Frenchman was staring at my mother's lap, at the splinter of ice that was melting in the groove of her skirted legs, until she covered it with her imitation pearl hand-bag and stared at me. Then her two index fingers scissored on my knee-cap and she gouged a blister precisely. When she held her nail varnish to the bottom of Mr Watt's brandy tumbler, the legs of the sucker magnified whitely to the root-system of a weed.

'I missed that,' she said, 'at the tick inspection.'

'Put it away,' said Mrs Watt. 'It makes me think of the house-dust mite. He showed me a picture of a house-dust mite when we married, and it made me bring up my Milk of Magnesia to lie there and realise they were eating me unbeknownst.'

'Speaking of which,' said my father.

'It's time to think about bed,' said my mother, and she blew out the match-flame on my knee.

'I wanted to walk to the jetty,' I said. 'It's still bright. It wouldn't take long.'

'It's dark,' she said. 'You'd drown. It would take forever.'

'Earth calling Timmy,' said my father. 'Over and out.'

'Then it's only another day until you meet Charlie Chaplin,' my mother said.

'The little man,' the Frenchman said. 'He is a great man because he is, par excellence, the little man.'

'You wouldn't say that if he was French,' Mr Watt said. 'You only say it because he's English.'

'I thought he was American,' my father said.

I knew he was Jewish because I had heard the projectionist

say so; but I was not supposed to talk after 'Over and out'. I squeezed past Mrs Watt and my elbow rubbed the bare knob of her shoulder. The skin was so soft there that you could write your name on its plump vellum as if you were writing with a ballpoint on a rotting banana.

'At Los Alamos,' said the Frenchman with the crewcut, 'the physicists watched Charlie Chaplin in the evening. They cut a hole in the wire around the compound so that the native Indians could slip in under cover of darkness and sit in their blankets on the benches among the tall scientists to watch the little man walk down a lane and turn and look back and disappear.'

Mrs Watt leaned up and put her mouth to my ear.

'Everything they say is a lie,' she said. 'Pass it on.'

*　　*　　*

When it started to rain the old gilly rowed to the island in the middle of the lake where there was the ruin of a church we could shelter at. He handed us ashore, my father and the Frenchman and Mr Watt, and the four of us huddled under a drystone overhang at the back of the building. In our hats and hoods and with our hands in the drenched koala pouches of our anoraks we might have been taken for monks. So I hunkered down among the sour smell of men's trousers and sheep droppings and I wrote the date out, between a corduroy leg and a Wellington boot, with one edge of the cube of pink chalk I had taken from the billiard-table in the games room: June 20th, 1965. But I wrote it with my other hand, in knuckled jerks, because I had been trailing my left arm in the water and my body was amputated up to the elbow.

'There you are now,' Mr Watt said. 'The sky was as blue as bedamned at breakfast. If you peed in the grass this minute, you'd see steam. That's how cool it's got.'

'There's always steam when you pee,' the Frenchman said. 'Even in Algeria. Don't forget that urine is ninety-eight degrees

Fahrenheit when it greets the world.'

Water was guttering in over the high gable like the silver
fringes of a christening shawl. But the gilly stood bareheaded in
the roofless nave of the church with his hat in his hand and
could not be persuaded to come into our pelted heronry. Rain
coated him like a caul.

'It's out of respect,' my father said. 'The Mass was said here.
The monks are buried around us. Everywhere we walk is a grave.'

'Everywhere we walk on the planet is a grave,' the
Frenchman said. 'The whole of Europe is a Jewish plot. The
whole of Russia is a Christian cemetery. That's why we have
the bumper harvests. It's not pesticides. It's the protein of exter-
mination.'

'Big Ears possibly listening,' said my father, blowing blue
smoke towards me.

'Be warned. Beware,' said Mr Watt.

'But it's true,' the Frenchman said. 'In the revolution we dug
up Carmelite skeletons and danced with them in the chancel of
the cathedral. That's the Great Rift Valley we come from.'

'Loire valley, more like,' said Mr Watt.

They stood in the smoke of their cigarettes and watched the
gilly pray.

'You could put it on a postcard,' my father said. 'It would
make a wonderful postcard.'

'That's why I come to Kerry,' said Mr Watt. 'I need to keep
in touch with the real world. I need to find time for timeless-
ness.'

'It must be a decade of the rosary,' my father said, 'though
he has no rosary beads. He's been too long for an Our Father.'

'He's foolish,' the Frenchman said. 'His income for the
entire year depends on how well he does in the three months of
the high season. He could get a cold. He could get pneumonia.
Then where would his family be?'

'He's not married,' my father said. 'He'll sleep with his
parents.'

'He's no fool,' the Frenchman said, and he sighed biographically.

'He's as bright as a button,' said Mr Watt. 'I hadn't spoken a word when he called me Skipper.'

'He's a navigator,' my father said. 'He'll survive anything.'

Then the rain lightened and the shiny world lined up for photographs: of the three friends from the three allied nations, of the three friends and the gilly; of me and the gilly at the cavity for the cruets in the east wall where the ancient altar once stood and the priest presided; of my father shaking hands with the gilly at a shallow, labelled font where ancient babies were ladled; and of the three men with their catch at the gravel shore, holding up their fishing rods like rifles over two trout in a tarpaulin. There was no picture of the four of us taken by the gilly because my father was afraid he would damage the camera.

'Don't look at me like that,' he said to me. 'Ask him when he saw his first motor car.'

But his mood changed when we reached the private jetty and climbed up the beaten fisherman's path among the ferns and the chortling ditches. My mother was standing at the stile beside the sand-dune where the golf-links petered out, holding the pelvis by the tips of her golf-glove fingers.

'Burke and Hare,' my father said. 'Burke and bloody Hare.'

'I didn't go there,' I said. 'I didn't.'

'A hundred years ago they would have hanged you,' said my mother. 'They strung up grave-robbers a hundred years ago.'

'It's not just a crime,' my father said. 'It's a sin.'

I looked down at my drying sandals that would squelch for fifty yards after you left the water and I thought of Charlie Chaplin.

'He's not normal,' my mother said to me. 'Normal boys are squirting water pistols at girls or having a crab massacre. Normal boys don't dig up dead people to play with.'

In the film where he was an undertaker who listened to the coffins with a veterinarian's stethoscope, Charlie had dodged the maniac's shovel by jumping in and out of the fresh graves like they were trenches on a battlefield; and when the priest had arrived in his biretta and bridal dress to read to the fissures in the earth from the book in his hand, Charlie had pretended he was a corpse come back and scurried round the churchyard kissing the holly and the altar-boys before hightailing it into no-man's-land and going to ground in the fancy-free credits. He would have twirled his brolly as my parents pulled at their beards like bellropes and drummed their frosted brassieres. He would have shaken his leg to let the penny drop through the hole in his pocket to the hole in his shoe.

'What is it?' said my mother, peeling off the glove and walking her fingers in the air.

'No idea,' my father said. He was holding it like a steering-wheel. 'Uterus, do you think?'

'I have nothing like that in me, anyhow,' said my mother. 'You can look if you like. I've kept all my X-rays.'

'Whatever it is,' my father said, 'it's a dislocated bone.'

'You'd better relocate it,' she said. 'I'm sure it's alive with things you can't see.'

Then she turned and walked up the hill to the hotel with a half-moon of sun-tan on her vanilla nape from her bunned hairline to about her second vertebra. But my father and I took the long way round by the sheds and the outhouses until we were at the great garbage containers behind the kitchen where someone had hung diamond-patterned socks beside a dart-board that the rain had swollen until it was warped.

'The point is,' my father said, 'it's part of a human. Part of a human being, what's more. This bone had a mother. It had a father. It may have had cousins. We're in the presence of someone who was christened, etcetera. This is not Papua New Guinea.'

'I know,' I said. My waterproof see-through sandals had walked into beans, and bubbles of brown were treacling into my toes. I was afraid that the beans had been regurgitated by a person or by a cat from the rubbery slip-knots of their stomach, but I was not sure if a cat would eat a bean and there was no-one in the world that I could ask.

'Earth calling Timmy.'

'Over and out,' I said.

'You don't say "Over and out". I say "Over and out". You say "Roger".'

'I know,' I said.

'I know you know,' he said. 'That's not the point.'

'Roger,' I said.

My father looked at me without blinking. He could do that for almost four minutes by the stop-watch, but my mother was afraid he would go blind. She would clap her hands in front of him like a hypnotist.

'Our Father,' my father said.

'Our Father, who art in Heaven, hallowed be Thy name,' I said. 'Thy kingdom come, Thy will be done on earth as it is in Heaven. Give us this day our daily bread, and forgive us our trespasses as we forgive those who trespass against us, and lead us not into temptation, but deliver us from evil. Amen.'

'Amen,' said my father.

The projectionist stood in the door-frame of the kitchen, looking at us. He wore his tall chef's hat and carried a butcher's cleaver in his wedding hand. His apron was the pattern of my summer pyjamas, stripes of prisoner's cerise. Two little mongrels had lost interest in him, and were moving toward me through a tractor wheel. But my father dropped the pelvis into the garbage drum like a woman would drop a handkerchief from a balcony.

*   *   *

Early in the morning, when the hotel van had left with all the children and two chaperones for Waterville and a picnic lunch on the lawn with Charlie Chaplin, I went down to the jetty and I sat on the shingle with my waterproof shoes in the water. The shallows were copper-coloured and clear to the bottom, as warm as urine. The dead invertebrates decayed there in their grey ghettoes. Little detonations of silt flowered quietly around my feet whenever I shifted them, like the beautiful concussions you would watch from a bomber, the brown soundless magnolias.

'There he is,' said Mr Watt. 'The man himself. I gather the parents had a bone to pick with you.' And he crouched down beside me like a Buddhist squatting, with his tackle and flies in his lap and his maggot box on the sand beside him which was once a tin of assorted Austrian chocolates you might gift-wrap for a grand hospital visit. But I could not think of anything to say to him.

'I heard,' he said. 'I wouldn't worry. Charlie Chaplin was nothing compared to Buster Keaton. If you saw Buster Keaton or Fatty Arbuckle, you wouldn't stop to look at Charlie Chaplin. My mother adored him, and what good did it do her? She died.'

Then we said nothing for a while, and I wondered if Mr Watt could smell my hair and my eyes and my breath the way I could smell his. So I twitched my toe in the bed of the lake and the silt puffed like a parachute.

'I was always in trouble,' he said. '"All watt and no voltage", the teachers used to say. I went to three schools before the war, and in each and every one of them there was a teacher who thought of that line. "All watt and no voltage".'

'Did you ever steal bones from a grave?'

'No,' he said. 'The worst thing I ever did was to hide my father's teeth on Christmas Day.'

I lifted my leg from the water and it was dead from the hive down. I could have lit a match under it. But if you were baptized in Scotland or America you had to stay underwater for ages like a swimming test for the Sea Scouts, and there the currents were so cold that fish had been known to throw themselves onto the bank as if they were humans walking into the sea.

'Why,' he said, 'is a mayfly called a mayfly?'

I thought about it.

'Because it may or may not fly.'

'No,' he said. 'A mayfly is called a mayfly because it flies in May.' And he opened the lid of the maggot box a fraction and I saw the drowsy heap of wet wings stir minutely in the metal detention.

'But this isn't May,' I said. 'This is June.'

'How are they to know that? It was May when God invented them, and it stayed May until the Pope in Rome reformed the calendar three hundred years ago. I had a friend, a fisherman, and he always called them Juneflies; but his face turned red one morning, and then it turned redder, until even his wife at the breakfast table was relieved when he stopped breathing. That was in May, too. Now nobody remembers what his middle initial stood for, and the mayflies are still mayflies.'

'What was his middle initial?'

'L.'

I rested my open palm over the crack in the tin and I felt the teasing fuselage of an insect pant on my skin.

'They live for one day,' said Mr Watt. 'Twelve hours of darkness, twelve hours of light. They fly in squadrons; they fly solo. When they land, they mate on the water in the creases of the ripples. Their eyes are as complex as the nose-cone of a Lancaster, but they have no mouth. Their life is too short, you see, for eating and drinking. And they have never heard of Charlie Chaplin.'

He got up then very slowly, first his shoulders, then his arms, his hips, his legs, letting the dead sensations drain out of him, the sediment of sleep in his limbs. He was not used to crouching for so long.

'The old bones,' he said, and he sealed the scratching container. 'They never let you forget. It only takes a few months to assume flesh; but it's taking me forever to assume bones.'

'Perhaps,' I called to him as he walked away in the high fisherman's boots that breathed like an accordeon air-pump whenever he took a step. 'Perhaps his name was Lazarus.' But his silhouette only waved to me or shooed flies at his face.

*   *   *

My watch was so loud the earwig shrank from it.

Animals could cross the entire country from left to right, from the coral beaches of the Atlantic coastline to the swimming pool in Sandycove, by tunnelling through the hedgerows. Even a fieldmouse enormously mourning a paw or a sweetheart could journey from the Venezuelan backwash of the Gulf Stream, say, along a system of trenches as intricate as the Somme, the interlocking rootwork of broadleaf and bramble, barbed wire and abandoned mattresses, and arrive in the fulness of time at my granite doorstep and green weatherboard, a survivor of headlamps and barn-owls and the lethal, laid ammonia like pollen around the silos.

'Timmy. Are you in there? Say Yes if you are and No if you're not.'

I knew that was true because I had heard it on British television the time my father brought a television into the house on approbation for Hallowe'en and Poppy Day, and I went walking round and round the living room among the chair-legs and the National Geographics like a radiation expert with his geiger counter, scanning the mounted mantelpiece photographs with the two tipped rabbit ears, testing the scuttle and the picture-railings to find the frequency of mercury, until deep in the woodland of the book-shelves the picture cleared like a crystal snowstorm, and the Queen of England frowned at the frowning clockwork artillery marching towards her, and my father told me that no feeling person was saying a word at this moment, and that even the perch in the rivers stood still under the shadow of the dragonflies.

'You'll be crawling with things when you come out,' Mrs Watt said. 'You'll be filthy. Filthy dirty. And your mother will be cross with me, you know.'

So I wormed deeper into the ticking wet of the bushes, into the slick pleats that shushed me as I entered them, into the damp tobacco undergrowth of the wild rhubarb and the shivery, chittering ferns, and I counted to sixty. I counted slowly, and between each number I said to myself the words Charlie Chaplin because that was a second in time.

Then I did it again.

'There's hardly any point in my talking to ladybirds,' she said. 'You're obviously not in there. But, since blood is thicker than water, perhaps those dreadful creepy-crawlies that feed on Timmy's flesh whenever he creeps into their crawly headquarters will pass him the message that his mum and his dad will be back for the buffet in about three hours; and while I know them to be holy persons, made in the image and likeness of the Lord, they are not yet saints.'

'Twenty-seven, Charlie Chaplin,' I said. 'Twenty-eight.'

'Goodbye,' she said.

'Twenty-nine, goodbye, goodbye,' I said. 'Thirty, Charlie Chaplin.'

Spiders came and went on the hard bats of the leaves without once stopping to stroke each other. A fly sharpened its legs like a cutler. Two snails climbed the white rungs of a stalk. My eyelashes were growing at exactly the same speed. When I blinked, I could hear my eyelids part like an apricot.

It was not until the hotel bus drove up the drive and skidded to a stop on the woozy gravel that I stood up and walked out of the jungle. The boy who had borrowed the billiard cue for a spear paddled toward me with a finger in his mouth and his feet at a quarter to three. Then he smiled.

'You missed nothing,' he said. 'He does not look a bit like Charlie Chaplin. He looks like Khruschev looks. He is an old fatso with wiggy white hair. All the sweets in his pocket were stuck together. We should have stayed here and had a crab massacre.'

Then I walked in my webbed feet through the smoked revolve of the hotel entrance and across the wicker cubicles of the tea-room down the corridor where the hacked stags snarled from the crucified plaques and their antlers hanked the strings of turf-smoke until I was outside Mrs Watt's room.

'Who is it?' she said. Her voice was tiled from the toilet walls.

'Me,' I told her. The antlers branched their shadows at me like a candelabrum.

'Come in, funny fellow,' she said. 'It's alright.'

There was one big bed and two small mirrors, but they had still paid more for No. 22 than my father had for No. 31 because of the sun all morning until eleven; and my mother understood that perfectly. I sat on the bed in the slump where Mrs Watt had been sitting, and the pouches of the quilt were still warm under the bare backs of my legs. Her private linen lay in the shape of a person beside me, first the brassiere and then the underpants, the dangly pegs and the rolled stockings, with the tasty, clear-headed smell of a bank-note that has never been tousled in a trouser pocket.

'I'll be with you in a tic,' she said. 'Wait a moment.'

She was in the bathroom, steeping her feet in the bidet with her slacks pulled up to her knees. I could see her through the fracture of the door and the door-frame though she couldn't tell I was watching because she'd bowed her head and her hair had fallen forward and extinguished most of her face.

'My feet swelled in my sandals,' she said. 'Now I can't wear my high heels. The hands are the first thing to go in a marriage. Then the feet. The feet are the second stage.'

'My mother says you have beautiful bone structure,' I said.

'What does your father say?' she said, and she eased her foot out of the bidet so that the water ran from it like wet wax as if it were an exhibit at an autopsy.

'He says that skin and bones is not as nice as flesh and blood,' I said; and she wooffed and towelled her foot in one of her husband's vests and came out then into the bedroom, half-hopping, and took a good look at me.

'I wonder if I ought to sit you into a bath,' she said. 'You're a bit whiffy.'

'Look,' I said, and I took off my shirt to show her the bites on my body. 'Look,' I said, and I pulled down my pants and stood out of them, with only my waterproof sandals on me and the tank-tread of my belt around my pelvis. 'Look,' I said.

'You're covered,' she said. 'You're covered all over.' And she kneeled down in front of me and touched me here and there, here and there, with her soggy, drowned fingertips. 'You've been through the wars,' she said. 'What possessed you to play in there?'

'They go into me everywhere,' I said, and I gathered my scrotum in my hands. 'Here, and inside my legs, and between my bottom. I can show you.'

'They don't jump, do they? Like fleas, I mean.'

'No,' I said. 'They go deeper and deeper and then they lay their eggs.'

She stayed squatting in front of me for a moment, considering. Then she got up suddenly and went to the dressing table. I watched the two of them, the woman in the room and the woman in the mirror, examine the instruments on the smoked glass surface like a geometry set, projectors and compasses, the clicks and chinks becoming thuds when a steel comb or a tweezers was placed on the solid blotting paper and not on the clouded rink. For a time they were absorbed in a silver cuticle scissors they found there, pricking the white slough of their finger with the edge of one shear. But I was content to sit there with my skin drying on my body like a warm apron of sand after the wave has withdrawn.

'*The Devil Rides Out*,' I said, and I bent over to squint at the other titles in the stack at the barleyscrew bedside table. '*Zero at Midday* by Saburo Sakai. *The Bible's Revised Standards*.'

'If you can't close your eyes,' she said, 'a good read is better than fine writing.'

The woman in the mirror said it too, but not out loud: she spoke it to herself, as if she had known the words all along and was waiting, listening for the line of the song on the wireless while she ironed. Her mouth motioned and smiled.

'My mother fell asleep once in the sun,' I said, 'and the book left a white square at the top of her ribs.'

Slow frog sounds spluttered from the bidet. Wafts from her cottons soothed me. The woman in the mirror had a more beautiful bone structure than the woman at the dressing table.

'So,' she said, turning to me with the bright scissors in her hand. 'Lie on the bed is best. We'd better make you presentable for your mother.'

*   *   *

When I reached the outside wall of the hotel annexe, where the odours of turpentine sharpened the sheepswool scent of the eighteenth hole, I could hear a woman's paid screams and the voices of Laurel and Hardy from the games room; so it was tea-time for the children, six o'clock or thereabouts, with at least three hours' light left. Across the lake the lamentation of one individual bird intoned the same phrase over and over, the same weakening treble again and again, like a tone-deaf idiot child practising a recorder; and it stayed with me at the shore and under the orange struts of the disused railway bridge and across the anglers' rope-bridge to the burnt-down boathouse where the farty bog would snigger as it clutched your gumboots. I trotted on with the hatbox under my arm, and the blowpipe darted over the water and the water feathered its flight; and I thought that perhaps the mate or the mother of the bird that was beside itself had been brought in a sheet of the Manchester *Guardian* to a taxidermist in town.

Where the dunes began I lay low. There were still people about, though the sun was stretching their matchstick shadows the way my mother stretched her imported stockings, and only a few adults were standing up to their waist in the sea, hugging their white abandoned torsoes over the jigsaw of their legs. I could hear the clapped calls, the barking of pet-names and, closer still, off to the left of me, in the crumbled gully where I rollercoasted on tea-trays, girls' voices going mad.

'You must have done a gallon.'

'I've more to go.'

Through the quills of stiff sea-grass I could see the two of them in a giggly conga churning the sand with their bare feet while the pee spread faster downhill, and laughing like gods as they yanked at their swimsuits under their skirts.

'Don't make me laugh,' one of them said. 'I've a weak floor.' And they rolled down the slope and lay at the bottom, screaming and crying.

I gathered up my hatbox and went on behind the gully and beyond the canvas windbreaks where the seminarians sheltered, bus-tickets for book-marks in their Penguin paperbacks and jam sandwiches with the crusts cut off them in a housekeeper's tinfoil folds; and farther again, where a woman was burying her husband in the grey, damp sand and patting his chest with the flat of the spade as she called her toddler.

'Look, Gregory, look. Isn't Daddy silly?'

'This is ridiculous,' the father said. 'He's a year behind his age.'

'How is he ever going to learn anything if he hears you saying things like that?' she said. 'You've been saying things like that since he was born. Look, Gregory. Stupid Daddy.'

But the father sat up straight and the sand fell off him in breastplates, and he had no hair on his chest and the same religious medallion that my own father wore except to the swimming pool. Then the mother kicked sand in his face and Gregory swung at her with the seaweed in his bucket as I jumped into a trench and ran along its length to find a windsock in the overgrown wire fence that would bring me into the fortified churchyard. Down where the land and the sea leaked into each other in a little denuded triangle of ground, the eroding ochre domain of wildflowers and metatarsi, of bumblebees and human remnants, were the rockpools of the hauled Uranian crabs, and the breakwater concrete slabs were still crunchy with the numbered armour of the smashed hostages from the last massacre before my parents had read me Ezekiel's lecture. Even now I could see fresh legs that the gulls had not come for. They lay where they had been pulled off during the day to handicap the fastest crabs in the derby.

There, when I parted the prickly, saline grass with my two thumbs, was a hole I could squeeze through.

Suddenly there was a noise, a rattling, and the bones came together, bone to its bone. I looked, and there were sinews on them, and flesh had come upon them, and skin had covered them; but there was no breath in them.

That was what it said in Mr Watt's service Bible on the page that I had worked loose from its binding with the edge of the cuticle scissors. I read it at the speed of the ambo where the elderly canon counted to four in an undertone at each colon, although it was difficult because the print on the opposite side of the cigarette paper piggybacked each gothic letter as if the real message were being deciphered at dead of night painstakingly over a floating wick.

Thus says the Lord God: I am going to open your graves, and bring you up from your graves, O my people; and I will bring you back to the land of Israel. And you shall know that I am the Lord, when I open your graves, and bring you up from your graves, O my people.

The pelvis smelled of potato-skin and spaghetti, but it was glad to be home. It twitched a bit in my hands like a water diviner's fork, sensing its underground source. I was not sure if it was a man's centre of gravity or a woman's or if it spoke English at all. It may have been washed ashore from a Hungarian shipwreck, or belonged to one of the Africans who had been adopted for a pound, ten shillings a week by the farmers with cattle-grids. But I blessed it and kissed it and stooped into the hole.

I will put my spirit within you, and you shall live, and I will place you on your own soil.

'How long more?' said a voice from the other side, from inside the churchyard, from deep within its prohibited, lumpy precinct; and I thought at once of the muslin sleeves of the rain

trailing across the gable of the oratory to where the old gilly
stood in the science-fiction thistles, rotating his hat-brim like a
rosary. It was the same muffled mouth, as if the flour of too
many scones had coated his gums. But the truth was, he had no
teeth: they had been strewn across the universe, and his diet
was down to pears.

'Eternity takes time,' said a second voice; and this voice,
frank and Yankee, the voice of Paramount and Universal, was
American.

'You're as long as the priest,' said the gilly. 'Do you know
that?'

'No, I don't know that. As long as the priest at what?' the
American said.

'At funerals anyway.'

'This is not a funeral. This is the opposite of a funeral.'

'It'd be my funeral if some artist turned up with his paint-
box. They're always coming here to paint. Then they do a
dance when it rains.'

'We're not grave-robbers. Do you see yourself as a grave-
robber, Kenneth?'

'No,' said a third voice, lighter, more lenient. 'I don't see
myself as a grave-robber. I see myself as someone who's filling
cradles for the dormitories of the Lord.'

'Amen,' said the other American.

'Amen,' said the gilly. 'Mind at the MacCarthy vault there.
There's a burrow that could sprain your ankle.'

I wedged the hatbox into a cage of roots and worked my
way forward on my belly until I could peep up over the
hedgerow where it sank steeply, suddenly, surprisedly, in a pink
dyke. Across the semi-desert of the cemetery among many
wall-fallen headstones sat the bareheaded gilly. He was leaning
his side and shoulder against the pillar of what had been a
stone cross or a megalith maybe, and you would have imagined
he was about to milk a cow or to hear a confession. He had
made himself comfortable.

But the two Americans were moving among the graves.

'How about this individual?' said one of them. In their creamed and gleaming skulls, their accurate, black, scholastic jackets, and the burly books they portered like brickbats in their right hands, it was hard to tell them apart.

'Who is it?' said the gilly.

'McHenry, Charles. Charles T. P.'

'Charlie was a great friend of my father's,' said the gilly. 'He ran away to sea at fifty, and he came back five years later. There was no other woman. It was ships and the sea.'

'Was he a relation?'

'I always called him Uncle Charlie,' said the gilly. 'After he came home, I called him Mr McHenry. My mother felt we owed it to his wife.'

'Was he bloodline?' said the American. 'We can only baptise the bloodline.'

'We've been over that ground a good few times,' said the other. 'It's not negotiable. We want to be sure that every cot in the dormitory is properly tagged.'

The gilly stared into the inside of his hat on his lap. My father had said it would go up like a Molotov cocktail if you threw a lighted match into it. It was as volatile as gelignite with the ancestral grease.

'He was,' the gilly said. 'He was a relation. He was immediate family.'

'Then we'll baptise him too,' the American said. 'There is room at the Lord's table for Charles McHenry.'

'Not just room,' said the other, and he seemed to be loosening the screw-top of a flask as the other balanced his book in the palm of one hand and let it spread its heavy halves like a conjuror's paper bouquet.

'Not just room,' said the American. 'A place of honour. Even for those who go down to the sea in ships the Lord offers a lasting anchorage.'

'Amen,' said the gilly.

'OK,' the American said. 'Then we're done.'

'It's just that they do come,' the gilly said. 'I tell them they should paint the sunrise, but they say, no, no way, not at all, you can tell a sunrise from a sunset even in a photograph. These are people who wouldn't stir until the middle of the day, do you know? It'd be easier to wake the dead.'

I reached back to the hatbox and lifted out the pelvis. It was already within ten yards of consecrated earth. If you could hear a valid Mass on the steps of a church without once going in, you could trust that the vicinity of a graveyard shared in the sacredness of the burial ground. I could do no better. Besides, any passerby or picnicker who discovered the fragment would be nearly naked for another day at the beach, all flip-flops and synthetic trunks and cooking fat for a swift tan, and they would be unlikely in that state to touch what might have been the jawbone of a mule or the backpassage of a pet camel. I lobbed it into the soft smother of nettles and stole away in the evil squelch of my sandals.

'Charles T. P. McHenry,' the American was saying. 'As you lie here today in this beautiful churchyard awaiting the resurrection of the flesh at the Last Judgement when the Christ of God will summon you before him to disclose the totality of your works and days, do you of your own volition, without coercion or constraint, proclaim the risen Jesus, Emmanuel Sabaoth, as your personal Saviour, and so seek baptism by water and the power of the Holy Spirit through the presence of a proxy of your bloodline?'

'He does,' said the gilly.

'Charles T. P. McHenry, your gravestone reminds us that your eternal life began about nine months before January 17th, 1878. Do you acknowledge that everything since then and so far has been corruption and darkness?'

'He would,' said the gilly. 'He was always straight.'

I went in a wide arc that took me down and around the foreshore and along the headland, over slithery kelp and a dumped Volkswagen to a village of soundless rhododendrons where a feeding bird could not have been bothered to glance at me as I passed him. Only the grass that I walked on made a sound, as slight as a smoker exhaling: only the grass, and the coal-fire fretting of scratchy heather, and the bubbly chuckles of my shoes if I forded wetness. So I slowed to a tramp until I could breathe through my nose.

'One, tick inspection. Two, tick inspection. Three.'

The gilly was standing in front of me with his hands in his pockets.

'Hello, Skipper,' he said.

'Good evening,' I said.

'It is,' he said. 'Thank God.'

And we stood there for a while, looking at each other. A planet of midges condensed in the shimmer between us. They flicked my skin like a party sparkler, but I did not blink or groom my face.

'When was the first car you saw in your life?' I said.

The bird who was mentally ill was still at it. I had come that far.

'It was before the war,' he said. 'It was before the Great War. I was walking in a Corpus Christi procession and a car stopped to watch us. Then we stopped to watch the car. Even the priest who was carrying the Real Presence turned around to look. It was a high, open car, with lamps like a lighthouse. The women were dressed like bee-keepers, with long veils that hung down to their laps. My father said to me: "You've seen everything. Go on now"; and I did.'

'Alright,' I said.

He took his hand from his coat-pocket and stared at it as if it was the embryo of a pigeon that had fallen out of a pylon and lay in its fossil swim in his palm.

'When I was your age,' he said, 'a man came to my town with a tripod and a projector, and the parish priest gave him the loan of a sheet from his own double-bed in the presbytery to use as a screen. But my mother decided to darn socks with a wooden mushroom while the whole peninsula carted church benches out into the open air to watch Charlie Chaplin trick on a tramcar. The way they were laughing would have woken the dead. I never in my life heard laughter like that. I was not myself, Skipper. I was beside myself. I hit the wall with my fist. It was the hardest blow I struck, then or later.'

The flies were in my hair, my eyelashes, my lips. I was being eaten alive.

'The little bones were never the same,' he said. 'My hand still hurts when the mercury sinks. Winter, it's a numb class of a throbbing; summer, a sort of a scalded ache. There are injections, of course.'

My shoulder was not itself. That was from throwing the pelvis the way I had. My armpit would pain me for three days now. It had happened before.

'I am not saying a bad word about my mother,' the old gilly said. 'She was a saint in her own right.'

He reached out in the smell of shag and vaselined spinners and brushed the flies from my face with the front of his hand.

'Go on now,' he said.

From there to the dirty foxhole where the buried father wrestled with the elastic of his underpants beneath his towel and stalked away in a pet from his child in tears I did not turn back; as far as the gully where the girls cavorted I did not look behind; to well within spitting distance of the rope-bridge and the boat-house I waded in my waterproofs without swerving or stopping. But then my sandals smarted and hurt me, and I sat down and unstrapped them from the criss-cross patterns of sunlight and moonlight that the weave of the plastic had imprinted. I inspected them like that for ages, the two shuddering animals that had landed me here, their alien, holy swellings. They had walked me into it, the sensible world.

I coaxed them into my lap and cradled them there.

Dermot Bolger

Father's Music

PROLOGUE

M Y LOVER lowers his headphones over my hair, then enters me. He thrusts stiffly and deep. Irish music swirls into my brain, a bow pressing down across a fiddle, teasing and twisting music from taut strings. My breath comes faster as his hands grip my buttocks, managing to rub his shoulder against the Walkman's volume control. The tune rises, filling me up. I close my eyes so that I can no longer see Luke, just feel his penis arching out and in. The set of reels change and quicken. I listen to a gale blowing across a treeless landscape, see a black huddle of slanted rooftops and drenched cows dreaming of shelter. The beat is there inside my head from childhood, in an old shoe striking the stone flags and the hush of neighbours gathered in.

Luke pulls my legs higher, positions a pillow under my tensed back. I do not want to ever open my eyes. The music is so loud and quick it seems sweet torture. It courses right through me. I can see his old face playing, that capped man with nicotined teeth and tufts of greying hairs in his nostrils. His eyes are half closed, his breathing laboured. He looks so infirm that he could hardly shuffle across the room, yet his hand flicks the bow back and forth without mercy. He squeezes the wild tune loose, an old master in utter control, coaxing out grace-notes and bending them pitilessly to his will, while the wind howls outside along sheep tracks known only to mountain foxes and stoats and to him. He is my peddler father, a lone wolf, that wandering tinker whom my mother never spoke of again. I don't even know which isolated graveyard must now constrain his restless soul.

My lover suddenly cries. I know that I have drawn blood with my nails against his back. But Luke's voice is lost beneath the reel spinning faster and faster. And I shout out too, no longer caring who hears in that cheap hotel near Edgware Road, with no will left of my own. My voice is just one more note lost in the frenzy of the Donegal gale blowing itself out among the rocks beyond the house where my father once played. Then my scream is suddenly loud, piercing the rush of white noise as the reels halt and I hear my lover come and feel his final thrusts before I twist the headphones off to look up. The same hairline cracks on the ceilings, a fly blundering against the lampshade and clinging insanely to life in late November, the map of damp on the wallpaper above the window.

'Did you come?' Luke asks. If I did it's my own business. I stare back at him till he looks away.

'You seemed to get off on the music. Was it a turn-on?'

'Does your wife like you to fuck her like this? Or is she more the Country-and-Western kind?'

We lie still after that. Why do I always need to hurt Luke? Is it to keep any prospect of tenderness at bay? In four weeks it will be Christmas, with children waking him before dawn. He gets his store manager to phone them from his tile shop every Christmas Eve. Afterwards they ask Luke, 'Why does Santa have an Irish accent?' I am not jealous. I have no wish to intrude or make silent phone calls to eavesdrop on their puzzled tones. Luke would bring me somewhere better than this hotel if I asked him to. But I feel safer here. It suits our relationship which started in that tacky Irish Centre across the road, where Luke had been vaguely embarrassed by his family over from Dublin for a wedding, dressed like overdressed extras from a gangster film, and I had been drinking by fluke, fag-hagging with a black queen. The only point my mother and Gran were ever united on was that I was never to marry an Irishman.

I listen to the sounds of an Asian family being bed-and-breakfasted by the Council in the next room and think of how the envious dyed-blond bitch of a receptionist gawks at us each Sunday. I had arrived early last week. 'Your friend isn't here yet,' she said. 'He's not my friend.' I eyed her up coldly, raising my voice. 'He's my lover!'

Luke turns over towards me now, half asleep as always after he comes. Sometimes I lie and claim that he calls me by his wife's name when he wakes. It frightens him in case he's doing the same with her. I like it when I can frighten Luke, especially when he frightens me so easily. Maybe this edge of fear has held us together all these weeks. I don't want to look further ahead but I know our affair cannot last.

I touch the scar below his left nipple. After all the fights he has been in, this is the only mark on his body. The Canal Wars, he called them. I looked it up in a book on Irish history in Islington Library. He laughed when I told him I couldn't find it, and spoke of rival gangs of Dublin youths fighting for possession of a canal lock where they could swim among the reeds and rusted prams in their underpants. Luke had been ten, sent out by his big brother Christy on a mission to spy on the enemy. A rival gang had caught him in a laneway and stripped off his shirt before a ginger haired boy with a deformed hand opened Luke's flesh with one slash of a bicycle chain. He came home with blood on his face and clothes. His mother sat with him in the hospital while the stitches were done. Weeks later an uncle had struck him across the face in the street for allowing himself to be caught by anyone.

'I was never caught again,' Luke told me once. 'It was the best lesson I ever learnt. Eleven years later I was in this pub in Birmingham. I glanced up in the jakes and recognised that deformed hand straight away. "Remember me, Ginger?" I asked. The man had grinned sheepishly. Jaysus, they were great oul' days all the same, Mr Duggan.' I couldn't hate a man with a grin like that. I pulled his jacket over his face so as not to leave scars when I kicked his head in.'

I had liked the way Luke said that, the genuine considera-
tion in his voice. But why bother doing it all those years later, I
had asked. What could it prove? Luke had shrugged and
claimed he'd no choice at the time. He might have been in
England, but he was still a Duggan and it was the least that
was expected of him back then. For years Ginger's fate had
been hanging over him and he had always known he would
meet one of the Duggans again. The man would have felt
slighted if Luke hadn't bothered to beat him up.

Luke claims that if they met now he would never touch the
man, but I don't know if I want to believe him or not. I trace
my finger across Luke's scar again. He's had it so long that the
stitch marks have faded into his skin. There's something
vaguely delicate and vulnerable about it. His eyes are open,
watching me.

'Why are you always fidgeting with that?'

I don't answer. I close my eyes and see Luke diving from the
rotting beams of a Dublin canal lock, his thin, white eleven
year old body splitting the green water apart. He sinks down,
his eyes opening in the fading green light. Bottles, reeds, and a
rusted milk churn. Something catches his ankle and he panics
from memory, splashing and floundering his way back up to
spit the oily water out. No boys are left to wage war on the
bank. His cheap vest flaps alone under a stone like a flag of
surrender.

'Tell me about the canal again.'

'No.'

'Go on, Luke.'

He rises on one elbow. Is he angry or scared?

'You're one mad bitch at times,' he says.

'Only at times? Go on, tell me about James Kennedy.'

I know he will tell me and he knows that I know. But not
for a while yet. The story must be drawn from him like a ritual.
Thirty-one years later the memory is still raw to Luke. Sixteen

months ago I had watched my mother die in Harrow, but I had
been prepared for that, with doctors in the background and the
cleansing scent of disinfectant as nurses discreetly waited to
change the bed. Her death had been so prolonged that I had
grown almost resentful of her. But what would it have been like
at eleven to see your best friend drown?

Up until then Luke's older brother, Christy, had been the
gang's natural leader, but, by the age of twelve, Christy was
initiating himself into the stronger currencies of adolescence:
the webs of factory skylights to be opened, the nods of silent
fences, the expanding limits of pubescent girls allowing themselves to be manoeuvred down alleyways. In that vacuum it
was James Kennedy who had become the Canal King, the
reigning monarch of their childhood who plotted wars and
conquests, with Luke happy to be his lieutenant.

Somewhere in Luke's memory it must still be that parched
July day, when thirty rival youths had been beaten back from
the water's edge and James Kennedy's gang had danced on the
rotten planks of the canal lock in Y-fronted celebration. They
had dived repeatedly from the wooden gates, raising a constant
spray of green foam as dogs shook themselves dry on the
towpath and an old tramp hunched down to watch, sucking on
his collection of butts. What madness made Luke dive from so
high up on the lock, and what choice had James then but to
climb even higher? The hush began before James's body had
even broken the water, as each boy counted the seconds, waiting for James' head to reemerge. Thirteen seconds, fourteen,
fifteen. Nobody wanted to admit that something was wrong.
Nineteen, twenty, the sudden rush of bodies instinctively diving
in. James was still alive when they gathered around him, his
foot twisted and caught among the spokes of an old wheel.
Lush reeds were twisted round his ankle. Some of the boys
claimed that the reeds were alive, wrapping themselves tightly
back round James' shin no matter how often they tried to prise
them away. The others were forced to surface for air, while

James' kid brother, Joe, screamed and wet his trousers on the bank. There was only James and Luke left down there, with James' face turning blue and his eyes curiously calm as if saying, 'You're the new king now, kiddo; it's all on your shoulders.' When the others dived again it was to pull their hands apart and bear Luke up into his new kingdom of barking dogs and sirens and the scorching sun.

Shortly Luke will tell me this story again beneath the blankets, his voice cold and emotionless. I'll feel his penis stiffen and know that soon afterwards he will turn me on my stomach, his hands merciless as he grasps my hips to drag me back and forth. I will raise my hands to pull the blankets tight, drowning under the blackness we are submerged beneath, as I listen to his hard excited breath and think of how his heart will beat, loud and fast as if still scared, in the silence after we have spent.

I open my eyes, surprised that I have slept. I can hear the Asians watching a Star Trek movie on television. The carpet is threadbare and cold against my feet. I find my tights in the street light coming through the gaps in the blind, hesitate and then pocket his Walkman with the tape. Sean Maguire is the fiddle player, he says. I think of Luke in jail that one time in Dublin, slopping out and being ridiculed for listening to music like that, as his family name alone protected him. He's been clean now for years, he claims, a legitimate businessman, but he never tells me why he served time, and there are things that even I know not to ask.

The hotel room is freezing. I find my skirt and shoes. Luke hates me leaving without waking him. That's why he has hidden my knickers. He will reach for them beneath the mattress in half an hour's time, fingering the material like some obscure consolation as he imagines me sitting on the swaying tube to Angel, being eyed by black youths in baseball hats. My legs will be crossed as I read the ads for fountain pens and jobs as office temps, while in my ears his tape will play on like a phantom pain, bringing back all the memories I have never been able to tell him about.

The small girl whom I had once been in my grandparents' house in Harrow seems like a stranger locked away in my mind now. By day she obeyed her Gran's clockwork ordinance, but alone at night she'd close my eyes to imagine rooftops huddled against a Donegal hillside and neighbours gathered to hear her unknown father play in hamlets and remote glenside farms. I can see her still dancing barefoot in her bedroom, while my mother and Gran argued about her future downstairs. Swaying to tunes that she could only imagine and spinning faster and faster until, finally, falling on to the bed and gripping the blankets dizzily over her head, she almost believed that his fiddler's hands were swaying in the shadow of the cherry-blossom branches against my window: my own dark father making secret music for the daughter whose existence he had never bothered to acknowledge.

Father's Music was published by HarperCollins in April 1997.

Molly McCloskey

Losing Claire

HER PARENTS didn't beat her. This story would be easier to tell if they had. But because she never came to school with bruises in impossible places, I don't know who to blame.

Claire would like to rewind her life, which is not an uncommon urge in the video age. If I could, I would rewind her life for her, and when I played it back, it would be filled with roses and pointed birthday hats and a shiny new bike lying on its side in her front yard. Fresh Oreo cookies for dipping into a sparkly-clean glass of milk while watching the *ABC After School Special*. A toilet that flushed. A house that didn't smell like wet dust. Parents who gave a shit.

The opening shot would go something like this. A girl who believes she's beautiful (she is) poses for a picture between her mother and father. They are all smiling. Her father is scanning the horizon, as if he might catch a glimpse of God and give a little wave of thanks or a thumbs-up sign. Her mother has what look like tears in her eyes – tears of joy – though they could be from the wind. Because the three of them are on a mountainside, out in front of a rented cabin, in the midst of a rustic family holiday. Tramping through the woods, spying deer, feeding rabbits, playing Hearts in front of the fire. Lots of bellyful contented sighs at bedtime. That kind of thing. And Claire, Claire is looking out over this vast valley scooping and swelling beneath her in the steely-hard October sun and feeling herself as big and as important as all the earth. She's loving all those little animals, all the different kinds of trees she can't name but her dad can; all the berries and toadstools and clouds and shadows of clouds, green grasses, blue mountain backs flat as slate, gulps of air. God's earth, she's thinking – for Claire goes to Sunday school in this life – it's not a bad place to be.

That's it then, the outline for her life. Because once you have the outline for a comedy-drama, it's very hard to develop a believable tragedy out of it. I could leave you with that photograph and I bet you could throw anything at that girl and she would surface, sorrow streaming off her as easily as if she were coated with that special wax people put on their windshields.

Claire is twelve in my rewrite because that is the age at which we met. She smelled to me like green beans cooking in my mother's steamy kitchen, so it felt like I'd known her forever. It felt right. Now, she is like a chunk of me that is slowly cracking off and the gathering crowd inside my head is horrified.

Claire was born in the poor end of town, on the wrong side of the tracks, and no doubt, under a bad sign. A wayward father, alcoholic, amorous and elsewhere, an unstable mother, unfortunately ever-present. And Claire. She worked her own way through college. Engineering degree, private school, *summa cum laude*, life of the party. That was Claire. The kind of person who never needed a map and never got lost. Her life was logic grown out of chaos, like dawn burst from swirling black vapours.

After graduation, we took an apartment together. Claire got a job in a bar like a lot of our friends. But then she stopped getting out of bed in the morning. Slept all day. Never let me open the curtains. She was like a bat. Then one morning, she got up and said, 'I'm taking a trip. To Jamaica. I want to be with Rastafarians, smoke joints and worship Haile Selassie.'

'Fine,' I said. 'Who's going to take over your rent?'

'Rent?' she said. 'I'm talking about the one true religion.'

She did hang out with Rastafarians and she did smoke joints but she didn't worship anyone, except a thug who beat her up. When I met her at the airport, she still had the jaundice-yellow spots of fading bruises. But at least she'd seen daylight. Her skin was tanned and freckled and in her hair there were blonde streaks that felt like shafts of sun on polished pine. Maybe she'll be brave again, I thought, but she just went back to bed.

Three months later, she said, 'I'm going to Canada.' She found herself a little snowed-in shack in Saskatchewan and a Mountie who taught her to fish through holes in the ice and build fires without matches. When the thaw came, she returned to me and said, 'Ownership of material goods is the path to spiritual ruin.' And then she went out to rent a video.

There were a few more Canadas – Morocco, Guatemala, Turkey, Goa. She became like a stitch threading its way in and out of my life. After Goa, she hardly spoke. But when she did, it was in torrents. One day she came home crying and said: 'I was in the check-out line in the Safeway today there were so many people I had everything on the list I was OK but the cash register started going THRING THRING a baby was scream- ing a clerk was smashing those big metal carts into each other I was shaking I couldn't swallow I had to squeeze out of line to leave the store only I forgot to put my basket down so the lady rang that bell that's like a siren the manager came after me so I dropped the groceries apples rolled out all over the floor people were staring at me and I ran out the door...'

Then she wrung her hands and said, 'And that's why we don't have anything for dinner.'

Soon after that, she left me for the sea. When the city had begun to confuse her and she started needing less of everything.

'I have to keep it simple,' she said, 'for my own sanity.'

'That's OK,' I said, 'that's good, in fact.'

She moved up north, to a small town hemmed in by pines. To where the locals swap sadness like a secret handshake, as if happiness were akin to selling out. And to where the fog rolls in off the sea, like a grey carpet unfurling towards the moun- tains, the sea's heavy warm breath on the back of her neck.

We wrote letters to each other. Small normalities began to accrue in hers, like bits of punctuation she was learning. I started visiting her on weekends. She was nice again and laughed at all the right times. Small muscles took shape within the smooth pods of her burnished legs and arms. I felt as though I'd spotted an old friend coming down the street. But she was a watered down version of the girl I'd known. It was as though she'd struck a compromise with God. In exchange for her sanity and a modicum of happiness, she had agreed to abandon what our parents used to call *amounting to something*. But at least she wasn't in bed all day with the curtains closed. And I loved her like I used to, in the way that reminded me of my mother's steamed-up kitchen.

She sent me madcap photos of herself. Claire in costume on Hallowe'en holding an orange and black drink. Claire taking a bite out of six-month-old bread she forgot was in the oven. Claire shaving her head. Claire dancing on her roof in the rain. She held up her happiness for the camera the way some people hold up blue ribbons they've won.

But something was wrong.

Those small normalities slipped away again and her letters stopped making much sense. She was disappearing back down into that black hole of swirling sand and sea and wind. Claire was losing her mind.

It was hard for me to believe because I knew her when she was fearless. I knew the girl who'd written in her college yearbook under Immediate Goals, 'Designing desalination systems in Africa.' I have a photograph of her on commencement day. A sunny afternoon in a Northern California town, her tasselled cap in mid-air, her fingers wrapped around the neck of a champagne bottle, Ray-Bans blacking out her eyes. If I didn't love her, I would've hated her because, in that moment, she threatened to do all the things in life that I would never be brave enough to do.

But then suddenly, life had stopped. She just didn't know

what to do. Some sort of malaise took hold, and her cherished goals began to quietly recede, like objects in the distance which had deceived her by appearing to be near.

By the time the accident happened, I hardly knew her at all. She was joyriding in a '64 Thunderbird and took a turn too fast. The G-forces swept her into the side of a mountain on one of those foggy days. She was three months in hospital, in traction, in the dark. In the darkness, it all came clear to her. How she hadn't really given up her dreams and was being punished for that. How she was the product of neglect. She realised that all the laughter and all the faith of those early years amounted to nothing but a pretty house of cards. That while I had foundations, she had only a false floor. And then she crashed through it, so that there wouldn't be any doubt.

Since she's gotten out, she can't seem to do anything. She can't even decide what to wear, and when she goes to the supermarket, she gets lost in frozen foods, paralysed by the sight of Tater Tots. They remind her of her childhood, which suddenly she is aware of never having had.

'Nobody comes to visit me,' she says.

I visit when I can but, to be honest, what I want to do is shake her, slap her face, as if it is all simply a matter of *coming to*. She splintered but she has been fixed. Modern medicine has knit her bones and sealed smooth her wounds. She is without scars. It is only when I come closer that I can hear her mind chattering, as though her skull has become a cold place to be. I can see the strain of hanging on in her eyes, in her crow's feet, even in her smile lines. Especially in her smile lines, which are etched deep, like fossils of footprints under frozen layers of earth. They are history lessons. Somebody walked here, they say. Somebody smiled widely.

She still has her brilliant flashes. Crystalline moments that glint like sun on champagne. But this blinding, unannounced joy of hers gets sucked back into blackness, and just as she laughed at nothing, so does she cry. Watching her fluctuate between exuberance and withdrawal has become as terrifying and as riveting as watching the magnified throb of an exposed heart.

The last time I stayed with her, I dreamt there was a giant capstan in her yard and I had to keep turning to reel her tears back in. When I woke I lay there thinking, I would, you know, I'd do it. I would rewind her whole life and all the tears would go backwards and we would laugh again like we had when we were kids in school. The way we had when the teacher rewound the video tape and Hamlet pulled the sword out of Polonius. All the blood raced back inside and the open wound closed. We thought that was funny.

Only Claire can't remember having laughed like that. She insists she never felt so carefree. She says she was like a tree in the city, imprisoned by wire, truncated and choked by fumes, but admired for her stubborn explosions of life. So now she is searching for a patch of innocence in which to replant herself. A bare new sapling to grow up straight and solid. It's a wild goose chase though, and it isn't funny anymore. Claire is sliding down into an eddy. I can see her hand reaching up to me, but the centrifugal forces are so strong, they're tearing bits of her off. I'm losing Claire. And Claire is losing her mind.

Philip Davison

Bag of Jewellery

CARS OCCUPIED the space reserved for the bus. Luke had stepped down from the pavement and was standing between fenders, steam pumping out of his nostrils. Would she take to sleeping in the middle of the bed after he was gone? he wondered.

He leaned forwards, both hands flat on the car bonnet like he had the Grim Reaper trapped under it. He was a small man, and now he had a stoop. Gravity had shrunk his spine.

Two overcoats, one worn under the other, that was the price he had to pay for being out in the streets on a bitterly cold day. Evidently, this supplementary weight ensured that the Grim Reaper remained trapped under the bonnet until the bus came.

He would have to get a bicycle, he decided. Not to ride, but to help him walk. You could wheel a bicycle most places. With legs as weak as they were he could not comprehend his feeling younger than his years. Feeling younger than your years served no purpose he could identify save to keep death a surprise. The bicycle would come as a surprise to her, his wife. And what of it? She liked to boast about growing up in a house where every-thing had to be on wheels – the kitchen table, the bath...

'We should have walked,' he said, looking down at his hands spread on the warm tin. When was the last time they were in a car together? The previous summer. Coming back from Brittas Bay with their daughter, her husband and their children. It was dark. The wind was up. The children whinged. The moon swung back and forth over the road they travelled. It was cold that night in spite of the crush in the back seat. There was a draught from his window. May felt it too, he was sure. She had poor circulation in her legs. Her legs were stiff. She was suffering now standing at this bus stop. It had been cold on the beach but it shouldn't have been cold in a modern car. May should have said something. He should have spoken out. Moreover, he should have gone to visit Johnny Mullens in hospital that Sunday instead.

'Is that Paddy Dumphy over there?' Luke asked his wife. It looked like Paddy Dumphy.

'No,' May replied emphatically, 'it's not Paddy Dumphy.'

'What number is that bus coming?' he asked.

'It's not our bus,' she said, 'you needn't worry.'

'We should have walked,' he said.

They were going to visit his brother and family. May was insisting on the visit in spite of his spoiling and his baiting. Luke had pointed out that this was the same brother who, all those years ago, had advised against their marriage on account of her ill health. May had been consumptive. Consumption was a young persons' disease. The streets of Dublin had been full of people in their twenties dying on their feet, herself included.

'He's still ashamed to have you in the family,' Luke insisted.

All those years ago May had refused to go to the sanatorium. She had pulled through by herself. Her love for Luke, her desire to marry the man, had made that possible. 'Personally, I thought you might be the sort to get well,' he had told her on their wedding day. He never did catch the disease himself. Here they were, forty years later, waiting for a bus in the cold.

'I'm sure that was Paddy Dumphy,' he said. 'I'll never know, will I?'

'We're late,' said May.

'We should have walked,' he said again, but she let it pass.

There was no way they could have walked. It was much too far for someone in his condition. Johnny Mullens could have walked the distance as late as last week. Poor Johnny.

'Poor Johnny Mullens,' Luke said, thinking about Johnny and himself.

'Oh now.' May managed to sound sceptical.

'God rest him,' Luke insisted.

'God rest him,' she agreed.

He left it at that.

The man Luke thought was Paddy Dumphy was now standing in the lane across the street. He had a cylinder of gas standing beside him, together with a youngfella who was holding two carrier bags. Luke and May observed a relay of youngfellas hand over money and get their quota of children's gas balloons inflated.

'It's a disgrace,' said May, 'making a fortune out of the children.'

'A disgrace,' echoed Luke, 'the price they charge.'

'You can't refuse a child a balloon at Christmas. They know it and they rub it in. It's hookery.'

'You need a hawker's licence for that carry on.'

'Don't try to tell me he has a hawker's licence. We should call the guards.'

'Never mind the guards. It's a bus we want. The famous number whatever it is.'

She let that comment pass. They looked down the street in anticipation of a bus. None was to be seen. Luke again looked to the man with the cylinder of gas.

'Are you sure that isn't Paddy Dumphy?' he asked.

'Why don't you go over and ask him?' May snapped.

That put an end to it.

The bus came.

On the bus Luke again attempted to discredit his brother. His brother's wife was also targeted.

'Fancy him asking me to buy a Christmas tree and hawk it out there on the bus. What does he take me for? What's wrong with her going out and buying a tree? She's in the Friends of the Sailor. She's well able.'

'Your brother isn't well. She has her hands full looking after him.'

'He won't get out of that chair. I know that. Christmas tree or no Christmas tree.'

'You can't have children coming to the house and not have a tree. You know he dotes on his grandchildren.'

'Dyin' on me feet, I am, and he wants me to lug a tree out there on the bus. We'd be a laughing stock.'

'Your own brother, and you won't lift a finger.'

'I'd never see the money.'

'You're a disgrace, so you are.'

'She went out and got a tree, didn't she?'

'No thanks to you.'

'God help any sailor who has her for a companion.'

'What are you talking about? She gave that up long ago.'

'That sort never quits. Can't you see her drivin' youngfellas off the Russian oil tankers into the arms of Our Saviour?'

'Some Christian you are, won't even lift the telephone to see if your own brother is alive or dead.'

'He'll outlive us all.'

May unwrapped the boiled sweet she had been saving for the bus journey, and put it in her mouth. 'I'm sure it's a lovely tree. I'm sure she did a good job decorating it.'

'Oh he'd leave it to her alright. Didn't he abandon his family for five years? Didn't he leave them high and dry while he acted the swank in London and sent back money for the children's birthdays and for the holy communion outfits? Now there's a Christian for ya. He isn't fit to decorate a Christmas tree.'

'Have you nothing good to say about anybody?'

'Poor Johnny deserved better. He died in the zoo. Can you credit that? He was taking his grandchildren around the zoo.'

Luke didn't want to say more. May knew he was genuinely upset over Johnny Mullens. She attempted to acknowledge the loss.

'It must have been awful for the children,' she said.

'You wouldn't have a chance in the zoo,' Luke declared.

'Were you showing your jewellery to those kids again?' Luke asked accusingly.

'Never you mind,' May countered.

'I told you about that.' He managed to make this reprimand sound like an acknowledgement of benevolence. He was annoyed with her, however. She was smug because she had enjoyed herself and the visit had passed off without major incident. The brother had made an effort. His wife had proved less willing in that department, but she had resisted the temptation to cause trouble. On this occasion she had presented Luke with the easier target.

'Did you hear her – "your plant is dying." "It's your plant," says I. "I gave it to you." "Well, it's dying," says she. "There wasn't enough earth in the pot." Earth! If it's earth she wants, I'll give her earth.'

'I said there wasn't enough in the pot meself,' said May firmly.

'According to her, that's my fault,' Luke countered.

'You weren't looking at what you were buying.'

'She doesn't deserve a plant.'

'I can't remember the last time I got a plant.'

'God love ya.'

' "I had to report it," says she. The cheek of her. Trying to get me monkey up, she was.'

'That wouldn't be hard.'

'Oh the voice of an expert. She got no satisfaction out of me – nor him, the lug, sittin' in his chair. A bloody tree they wanted this time!'

'You should hear yourself.'

'I'm glad to get out of there,' Luke declared. 'Me ears are ringin'. I need to sit quiet for a while. Will we go in here?'

He took her silence for tacit agreement. She let it pass. She followed him into the public house. Everything about his brother's local public house reminded Luke of his brother. Another token of disapproval was called for.

'Bit of a kip wouldn't you say?' he said once they had

crossed the threshold. They both had been in here before and he had said the same thing. 'What'll you have?'

She asked for a gin and tonic, with ice and a slice of lemon. Luke went to the bar and ordered. The gin and tonic arrived without the lemon. He again asked for a slice of lemon.

'This isn't a fruit shop,' he was told. 'There's no lemons here.'

Here was a reply Luke could savour. There was capital to be made out of such a remark.

He handed May her drink. 'Get that down you, 'cause we're leavin'. Nobody's got a civil tongue in his head around here.'

May scoffed. 'Where's me lemon? I asked for lemon.'

'Lemon? Lemon is it? There's no lemons out here. Oh he's in his element here, that brother of mine. He has his own children destroyed with his meddlin' and his selfishness... and those kids you're so fond of showing your finery to probably never see a bit of fruit from one end of the year to the other. None of that lot knows anything about bringing up kids.'

'Oh, and you're the expert?'

'Sure you only have to look at them. Their skin is grey. A child should have a bit of colour in his cheeks, for God sake.'

'What do you know?'

'Christmas how are ya,' he said, looking at the bar. 'He's in his element here alright. Are you drinking that or not?'

The wind was up. It had been increasing steadily throughout the day. It was colder now that it was dark. Too cold to wait at a bus stop. Luke insisted she stand inside while he hailed a taxi. To please him-in-his-two-coats, she waited inside.

In the taxi Luke took a strong interest in what movement there was on the streets through which they passed.

'Did you read that in the paper – about the youngfella having his nose clipped off his face by a gang of hooligans? That was out here.'

May had read the article. The incident had occurred on the other side of the city, in a street not far from where they lived. She let it pass.

'Let's not go home yet,' she said, 'not directly.'

They were together again in the back seat of a car, this time paying for heat. The fare was something they could ill-afford. May insisted on paying the fare herself. To please her-with-her-bag-of-jewellery, he let her pay. There was not much light in the back of the car. She opened the bag wide.

'Careful,' he said with a little nod.

They had stopped at a late-night grill bar. May paid the fare and gave a generous tip.

'There's Paddy Dumphy,' May announced, peering through the window before entering. 'Look at the trousers on him,' she commented disdainfully.

It was about eleven o'clock. The place was jammed with the young, with misfits, with the insensible. Paddy Dumphy was standing at the end of the counter waiting for his hot plate. When Luke called across the room Paddy lifted his cap on a fat, colourless face. His expression suggested he had been caught in some shameful act.

'Are you sure it's him?' Luke asked out the side of his mouth.

'Face on him like a bar of soap,' May observed without pity. 'I'd know it anywhere.'

Luke remembered May's white face. 'Don't buy the girl new clothes,' the doctor had advised her family, it would only serve to make matters worse. It was God's will, the family had decided. Germs got a welcome in this city. After forty years May still believed it was a sin to admit to having had tuberculosis. She had survived in spite of the disease. Here they were, her showing off in her Sunday best, him chilled to the bone in his two overcoats.

The couple pushed their way to Paddy. They exchanged greetings.

'There's a gale for ya,' exclaimed Luke with a jerk of his thumb over his shoulder.

'Don't talk to me,' retorted Paddy. 'Destroyed, I am. The balloons was a dead loss today.'

'Balloons, you say?' Luke said, triumphantly engaging May's critical gaze.

'I've been selling the gas balloons,' Paddy explained.

'There's no stopping you, Paddy Dumphy,' Luke declared.

'It was alright up until about two o'clock,' Paddy said. 'It was a dead loss when the wind got up.'

'You're looking well, all the same,' said May. She made it sound like it was a surprise.

'People have been saying that,' Paddy replied uncomfortably.

'The fresh air is no harm,' May said matter-of-factly.

'Aye, well...'

'There's no stopping him,' Luke said with an affirmative nod.

There was a pause. May placed her order at the counter without consulting her husband. He followed suit.

'You heard about Johnny Mullens?' Paddy asked respectfully.

'I did,' replied Luke in a solemn voice. 'He died in the zoo. Can you credit that?'

'Poor Johnny.'

'You wouldn't have a chance in the zoo.'

'It was his time to go. That was all. It doesn't matter where you are.'

'I seen him in the hospital some time back,' Luke said filling the space with a lie, 'after the last belt.'

'And how did he look?' Paddy asked.

'Johnny never looked any different.'

'True...'

'Was there many at the funeral?' May asked.

'A great number,' Paddy replied. Johnny's wife could take solace from that, he assured them.

'We only heard yesterday,' Luke interjected. Though Johnny Mullens had not been a close friend, Luke was heartily sorry.

'God rest him,' said May.

'God rest him,' agreed Paddy.

There was another pause. They looked expectantly towards the kitchen.

'We were out with the brother, God help him,' said Luke.

'And how is he?' Paddy asked.

'Confined to a chair,' Luke explained.

'He didn't look at all well,' May added.

'I'm sorry to hear it,' said Paddy sincerely, though he had never met Luke's brother.

'Not that you'd want to go out of your house,' Luke went on, 'not out there. Nobody has a good word for you out there. And the violence...'

Paddy asked where that might be. Luke gave his answer and followed with 'He's stuck out there, in the middle of nowhere, stuck in his chair.'

'It's not safe,' May added.

'Did you read in the paper about the youngfella who had his nose clipped off by a gang of hooligans?' Luke asked.

'I did,' said Paddy. 'And the police finding it and the surgeons sewing it back on. Can you believe that?'

'That was out there,' Luke said flatly.

'There's no bread delivery out there anymore,' May said.

'That's the same all over,' Paddy said.

'I've been telling the brother and his wife they should get out of that place,' Luke said. 'Aren't they building houses for old people down on the docks? He should be on some sort of a list.'

'The milk'll be next,' May said. 'There'll be no milk delivered. Under siege, they are.' She caught her husband staring at her enquiringly. She looked away, towards the kitchen door. 'The service here is a disgrace,' she declared.

'She shows her jewellery to everyone,' Luke told his friend. 'That's the latest.'

'I do not,' May retorted.

'There's no telling her. It isn't safe to leave them at home, she says, so she carts them around in the handbag. She shows them to anybody who cares to look. Can you credit that?'

'And what if I do?' said May hotly.

'Couldn't put them in the bank – ho no. Not that they're worth a fortune, mind.'

'Listen to the expert.'

'Let the kids have a good root in the bag, she did.'

'He's always complaining,' May told Paddy in a purpose-fully tolerant voice.

'For a woman that has a running dispute with every shop in the neighbourhood, she's awful quick to criticise. I wouldn't mind but there isn't a shop in the shaggin' city I can go into without there being something wrong with it.'

'Always complaining,' May echoed.

They were both looking at Paddy. For want of something helpful to say, he asked to see the jewellery.

This grill bar was not a usual haunt for Paddy or for Luke and May. Both parties had come here having changed their minds about going home. They would not have met otherwise. Paddy would not have found himself lost for words. They had made much of their chance meeting. For the most part people changing their minds ensured the continuous programme of events. For better or for worse, what was left kept them strong.

'I'm not perfect,' Luke said.

'You used to be,' May replied. Turning to Paddy, she opened her handbag. She started by identifying those bits of jewellery her husband had given her.

Glenn Patterson

Roaches

IN AUSTRALIA she was a pest controller for a time. Roaches, mainly, but you never knew what you were going to find when you rang a doorbell. Householders would look at her sometimes, standing on the front step, look down the path at the van, then back at her, like They sent me a *girl*? But mostly these people were in too much of a state of shock already to protest. One woman opened the screen door with the roaches crawling around the hem of her dressing gown. She stood aside sobbing and Aine walked right in and got to work.

By the end she had three guys working under her, and then all she had to do was go into the houses and see what the nature of the problem was and leave one of the guys to deal with it. She made good money in that job. This was in Perth, on the western side. She had landed in there one day and had seen the ad in the evening paper. She called at the address the next morning, out of curiosity, but it turned out she had a natural aptitude for the work. Well, the vermin a woman met travelling alone, you developed a strong stomach. After four months though it was time to move on. She had heard of jobs going on a floating casino somewhere off the north coast, so she handed in her notice and headed that way. Stopped off in Darwen a couple of weeks, working behind the bar of a hotel. Before she left she got rid of the roaches in their kitchen for them with a spare canister she had brought with her from Perth.

There wasn't a restaurant or hotel kitchen in the world didn't get them at one time or another.

She spent a month on the casino ship as little more than a cloakroom attendant before she was let anywhere near the tables. The gamblers were for the most part Malaysian Chinese, though there were always plenty of Americans and Arabs there too. Aine was a big favourite with the Americans, who only had to hear her voice to decide she was a good luck charm. 'Hey,' they would say, trying to read her name tag, 'Aynee, come over to our table for a while.'

She made a small fortune in tips. She could have made a much bigger one, but she wasn't that interested in the money. Eventually the offers were getting too insistent and it was no fun any more. She stayed on the ship a few weeks longer, counting the takings and driving them into the bank onshore. She was given a gun for this. There were three of them in the car: Aine, Terry, who was from Sydney, and another woman, Meg, from Canberra. They talked on the drive about how their lives had worked out that they were up here employed on a casino ship. Meg said it was bizarre; when she was a teenager she had imagined herself doing aid work somewhere. Later, she had rowed with her parents about turning down a job in insurance and had left home looking for, I don't know, a *circus*, and here she was counting tens of thousands of dollars every week and packing a gun to take it to the bank. She was, she said, perfectly content. Terry had travelled the world in the opposite direction to Aine's four or five years back, and on his return had got into drugs in a bad way in Sydney and had come up here to get himself clean. He was clean now alright. In fact he was maybe the cleanest person Aine had ever seen. He was friendly with the on-ship beautician and she would spend whole hours at a time restoring his ruined fingernails.

Meg and Terry asked Aine about Ireland. She told them the bare bones and thought again how bare indeed the bones had been, growing up in a small town in County Cork. Only this stood out. The summer of her fifth birthday she had gone with her parents in a hired car to meet an aunt flying into Shannon

Airport from the United States. The plane was delayed for
hours and there were police and soldiers carrying guns everywhere Aine looked about the terminal building. What it was, a
plane had come in earlier that day with a hijacker on board.
The hijacker, a soldier, had been on his way from somewhere to
somewhere else in America and had held up the plane with a
rifle. Aine was still convinced she could remember the plane
taking off again, lifting up into the sky. The soldier said he
wanted to go to Egypt. His father was an old man, living in
Italy, and the plane was going to stop there first and pick him
up. Aine was sure she watched the plane and told herself that
was the direction Italy was in. Her aunt arrived at last and
complained bitterly about the soldier who had taken the plane.
Aine sat beside her on the front seat of the hire car and her
aunt stroked her head while she talked. Aine's aunt was her
mother's sister; she was older than Aine's mother and had not
been back to Ireland for fifteen years. There was a party that
night at Aine's grandmother's house. Cousins and second
cousins and cousins of cousins Aine had never met.

In Cork city next day Aine saw a photograph of the soldier
who had hijacked the plane and asked to go to Egypt. The
police in Rome had arrested him and he was on the front of the
newspaper smiling and smoking a long white cigarette. Aine
never forgot that photograph and even years later she would
see someone who looked familiar and wonder who it was they
reminded her of and it would be the American soldier. His
name was Raffaela. Aine's aunt said that if they sent him back
to the United States they could put him in the electric chair, but
Aine never did hear what happened to him. Her aunt returned
to Boston and a little while later Aine went to school and
stayed there fourteen years.

She got a job in an estate agent's in the County Cork town,
selling cottages to rich Dubliners and old water mills to devel-
opers who made them into hotels for American tourists. After
a time she became engaged to another estate agent whom she

met at a Christmas dinner. They looked at property coming into their offices and phoned each other whenever they saw something that took their fancy. 'Youghal?' he might say one day. 'Converted farmhouse, three bedrooms, oil, 60.' And she might say, 'Bandon. Four bedrooms, quarter of an acre, 65.' They were still trying to reach a decision when Aine said one night she wanted to go to Italy. He told her they might not be able to afford a holiday with the wedding to save for and the house to buy. She told him she wasn't thinking about a holiday. 'I want to take a year, see things, before I settle down.'

But our jobs, he said. (He was already very nearly a junior partner.) And then she told him she hadn't been thinking of him coming with her. They were sitting in his car, a new Saab, they had just finished making love. What was he going to do while she was away? he wanted to know. What was *she* going to do? He was afraid of her doing with someone else what she had just been doing with him in the back of the Saab. She said he would just have to trust her. He put his head against the steering wheel, unable to believe what he was hearing. Aine touched the back of his head and realised he was crying.

She crossed Europe by boat and train. In Italy she would hear the name Raffaela spoken every so often and she would look up from what she was doing, and once she saw a handsome young man smoking a white cigarette and smiling, but of course it was all nonsense, because more than twenty years had passed since the photograph she had seen in Cork city was taken. She entered Egypt by way of Cyprus where she had found work for a short time in a bar popular with British soldiers. She received long hurt letters from her estate agent fiancé and wrote back asking him to try to understand. She did not stay long in Egypt. She met a man there, an Australian, as it happened, who offered her a lift on the back of his motorbike as far as Israel. In the end she stayed with him right through to India, six weeks altogether. For the first time on her trip she lied to her fiancé. She invented a second traveller –

another woman – and a second motorbike. Some things are harder to explain than others. As it was her fiancé was beside himself. When she phoned him from Bombay he shouted at her and said she was to come home straight away, then he cried again, then he told her he didn't want her to come back, then he hung up, she cursed the neutral line, he changed his mind, picked up the phone, asked was she still there. Yes, she said, just before her money ran out.

From India she began making her way towards Australia. She had some addresses there that Michael, the motorbiker, had given her. They had parted in Bombay from where he was intending to travel to Sri Lanka. He had left her to the door of the post office minutes before she'd phoned her fiancé in Ireland. When she had gathered together all her belongings she held his face for a few moments and placed her lips on his. It was the first time she had kissed him in all those weeks and miles they had been together. Some things are harder to explain than others.

By the time Aine arrived in Perth and started to work killing roaches, she had not heard from her fiancé for nearly three months and she began to consider herself no longer engaged. When she had been working a few weeks and had a flat with a phone, she called his house and got his mother. Aine's fiancé was in England with friends, watching rugby. It was five-thirty in the morning where Aine was, she had set her alarm for five-fifteen. His mother asked Aine did she think she'd proved her point now.

'What point?' Aine asked her.

'Good question,' her fiancé's mother said. 'Whatever point you were trying to make.'

Meg and Terry laughed out loud when Aine told them this on the journey in from the casino ship to the bank.

'What*ever* point you were *trying* to make,' Meg said, over and over.

There was a party on board the ship the night before Aine

left. Some of the regular customers were invited along and they brought her presents, underwear and fluffy toys. One man, a tall middle-aged Malaysian, who had often pestered her to come home with him at the end of his periodic trips, drew her aside during the night and removing a key from his keyring said that if she ever changed her mind there was a house whose door that key opened and it would be all for her. Aine added the key to her own keyring. She had been drinking champagne and tequila slammers. She was twisted off her tits, but even allowing for that she was touched. She laid her head on his shoulder and let him stroke the back of her head, while he spoke to her quietly in Malay, and she thought that whatever happened in the future she was happy that her life had contained these minutes.

She flew to Hong Kong for a last week's holiday, from Hong Kong flew to Manchester, from Manchester to Dublin and from Dublin finally to Cork, where she was met off the plane by her father and mother.

'You've lost weight,' her mother said.

'She hasn't been getting her sleep,' said her father.

Her fiancé wasn't in any time she rang and didn't return her calls. She had heard that he was going out now with another estate agent, from his own office, and that they were buying a place in West Cork. Aine didn't bear him any ill will, she had just wanted to talk to him.

She had been home a week when the stories started to circulate. She ignored them, but they kept circulating just the same. Snatches reached her ears as she walked past the boys who killed their workless days in the bus shelter and at the gates of the park. 'Half of Australia... Anything in trousers... *Fuckwad.*' The stories spread all the way to the city where she moved at length to look for work. She was waiting table in a restaurant one night: a party of five, all men, all drunk, their faces coarse and empurpled, like turnips. The usual smart comments to begin with. What was it about drink and men in groups that even words like stuffed mushrooms became snortingly funny? What was it about drink and groups of men that all women instantly became fair game? Aine was asking herself this as she was waved over to their table for the eighth or ninth time.

'These bottles are empty,' one of the men said, then as she leaned across the table: 'So is it true what they tell me?'

She looked left and saw him fold a twenty pound note before his raw-turnip face. She was trying to work out if she knew him and, if she did, where she knew him from. The faces around him were too excited even to laugh.

'Well, is it?'

How she gathered up the bottles she didn't know. Max took over the table while she sat in the kitchen and the men shouted out her name.

She shared a flat at the top of a steep hill with a woman called, though not named, Bo. Aine told her about the stories and the turnip faces in the restaurant. Bo was phlegmatic. Men, she said, had little brains and little room in them for anything other than their little dicks. She told Aine she should go and see her ex-boyfriend. Put a brick through his car window.

Aine called his mother. And of course it was all oh-no-not-my-baby. If people talked, people talked. People weren't stupid, they had eyes, they didn't need her son to tell them...

'Tell them what?' Aine said.

Her fiancé's mother didn't reply.

'Tell them what?' Aine asked again.

'Oh, you think you're so clever.'

'It was his mother all along,' Aine told Bo. 'Can you believe that?'

'I can believe anything here,' Bo said.

A month later, out of the blue, Meg wrote from Australia. She had been signed up to manage a new casino in – wait for it – Bucharest. She wanted to know if Aine was interested in working for her out there. Admitting Romania to the Commonwealth of Gambling Nations. Aine thought about it for all of thirty seconds and posted her reply as she walked down the hill to work.

Her parents, when she told them, despaired.

'What is it with you, Aine?' her father wanted to know. 'Are you going to go chasing ships all your life?'

Aine lit one of the long white cigarettes she had taken to smoking in Australia.

'It's not a ship,' she said. 'But say I was to, who exactly am I supposed to be harming?'

She worked out her notice, hoping against hope that the turnip-faces would come back into the restaurant, but in the end she had to content herself with the boys in her town. She took up position among them in the bus shelter one afternoon.

'You've a long wait,' someone said and they all sniggered.

Aine smiled, said nothing.

'There's no bus for another hour and a half.'

Still she said nothing but stood there anyway, and when the bus had been and gone and she hadn't got on it, went on standing without a word until the boys dispersed in embarassment. Later, passing the park gates in a taxi, she asked the driver to slow down while she threw the boys there handfuls of change.

'Get yourselves some sweets, lads.'

Her last appointment was with her former fiancé's mother. The night before she flew out to Romania, Aine paid her a visit.

'What are you doing here?'

'I'm going away again,' Aine said. 'I didn't want there to be any more bad feeling.'

'You made a laughing-stock of that boy.'

'I didn't mean to,' Aine said. 'I'm sorry.'

Rain had started to fall.

'Can I come in a minute?'

Inside, sitting opposite the woman who had almost been her mother-in-law, Aine took from her bag a box containing her engagement ring.

'I'd been meaning to return this.'

The older woman accepted the box and set it on the side-board on which stood a photograph of her son and his new girlfriend. There was, Aine was not entirely surprised to dis-cover, little to tell the two girlfriends apart. She felt an affection for her replacement, imagining her arriving back at the house in West Cork, and thought how, for those who chose it, this was no bad life at all.

'Well, it seems everything has worked out for the best,' she said.

'Yes,' the other woman said, smiling grimly. 'It has, hasn't it.'

Before leaving, Aine asked to use the bathroom. There she withdrew a second box, a little larger than the first, and, in a hole behind the radiator pipes, freed a pair of cockroaches.

Ciarán Folan

Start of a Great Adventure

THE FIRST time Frank saw the new tenants they were kissing on the stairs in the dark. He was on his way in from work, and as he shut the hall door, he heard a low moaning sound coming from the landing. He turned and saw two bodies outlined against the glass panels of the door to Miss Fanning's office. They hadn't noticed him, and he slipped down to the basement without putting the light on. Frank never mentioned this incident to Brenda, but despite all that happened later it was the most persistent memory he had of Peter and Nadine.

When he did bring up the new tenants in conversation the next morning, Brenda said, 'They're nice, I suppose. They're only kids, though, and I'll tell you one thing, there isn't any way they're married.'

'Not that it matters,' Frank said.

'Oh Frank, it doesn't matter in that sense,' Brenda said. 'It just means that they're not telling the truth, that's all.'

Since Brenda became caretaker many years earlier, the tenants in the top-floor flat had changed almost yearly. They were usually students or student-types with jobs in advertising or journalism, and Frank never cared much for any of them. His job as a projectionist in a small city-centre cinema meant he worked irregular hours, sometimes leaving home at eleven in the morning and returning after midnight. He hardly ever met any of the tenants and he kept what Brenda called 'a safe distance' from the goings-on in the house.

Brenda's work was basic maintenance. She hoovered the

stairs, washed the hallway, sorted the post, left out the rubbish for collection. She had keys to the offices and cleaned them during the slack midweek evenings. Generally, she kept an eye on things, and Frank soon began to hear details on the new tenants.

Peter worked for a video production company and Nadine did something in computers. Nadine was cheerful. She would always stop for a chat. But Peter was moody and would hardly ever say a word. They came and went at all hours. They had the life of Reilly and probably didn't know it.

All this was of little interest to Frank, but occasionally he would remember the two people on the darkened landing and wonder about their secret life together.

After some weeks, Brenda began to complain. One morning she found three overflowing refuse sacks stinking out the top landing. Someone kept leaving the hall door open at lunchtime and the people in the offices were worried about bag-snatchers and thieves. And what's more: Peter's bike was an almost permanent eyesore in the hallway.

At work Frank spent most of the day in the projection room, running films, loading and reloading reels, servicing out-of-date equipment. In between shows he would run across the street and buy coffee and sandwiches to take away.

Sometimes he would meet his employer, Trench, on the stairs, and Trench would ask him into the office. 'Have a barney,' Trench would say. 'Get it all off your chest.' And Frank would talk about the weather for a few minutes and leave.

Trench's office was an old storeroom built into a corner of the stairwell so it had only three walls and no window. There was a broken-down projector and a pile of empty reels and then a desk and two straight-back chairs. Trench never seemed to stop smoking, and the smoke seeped out and gathered in the stairway. Everytime Frank went by the office, he would cough loudly and hope Trench might get the message.

One afternoon Frank was passing through the foyer on his

way in for the first show of the day. Carol, the girl who worked the ticket desk midweek, called him over and asked him to stand in for a second. She came back ten minutes after the programme was due to have started and said, 'Don't worry, it's alright. Honest.' She smiled, and as she brushed past him Frank got the fuggy smell of Trench's office mixed in with Carol's skin smell. Trench was about Frank's age, maybe a bit younger. He was married and had a few children. Frank wanted to let him know he had him sussed, but he doubted if something like that would bother Trench.

Peter and Nadine had been in the flat about a month when, late one Friday night, Frank heard a loud sound from upstairs. At first he thought it was thunder.

'My God,' Brenda said. 'A herd of elephants, if you don't mind.'

But things got worse. All that night doors slammed and people came and went, shouting and laughing. A dull beat pulsed through the house until the early hours. Sometime after six Brenda got dressed and said she was going to take a look. She found half-empty bottles and cans scattered along the stairs. Someone had vomited just inside the hall door and somebody had managed to scrape pizza topping along the entire length of the banister. A used condom hung on the rim of the bowl in the second floor toilet. Brenda said that this was the straw that broke the camel's back.

The following afternoon, Brenda took Frank up through the house. Nothing had been touched. 'You see,' she said. 'This is the kind of people we're dealing with.'

Then she called up to the flat. Peter stuck his head around the door. He was really sorry, he said. Things had just gotten a bit wild. They would make sure everything was spick and span by the morning.

'He looks like he's on drugs or something,' Brenda told Frank. 'He looks weird.'

'There's no law against that,' Frank said.

The next day Nadine presented Brenda with a big bunch of flowers and a box of chocolates, but months later Brenda was still finding fragments of dried-in pizza on the carpet on the stairs.

Sometimes, as he watched people wandering in for the afternoon shows, Frank would spot a boy sauntering down the aisle or sitting with both legs thrown across the seat in front and be reminded of his son. Once he had followed someone out of the cinema and across the street to the coffee shop. But the boy had changed his mind and left while Frank was ordering.

One day, when his son was fourteen years old, Brenda said, 'I have to tell you that boy is a thief and a liar. I'm telling you because more than likely you'll never find out for yourself.'

Frank was shocked that his wife should think of himself in this way. But she was right. He had as much idea about the boy as about the motion of the planets. His son was a well-kept secret to him.

For months he watched in silence as the boy's room filled up with stolen items – pieces of stereo equipment, books on chartered accounting and chemical engineering, pairs of outsize jeans and expensive runners – and he felt he had been hard done by. He said to Brenda, 'What do you expect a person to do?'

Eventually Frank tried to talk to his son about it, but he couldn't finish a sentence without flying into a rage. When, unknown to Brenda, he went to the Gardaí, he believed he had done something positive at last. The Garda sergeant didn't seem to take the matter very seriously. 'He'll grow out of it' was what he said.

Then the boy started missing days at school, hanging out in amusement arcades in town, coming home smelling of cider and cigarette smoke. The school principal called Frank and Brenda in.

'It seems your son is angry at the world,' the principal said.

At night Frank would listen to his son moving about his bedroom or hear him crying out in his sleep and he would sense his own strength and hope draining out of him.

When he was sixteen the boy left home and went to live in a squat in London. A year later a friend of his wrote to say that he had joined a religious sect and was living in the south of Spain. Every Easter since an unsigned card would arrive, asking if they would like to make a contribution to the upkeep of the community. They never discussed these requests, but Frank was sure Brenda posted money out a few times a year.

Whenever Frank heard the word Spain he would think of a flat landscape with a shaven-headed boy in a long bright robe hurrying through a distant haze of heat.

The problem with the water started in October. Brenda told Frank that someone had been messing with the pump which had been installed four years earlier to get water to the top of the house whenever the mains pressure ran low. But the pump made an annoying high-pitched sound and Brenda had always arranged with tenants to have it on for a few hours every morning and evening when water was most needed. Now, she said, it was being put on at all hours – at lunchtime, in the middle of the afternoon, at ridiculous times. The people in the offices complained about the noise. All Brenda could do was turn it off. But then Peter or Nadine would come back down and turn it on again. 'What are they doing up there at three o'clock in the day?' Brenda asked.

She began to find notes on the hall table in the morning or pushed under the door late in the afternoon asking her to please leave on the pump.

She showed the notes to Frank. He thought they were reasonable. 'After all,' he said, 'it is very high up.'

'That isn't the point,' Brenda said. 'It isn't only about water.'

Late one night, Frank heard the basement door creak open

and then the pump came on. He checked the time; it was half-past two.

'See what I mean?' Brenda said. 'They're trying to provoke me. They want to force me out of the job.'

'Not at all,' Frank said.

'Oh, yes,' she said. 'Of course, you never see anything. Even what's right under your nose.'

Frank lay in bed, trying to sleep, but the whine of the water pump seemed like a warning of trouble in his life.

At Christmas the cinema shut for a few days and the offices took a week's break. On Christmas Eve morning Frank saw Nadine hauling a large suitcase along the street. He waved to her, but she was searching the traffic for a taxi and didn't see him.

Frank went to the pub at four o'clock. He wanted to get drunk, but he wound up talking to a fat man in a suit at the bar who insisted on buying him a gin and tonic.

'You know, every Christmas I start drinking at precisely five o'clock on the twenty-third and I never stop until it's all over. I never stop,' the fat man said. 'And I'll tell you something. It works. It bloody well works.'

On St Stephen's day, Brenda went to visit an aunt and Frank stayed in and watched *Casablanca* on the video. Late in the afternoon, he thought he heard a noise from the top of the house. He took Brenda's bunch of keys and climbed the stairs, stopping on every landing to listen and to check under the doors for light. When he reached the top landing he sat down on the steps and lit a cigarette. The house was empty. He could hear the attic door rattling in the wind and the sound of an alarm from somewhere on the street. He sat there for a while and finished another cigarette. Then he went through the keys in the bunch and found the two for Peter and Nadine's flat.

When he opened the door he got the stench of rotting rubbish. He pulled up the window in the lounge and turned on the light. The place was in a mess. In the bedroom two single beds had been pushed together to make one. There were clothes everywhere. The bedroom walls were covered in some kind of painting that looked faintly unpleasant to Frank, though he wasn't sure why.

He went into the bathroom and had a piss. He flushed the toilet. He ran both taps in the bath and rinsed it out. In the hallway he found the immersion switch and flicked it on. Then he went downstairs to get a bathtowel and soap. Back in the lounge he examined the things that were scattered about on the table. He found an unopened Christmas card from Australia and read it. He took a glass from the draining board and poured some brandy from a bottle on the sideboard. Then he sat in an armchair by the fireplace and waited.

As he was leaning down to pour another drink he noticed something white and crumpled on the floor near one of the dining chairs. He reached over and picked it up. It was a roll-your-own cigarette. He broke open the paper and smelt the contents. He spread some on the palm of his hand and examined the thin dark fibres scattered through the lighter-coloured tobacco. Frank had seen the college boys who checked tickets on the late shows smoking joints. He had watched them grin at the customers as they came in and he had heard them giggling in the foyer after the film had started. He shoved the mixture back into the paper and stuck it in his box of Rothmans.

He sat in the bath for half-an-hour, topping up with hot water every so often. Afterwards he checked the taps in the kitchen. He rinsed the bath and flushed the toilet again. There didn't seem to be any problem with water.

When he had all but finished the brandy, Frank took another quick look around the flat. He washed the glass and put the bottle back on the sideboard. When he was satisfied that everything was more or less as he'd found it, he shut the window, switched off the lights and left.

Frank was in the projection room one night when he remembered the roll-your-own cigarette. He had hidden it behind a stack of spare reels, just in case Trench was snooping around. The film had started and there was time to kill. He twisted the torn end and lit up. He watched the smouldering paper and waited for the sweet smell to reach him. When he took his first drag, he inhaled deeply. He watched the smoke curl and diffuse in the white beam that shot out into the auditorium. He felt something rise in his chest and then stop. As the foreign voices on the soundtrack grew clearer, he tried to piece an image to each sound. But soon he lost interest in the film and stared up at the smoke particles shifting in and out of the light. He waited for something to happen.

Suddenly the room seemed warm and clammy. He opened the door and brought his stool to the doorway. Trench and Carol were down in the foyer, talking. He felt no sensation now except tiredness as he listened to the voices falling and rising.

When Frank woke, the reel was spinning wildly and the house lights were still down, though the auditorium was empty. The smell of cannabis lingered in the air and he emptied the ashtray on his way to the foyer. There was no sign of anyone out front and the main door was locked. Frank knocked at the office. Carol answered. She was smiling, and when he told her he was locked in, she said, 'Well now, that's terrible,' and smiled again. Then Trench appeared and went down to let him out. 'Get a good night's rest,' Trench said, but Frank pretended he hadn't heard.

The next afternoon, as he was passing through the foyer, Carol winked and said, 'Woo, Frank, you're a dark horse.' Frank tried to work out why he was the one who could be made to feel guilty over the whole business. He wondered if perhaps things were getting to him. He was nearly fifty years of age and most of the people he knew seemed to be dope smokers and liars.

For months there had been no trouble with the water. Brenda hardly ever mentioned Peter or Nadine. She complained about the weather instead. She ate a lot and began to put on weight. Occasionally, Frank would see Peter at the supermarket check-out or get the scent of Nadine's perfume in the hallway in the morning.

One night after work he met Peter at the hall door. Frank said good night and Peter mumbled something and started to climb the stairs. Suddenly he stopped and turned. 'How about coming up for a drink, Frank?' he said.

Frank could see Nadine further up, leaning over the banis-ter. 'No, I don't think so,' he said. 'Not tonight.'

'No, seriously. Come on. You mightn't get the chance again.'

Nadine waved. 'Hi,' she shouted. 'Hi, Frank.'

'Come on,' Peter said.

'Alright,' Frank said. 'Just for a minute. I'm bunched.'

'Great,' Peter said. 'Nadine, make waves. We have a guest.'

In the flat Nadine told Frank to sit down and Peter began to fix the fire.

'What's your poison?' Nadine asked him. 'Let's see, we have beer, gin, whiskey.'

'Promise us one thing though,' Peter said. He turned and looked at Frank for a second. 'Don't ask for water.'

Peter laughed and Nadine made a strange giggling sound.

'No,' Frank said. 'I get the joke. Beer will do grand.'

Nadine handed him a can of Heineken.

Frank noticed some black-and-white photographs scattered about on the coffee table. They were pictures of Nadine, close-ups of her face, and they had the grainy quality of old magazine prints.

'What do you think?' Peter asked. 'In your line of work and all.'

Frank picked up a photograph. 'They're good,' he said.

'They're chronic,' Nadine said.

'No they're not,' Peter said.

'They're bloody awful,' Nadine said. 'Tell him what you really think of them.'

Frank picked up another print.

'Don't mind her,' Peter said. 'It's PMT.'

Nadine lay back in the chair and stretched out her legs, trying to aim a kick at Peter's knees. 'You bastard,' she said.

Peter grabbed both her feet and twisted them slowly.

'Peter, stop,' she screamed. 'Peter.'

'Tell him the truth,' Peter said.

'OK. He's really a genius,' Nadine said. 'Now, please let me go.'

'That's it,' Peter said, and he let go of her legs.

Nadine sat up straight. 'And he loves me. Isn't that right?'

'No,' Peter said, 'I don't.'

'Oh yes, you do. You liar.'

Peter looked at Frank. He was grinning. 'Nadine, where's the stuff?'

'What stuff?'

Peter had moved behind Nadine's chair and was running his fingers through her long dark hair. 'You know, the stuff Shane brought us.'

'Oh shit,' Nadine said. 'Not now, Peter. We have company.'

'Frank will join us. Won't you, Frank?'

Frank shrugged his shoulders. 'Maybe I'd better be going.'

'Oh, no,' Nadine said. 'Stay. Do. Really. Don't mind us.'

'Of course Frank'll stay,' Peter said. 'Now, get the stuff.'

'Alright,' she said, 'but only if Frank will too.'

Nadine got up and went over to the shelf by the stereo. When she came back she dropped a tobacco pouch and a packet of Rizlas into Peter's lap. 'Another one of Peter's many skills,' she said. Then she sat on the arm of Peter's chair and started to hum.

Peter rolled two cigarettes and handed one to Frank. 'Peace pipe,' he said. 'Kind of.' He lit the other one and took a slow drag before passing it across to Nadine who now sat on the chair opposite with her legs curled up beneath her. She smiled at Peter and closed her eyes.

After his fifth or sixth drag Frank realised that the cigarette he was smoking wasn't having any effect at all. He held it to his nose. It smelt just like an ordinary cigarette. Peter was bending down, whispering something to Nadine. She smiled and opened her eyes and looked over at Frank.

'Well, Frank, what do you think?' Peter said.

'Fine,' Frank said, sitting back in his chair.

'Start of a great adventure,' Peter said, grinning.

Frank took another drag. Nadine was watching him now, though her eyes were like slits, and Peter was staring into the fire. He could smell the drug in the room and he remembered the wave of calm that rippled through his body that night in the cinema. He shut his eyes but it made no difference.

Peter stood in front of the fireplace with both hands shoved deep in the back pockets of his jeans. 'I know,' he said. 'We'll play a game.'

'Oh, lay off, Peter,' Nadine said, her eyes still shut.

Peter was looking at Frank. 'Charades,' he said.

'Peter, no way,' Nadine said. She drew her legs up tighter and rested her head on her knees.

'Listen,' Peter said. 'I have it. We all describe someplace we've never been. It could be any place. It could be real or out of your head. That doesn't matter. What's important is that you convince everyone else it exists. Then everyone asks questions and you have to answer them as best you can. And even if it's imagination you can't tell lies. Does that make sense, folks?'

'Sure, Peter,' Nadine said. 'Whatever you say.' She shifted her weight in the chair.

'Come on, Nadine,' Peter said. He reached for her arm but she pulled it tight against her side.

'Fug off,' she said.

Peter waved the half-smoked joint in front of Nadine's nose. 'No more big bad cigarettes for Nadine if Nadine doesn't play.'

Nadine opened her eyes, shut them quickly, then opened them again. 'Oh, alright,' she said, reaching lazily for the joint. 'Just for as long as this lasts.'

Peter winked at Frank. 'Right,' he said. 'Frank'll start.'

'Yeah,' said Nadine. 'Peter's a bastard, but guests first anyway.'

Peter turned off the light and sat down on the floor beside Nadine's chair.

'Now, Frank,' Nadine said. 'Go on.'

'I'm not sure what I'm supposed to do,' Frank said.

'It's dead easy,' Peter said. 'OK, I'll try something just to get us started.' He closed his eyes.

'It's all very, very serious,' Nadine said, grinning at Frank.

'Nadine, shut up,' Peter snapped.

Nadine stuck out her tongue and reached over and took the joint from his hand.

Peter said, 'Now, listen. I see a white ocean and a blue mountain. Actually there are loads of mountains and they're all blue and they seem to go on for ever and ever.'

'And ever,' Nadine yawned, loudly.

'Be quiet,' Peter said.

'Question,' Nadine said. She was leaning over the arm of the chair, the joint held loosely between her fingers. 'What kind of blue are these mountains, anyway?'

'Jesus, I don't know,' Peter said. 'They're just your ordinary blue.'

'I mean, are they sapphire-blue, or turquoise-blue, or indigo-blue, or what kind of fucking blue?'

'You tell me, Nadine. Whatever blue you want.'

'No. You tell me. You're the one who started it.'

'For fuck's sake, Nadine.' Peter stood up and went over to the fireplace. 'Just shut up.'

Nadine looked over at Frank. 'Maybe you can help us,' she said.

Peter had turned his back and was staring into the fire.

'Go on,' Nadine said to Frank. 'Don't mind him.'

Frank waited and it seemed like he would never say a word.

'Go on,' Nadine said again. She had raised her voice.

'Sometimes, nothing ever prepares you for what people will do,' Frank said. 'Sometimes, I just wonder, that's all.' This is how he started but he didn't know how he would tell the story or if the words would make any sense.

Peter and Nadine were both looking at him now. 'What's the story, Frank?' Peter said, starting to laugh.

'Ssshh,' Nadine said. 'Shut up, you.'

Frank looked at Nadine, and then at Peter. They each seemed younger than he had realised. They sat before him like children, their faces lit by the pale flames.

Then he heard his voice begin again. 'Once,' he said, 'I had a son.'

Evelyn Conlon

The Long Drop

THOMAS McGURK knew that people got more confident with age, that they were able to tackle the small matters in life as if they were what they were. Or he thought he knew. But herein lay a problem: he wasn't sure anymore if what he knew or thought he knew was right. Indeed he knew nothing for certain these days. Here he was waiting for the dentist thinking that if Mr Rattigan said to him this time, 'Oh dear, there is no problem with your teeth, but your gums, your gums! Your teeth will last you your lifetime, but your gums! Mind you, your lifetime... hmmm, still smoking, I see, hmmm...' he would say.

'Look here, you're my dentist, that's all, and I'm paying you to look after my teeth, to service my mouth so to speak, so stop your lecturing and get on with the job.'

But he only wanted to say that; he wouldn't, he hadn't got the nerve. And he used not to mind what the dentist said, but today he was actually afraid of that lecture. If he was in heaven, or hell for that matter, he could write a letter back.

'See here you, Mr Rattigan, I do not think it's any of your business what I do with my mouth or any other part of me. Stick on your gloves and your protective mask, and floss away to your heart's content. And by the way, could you cease making provocative statements while my mouth is being held open by the mini-walking-stick that you've just thrown over my teeth.'

Dead, that's the only way he'd ever say it. For the last six months he couldn't say boo to a goose.

This might be a problem for any person, but for Mr McGurk it was a disaster because his job was in PR. 'That's right,' he thought, 'I'm supposed to be a PR man. A man who knows everything, a decisive, in-a-hurry, important man.' But he wanted the queue to dwindle slowly, and yet he wanted to be out of here. Decisive. He was also having nightmares. Last week he had been on a simple quiz on television and he had known only one out of thirty-five questions. All the country was watching him, including first girlfriends and unrecognisable girlfriends that he never knew he had. Waking up had not brought him consolation, had instead worried him further. A PR man. A man who knows everything, a man who is too busy to notice the unimportant goings on of the ordinary unimportant people who walk up and down his road. So what had this exceptionally important man achieved so far that day?

Breakfast had been eaten quickly, the less said the better being his motto at that hour in the morning. On one side of him was his good-looking son, who picked his way through breakfast, and everything else, as if he owned the world and had bought the table. Yes, the less said the better. On the other side of him his aging, his old father who was visiting for a week. Thomas McGurk was being storm destroyed, youth and senility were filling his arteries this morning, leaving no time for his own age.

He had then gone to Foreign Exchange at the bank. The customer in front of him was talking twenty to the dozen, telling all her business. Maybe she was a widow and had no-one to talk to at home? The bank teller appeared to be listening. She told him loudly, cheerfully, at the top of her voice range like a chorister, that she wanted separate pesetas for the two children – for their own pocket money, you know what I mean, plenty of notes if possible, preferably not the ten thousand ones – this by way of explaining that she did know roughly the denominations in question. Or that she had children, or that she was going, could afford to go, on a holiday. What was he doing listening to this claptrap, what was he doing coming into the bank in the first place, when he had more important things to be doing?

'That was a terrible accident,' she said; 'of eleven of them only seven were found, they were killed as well as drowned.'

He was in the bank getting sterling for his trip to London; he could easily use his card and get it out of a machine at the other end, but banks could be comforting. Going to Foreign Exchange marked the importance of country leaving, set differences between one journey and another; it would be a terrible thing if they ever brought in the ecu. Or he could easily have asked his wife to get him the money; for some reason she had the height of respect for him, the last person to suffer from that, he hiccuped to himself. He went to the counter, did his business, chatted amicably enough to the clerk, got his changed money. Such a transaction! This paper is worth that. Now can you give me someone else's paper worth the same. And different people accrued different amounts of paper for living the same lives. There was a lot to Marx.

He should be looking at the ads on the wall; he was a PR man, he should be interested. But he could only look at the woman sitting at the back desk in the office, not that he thought her good-looking, but because she seemed so organised, so engrossed, she must be content. There was a flawless rhythm about the way she lifted the telephone, tapped her computer, put down the phone, reached for papers, for statements, and it was herself who had worked out that rhythm. Yes, he should be interested in the ads, maybe he could make an ad out of her. He didn't make ads as such, but keeping the new successful ones just under his skin at his temple was part of his job in PR. The successful ad would tell you how to pitch your next product. A good PR man could sell anyone anything, could make anyone believe. He used to be able to do so himself. And now. Now he had to hesitate before having a conversation with his wife. This would have to stop. After seeing the dentist, he would go to the office, find out what his duties were to be in London, some new contract. He would cheer up, cheer himself up, take his wife out to dinner, pack his clothes for tomorrow, sleep well, have no dreams.

That must have been three months ago, no longer than that, because it was while in London that it had really started, or maybe that's when he noticed just how smack bang up against the wall he was. The day had been ridiculously hot for May; from his window the street looked like a cramped smoky pub; there must have been a shortage of air because people stopped along by railings, when they could find them, and gasped as if they were in hospital corridors. He left his hotel to go see De Kooning at the Tate – almost rhymed with 'Beckett at the Gate', a poem he'd just read. He'd started to do this recently, first it was to impress clients, or co-PRers. De Kooning at the Tate would sound good. But there was a danger that some of it could seep in, that he would find himself standing in front of a picture longer than was necessary, that he would begin dropping into bookshops casually, that he would begin to believe poems. He'd read about the De Kooning in the *Independent* – the English one – on Sunday. At home in bed. He came to the arts pages last, usually at twelve-thirty or so – that's Monday really, but it still feels like a Sunday night. Tight, choked, a hot London street. A few minutes after the arts pages comes the 'How We Met'; he hated it, just as much as he used to hate 'Family Ties' in the *Sunday Tribune*, where one family member waxed about another, shone up, glossed. He knew a man who had done it once: he had tried to be analytical, he said, but they had managed to change the tone by letting a word or two slip, or so the man said, but Thomas didn't believe him. He happened to know that the man hadn't spoken to his brother for years, that there was a rotting thing between them, a thing that would have been smellable from the next townland if they'd lived in wide open spaces where smells could be separated. Thomas didn't know much about De Kooning, nothing in fact, he didn't mind admitting only to himself, but he liked the name and got fixated for the few moments that it took him to read the article. He checked the dates; he would go see it on his next visit to London, it would fit in. He considered these fixations to be every bit as reasonable as love.

So there he was now on the tube, reading the bad thriller he'd bought at the airport. Even his wife had done more dangerous things in her life than the woman who had got herself murdered in the book. He lifted his eyes too often to check the next station, the names not staying with him, making him look like a stranger. He was a stranger. Last month he'd gone to the hospital with his father, supposedly to find out for the rest of the family what these tests would say, what exactly the matter was, but he had skulked in the waiting area for as long as possible, not wanting to be told about body parts nor hear his father talk about this and that and sigh that ten years ago there hadn't been too much wrong with him. Before setting off for the appointment he'd had a moment of caring and had offered to bring breakfast to bed for the old man, but of course his father had insisted on getting up to have it with him, stealing his privacy, telling him to lift that good coat, making him a child in front of his own child, who didn't notice either of them. There was a nightmare that came often, the coat hangers rattling on the back of their bedroom door, signalling his father walking in on top of them. In the hospital his father had looked at the man across the room.

'Put you in mind of Mary's Liam.'

'I don't know,' Thomas had snapped and then tried to take the sting away by attempting to laugh, 'and couldn't care less.' How brave of him to be bullying an old man. He was nearly overcome by the grief of not caring. He knew that the old man's neighbour took two hot water bottles to bed but kept the windows and doors open for fresh air. Very important that. How he knew was obvious, he had been told. Many times. For what reason he didn't know. Ridiculous, womanish things that the old man would have told his wife if she had still been alive; most likely it was she who had said them in the first place and he was repeating them now in his dotage. He'd been told lots of other things too, of no importance any of them, clogging up thinking space and the telling of them clogging up time. He needed a personal drainage system from his brain, he knew so much useless information. When your head got full of useless information did you keel over? Did old really mean a head more full of memory than expectation?

His father had made a county council cottage into a thing almost resembling a bungalow, so surely Thomas could be a PR man. He would PR his way out of every corner. But like the brave boy who jumped into the dying bus driver's seat and slammed on the brakes in time to stop a catastrophe, he couldn't be brave again and it was expected of him. Thomas had lost his PR skills. In the ward, where they were now settling his father into a bed, more tests to be done, he prattled away the nervous waiting and Thomas knew not of what he spoke. He was a stranger indeed.

He got off at the right station and went to the art gallery where he saw a woman who walked around beautifully, the trousers clinging to her like silk does to a woman. Watching her was almost unbearable. In truth he was glad to get out of the De Kooning. The painter neither upset nor pleased him. He went to the café where he watched his accent and allowed himself to get sad for himself. Could loneliness get worse than this? He was growing for his grave, waiting around to have his name fitted on a headstone. Of course he was a PR man, but what did that mean? When he was young a woman had disappeared from his parish, a woman not quite right, leaving behind a brother who was even less right. A telegram arrived: 'Mary Bell, alive and well, in Belgium.' Her brother repeated it like a mantra down through the years. A man his own age who became a European saw the same Mary Bell, destitute in Brussels, at the age of sixty. He decided to tell no one, except

Thomas. It would be better to think of her as alive and well.

After the café, Thomas went to his meeting. The client wanted to advertise in Ireland – the economy was doing well there, the papers said so. He wanted a space theme: what did Thomas care about space; he couldn't cope with his own sitting-room. The client had been in Ireland ten years ago; he asked questions appropriate to that experience and for a few moments Thomas was fine. The tricks of happiness include explaining to strangers the politics of one's country to one's own satisfaction, leaving out the aggravating truths. In Berlin and Jerusalem this is allowed, places where it is clear that there is no such thing as the truth, that all truth depends on perspective. In the client's office, for five minutes, Thomas talked like a citizen of one of those cities, or Belfast. In hotels at night, in strange countries, you can draw maps to show the bar staff where you were born in relation to Dublin and the Border. They won't know that you've got the shape of the country all wrong.

The client looked like his brother-in-law, the one who had ME. All those years in bed had given him a young look; had this man had ME, or was he in fact just young? What did this client know about Ireland: did he know that now they were growing pot plants in the country for God's sake? Thomas had noticed them on his last journey to the Midlands, where he'd stayed in a damp hotel. The local radio station had blared over the system at breakfast, he had been forced to listen to the funeral arrangements for the coming two days. Soon he wouldn't have to worry about his teeth being gone, they would just be gone. When he was young he was always out making things happen. There had been a vastness of time in front of him: he could have been anything, he could have become gay, could have become a light person.

'We will go out and make things happen,' the client said.

'Indeed we will,' said Thomas, buttoning up his coat, snapping closed his briefcase, backing out the door, afraid to walk face-first. Going through the swing doors, he thought, 'I don't want to actually *be* a bird, I just want to fly.'

On the street a church bell rang continuously as if six funerals were arriving. A singing busker looted her life for the emotions of her song. If she were on a real stage could she have ambition? Thomas used to have that, an exciting desire to master the next goal, to get the next most important job, to meet important people. And he had met them, but the trouble is that when you know hordes of people you know more people who get sick, and more people who die. He had been good at his job, very good, so good he was hated. Not for him the useless pity of the encyclopaedia seller who tells the destitute pensioner that, on second thoughts, she cannot afford his books. If there was a man in the room who might be useful some time he got buried in him in two seconds flat. And made sure that no one else got near him. Now getting a taxi was an achievement. But if he got one maybe he could stay in it. Not yet. He saw a church and went in. He sat in the back row and fell asleep. If he expired here, he hoped they wouldn't say at home, 'He died in the chapel.'

Bernard MacLaverty

A Legacy and Some Gunks – An Entirely True Story

THIS MORNING your man arrives in the kitchen to find a scattering of letters on the breakfast table. A visa statement, a request to read at a festival, some papers for a meeting and a letter postmarked Neustadt-am-Rübenberge. Your man opens the German letter and reads:

Rainer Böhlke
Gartenstrasse 35. 31535 Neustadt
Germany

Dear Sir,
 As a man living alone one thinks not only of one's past but also beyond one's own being.
 In a word, I have a considerable fortune and I would like to name you as my heir in my testament.
 This is a great honour for me because in this way I want to express my appriciation of your work.
 It would be a great pleasure if you were to accept this inheritance after my passing.
 I hope that with this help you would be able to attend to your important literaric work more intensively.

 Please answer very soon!

 Sincerely yours

P.S. If you would like to give me a little present, please send me a few handwritten lines from your latest novel with a dedication and your signature.

The signature on the letter resembles a small, but not too regular, heart trace in blue ink.

Your man immediately thinks it is from his mate, McWilliams, who likes to play elaborate practical jokes. But would he go to the trouble of printing Rainer Böhlke's notepaper? How could he get it posted in Neustadt? He holds the page up to the light. There is a German watermark – ZETA MATTPOST.

Then your man remembers that before Christmas he was in Germany and, on headed notepaper from a Leipzig hotel, had written to McWilliams in the following vein: that the hotel was offering him a free holiday if only he would sleep with certain beautiful frauleins. He need do nothing in return except give permission for the filmed encounters to be video-taped and broadcast. Stills would also be sold to magazines and it was up to him whether the black letterbox covered his eyes or his gentles. Could this be McWilliams' revenge?

Your man shows the letter to his wife. Your woman goes daft and immediately gets out the atlas to see where Rainer lives. There turns out to be about twenty Neustadts. Some of them are in former East Germany and she discounts these because Rainer has 'a considerable fortune'. She is driven to look at the postmark. NEUSTADT AM RÜBENBERGE. This is no help in finding it on the map.

'What if he is younger than you – and you die first?' she says.

'He sounds old.'

She nods. She makes up her piece with almost stale bread, left-over cheese and tomato and goes out to work, her eyes shining with hope.

It could be a case of the Henry Root letters. 'Henry' wrote to anyone of any importance in public life and teased a reply out of them which was polite and therefore made them appear foolish and gullible. Maybe Rainer has written to hundreds of writers (writers seem to think only of two things – writing and money) and offered to leave them his 'considerable fortune' in the hope that they will grovel and reply – indeed, arse-lick him for the rest of his short life. Then he will publish an anthology of the most subservient and greedy letters and your man's will be in pride of place. The frontispiece probably.

The words 'considerable fortune' strike him as odd. It reminds him of hearing a friend of his mammy's: 'I knew a man who drank himself out of a fortune.'

'What are you talking about,' says the mammy. 'I knew somebody who drank himself out of TWO fortunes.'

His mammy's idea that you could drink two fortunes told more about her concept of a fortune than it did about the amount a man could drink.

[A bottle of ordinary upside-down whiskey is about £12, and if a man was to be really extravagant and drink two a day that would be £8760 per annum. The occasional pint and small vodka and gin and tonic before a meal – and some wine with the meal – and even, in extremis, being forced into buying his round, would bring his drink bill to £10,000 a year. Given that his liver would not last more than 5 years, then a fortune is £50,000. This is the salary of a headmaster of a large comprehensive school. Any judge in the country will earn twice this every year. But your man's mammy never knew any judges or headteachers.]

Your man has books to leave back to the local library, so he scouts through the reference section. He looks up *'am'* in a German dictionary. He thought it meant near or 'in the district of' but it means 'on'. Like 'West-on-Supermare' or 'Lond-on-Thames.'

So, Neustadt is on the river Rübenberge.

He looks it up in the atlas and there it is – Neustadt – just outside Hanover. He imagines Rainer sitting, brooding in his castle above a bend in the Rubenberge. At his feet, a copy of your man's latest novel, the pages flittering in the draught. He owns everything as far as the eye can see. His factories belch smoke and manufacture things and accumulate further wealth. The sky is yellow-grey with the haze of burnt lignite. In his castle Rainer has no other dependents except for some mice. He puts his hand to his leonine grey head – his forehead, steep with intellect – his eyes dark with sympathy and maybe empathy for the poor of this world. His hand moves to his chest – his breathing irregular....

It occurs to your man that there is one possibility which he has not yet considered. That it is true. This German may have been touched by your man's writings and decided to leave him a vast fortune.

Jesus – he may never have to write another word.

The other picture your man has is of Rainer Böhlke, mad as a dagger and flat broke, slipping out past his distraught wife and children. He is going to post a letter to someone whose name he has seen on the spine of a book. In the hallway he stands licking a stamp with such thoroughness that the gum is all but gone, then he waves *auf wiedersehen* with the little white envelope which now lies on your man's desk, its stamp slightly askew.

That night your man and his wife go to the pictures – *Remains of the Day*. Jokes are whispered about how little remains for poor Rainer. After the movie they meet friends and all six of them go off for a drink. The only place they can get in on a Saturday night is the lounge of a prohibitively expensive hotel – the kind of place Rainer would stay for months without a second thought. Your man, being in the position he is, feels obliged to buy the first round. After a respectful pause – he certainly does not want to appear greedy – he explains the reason for his largesse. He tells them about Rainer Böhlke. They are aghast. Mouths open at the words 'considerable fortune'. Eyelids are batted. One woman – Fiona from down the street – believes it absolutely. Your man buys the second round as well. The company agree he can afford it.

In bed he casts his mind back. It wouldn't be the first time your man has had communication from a daftie. Some years ago he had a letter, passed to him through his publishers, from Copenhagen. Not only did it have the date on it but also the time.

18.40–19.00. It took the guy twenty minutes to write, although it wasn't obvious why he took so long.

Informationscyclist
Jørgen Andersen
København

ACCORDING TO THE AUTHOR AND HIS CONNECTION TO DENMARK.

I can offer the author a wealthy payd job in Denmark if he will come and visit my country. He will get around £3695 = Kr (crowns) 42,500 for a week in Denmark + free hotel and free travel in a Volvo 760 Turbo. The job will include:

6 lectures [4 universities + 2 Gymnasiums]
1 TV programme – about 45 minutes
1 Radio Programme – about 1 Hour
2 Chronicles in 4 newspapers

And I will get a professional chauffeur – who is also a professional photographer. His name is Bent Newmann – aged 66. Please take this letter seriously and please let your man answer on behalf of his own will. With love and hope for a better future,

Yours sincerely

Jørgen Andersen

NB! Notice that a big exhibition called,
'Karl Marx uses the library – do you?' is under prepa-ration in these months and will be set up in USA and Great Britain in 1988. The start will be Middlemarch 1988 – and the rest of 1988 /1990 – 300 years anniver-sary of the Battle of the Boyne in 1690 – 91.

Please answer quickly. That will be a help for my prepa-rations of the exhibition which will save thousands of mens, womens and childrens in Ireland & throughout the world.

Your man thought it better not to reply to this gentleman. Indeed he felt more than a little sorry for his mental plight. But that was not the last of him. One night at 4 a.m. when your man is lying in an alcohol-induced slumber the phone rings. Your woman kicks your man awake to the point of bruising.

'The phone's ringing.'

'Wh-why?'

'Because somebody dialled our number.'

Your man tries to exit the room through the wardrobe door, then the bedroom door and still the phone rings. Someone dear to him must be dead, surely. In the dark of the office he lifts a stapler. Probably the mammy. Murdered in Belfast. He puts down the stapler and lifts the phone.

'Hello?'

'Jørgen Andersen here. I am trying to arrange a tour of Den-mark for you. You will be able to do readings and speeches...'

'Do you know what time it is?'

'I'm sorry – am I too early for you?'

'Or late – I dunno which – Now fuck off and don't EVER phone me again.'

But he did – a couple of weeks later this Informationscyclist phoned at 4 a.m. again. The mammy was kidnapped by the Loyalists and she wouldn't stop talking and they were phoning your man to get her to shut up. On his blunder to the phone he stubs his toe on the metal filing cabinet and has to hop the last few steps.

'Hello?'

'Jørgen Andersen here. I am trying to arrange a tour of the United States of America for you. There will be no problem with the accommodations....'

When your man wakes, his first thought is of his new-found inheritance. When he sees the mail he considers his luck is in – he has won a prize, two books of short stories and a bottle of malt from *Scotland on Sunday* for identifying the opening paragraph of Hemingway's 'A Clean Well-lighted Place'. He rips the parcel open. Fuck the stories, where's the bottle of Macallan's best malt? It will follow under a separate cover, it seems. Your man was so bustin to win this whiskey he sent in the answer six times on six postcards with six stamps and, of course, whose card is drawn as the winner? Your woman's. Her that has never let whiskey pass her portals except she's dying with the flu. And the glass is filled with sugar and cloves and lemon and God knows what other shite to take the taste off it.

Other things bode well. The unemployed graduate daughter emerges from her bed and speaks. Last night at a quiz SHE won a book – a guide, *Central America on a Shoestring*. The fact that all six fellow contestants at her table had refused it does not put him off his notion that he, or at least his family, is on a roll.

There is one more omen which shakes your man to his foundations. Your woman has a notion that she wants to show an oul photograph of a faded film star to a friend in work. It is stored in your man's filing cabinet and reluctantly he gets it out for her. A poster of a previous engagement falls on to the floor and, idly, he opens it. It is a big photocopy of your man as a younger your man – doing a gig at the State Library WHERE? Your woman leaps over to see. Neustadt. AHHHHHHHHHH. NEUSTADT. Jesus, he's been there. He has done a reading at Stadtbibliothek Neustadt. Your man has been to the town where Rainer Böhlke lives. Has he slept with him? Maybe drunk on Weizenbier and Schnapps – he would never remember a thing about it – your man, that is. Or his wife – Old Missus Böhlke – has he bedded her? With her earphones of carefully plaited hair and tight lederhosen?

The next day your man and your woman are hot footing it down to the reference library when a guy walks past them on the Underground. He looks very distinguished – faintly greying hair, rimless spectacles, expensive loafers, navy Bavarian-style coat with the belt tied continental fashion. Says your man, 'That looks like our Rainer.'

'Jesus, I hope he's older than that.'

In the library they ask for a copy of the German *Who's Who*. It appears in two fat red volumes, dated 1992. There is no entry for someone called Rainer Böhlke.

'What a gunk,' says he.

Your woman has the idea of looking up the German telephone directory. There are hundreds of volumes. They get the one for near Hannover and there is a section for Neustadt-am-whatever. Böhlke has about five or six entries. Karl-Heinz, Gerhart, Heinrich, Gunter...

'Rivals,' says your woman. 'Extended family – they'll not get a penny, no matter how much they plead.'

But there is no sign of Rainer. Nor Gartenstrasse.

'A quare gunk,' says she.

'He must be ex-directory,' says your man.

'Is that good or bad?'

'He's an eccentric billionaire who doesn't like to be phoned by the general public. Or to be disturbed reading my books.'

They look up the equivalent of German Yellow Pages. Dry Cleaners – Undertakers – Lawn mowers – Fly-fishing. All this they can tell from the little advertising drawings. But still no Rainer Böhlke.

The whole thing is a practical joke – it's McWilliams. Your man has a vision of the joker laughing. When he laughs he tries to speak but can't. Tears flood into his eyes. His face is red and his body is shaking and he is trying to say something like – he completely fell for it – and me getting the paper printed and making those mistakes and you falling for them and me knowing a guy who was going to Germany and looking up the phone books to get a German name and getting the letterhead printed and making up the text and giving it to the guy to post. He is still laughing; he slaps his thigh as he remembers phrases he has slaved over – 'considerable fortune', 'as a man living alone', 'in a word'. It was a work of art to make it seem Rainer had good, but not excellent, English. McWillams is the kind of man who laughs so much he slides down the wall and ends up on the floor. All but pissing himself.

Your man voices this picture to his wife.

She says, 'If WE couldn't find him in the phone book, how could McWilliams?'

Your man considers this and nods. In a voice husky with emotion he says, 'I love you.'

Throughout the day the name of the German philanthropist/lunatic/joker occurs frequently in their conversation – almost as if he is one of the family. In a callous and greedy development, by late afternoon he becomes known as 'Rainer, God rest him'.

The next day is decision time. A letter will have to be written. The lure will have to be taken. It is the only way to tell whether it is a juicy morsel or a barbed and empty hook attached to McWilliams's line.

Your man sits down to the wordprocessor. The phone rings. 'Hello?'

'Fiona from down the street here. I'm afraid I have bad news for you about your inheritance.'

'Don't tell me he's dead.'

'No – it's worse than that. I was telling a friend of mine about your letter – this friend is a composer – and he stopped me. He just said Rainer Böhlke. He got a letter too. Wanted to leave him a considerable fortune. And all he wanted was a compact disc – signed by the composer.'

Your man puts down the phone, feeling he has been kicked in the gentles. All that need happen now is for the bottle of Macallan to arrive broken or be cancelled,

'What a terrible fuckin' gunk.'

He calls out for your woman who is in the other room throwing out her cheap jewellery. She comes in polishing a marcasite brooch.

And he tells her.

After a long silence she says, 'Jesus, Mary and Joseph. Haven't some people little to do with their time.'

Brian Leyden

The Family Plot

T HE WAY to the surgical ward is an obstacle course of confusing elevator stops and misleading arrow signs, pointing to dim corridors with hospital equipment, spare beds and trolleys pushed back against the walls. There is a grubby, seated area where the smokers congregate. Then a medical-dispensary waft from the nurses' station; and that all-pervasive stink of disinfectant, a chemical reek I can't help thinking is used to mask something worse.

I know the route by now, and I have learned to avoid the sweaty discomfort in which I normally arrive for hospital visits: my head throbbing, mouth dry, shirt damp and underwear glued to my crotch, clutching some useless offering in a crumpled bag.

The ward is an open-plan room crowded with temporary beds and screen curtains, hot radiators, tightly shut windows, the November evening rain weeping down the glass. The atmosphere is stuffy. Suffocating.

The bedclothes are barely disturbed. My father is asleep, his eyes mercifully closed. The seal has been broken on the cap, and there is a glass of 7-Up on the locker top next to the bottle I brought yesterday. But he drinks little now.

A young nurse goes by, wearing a minuscule folded cap and a watch like a tiny medal for valour pinned to her breast. I catch her sidelong glance at my father and me, standing beside the bed. She returns a minute later and inspects the mixture of gases, but tries not to disturb the patient or his wordless visitor. She moves off again. Her soft-soled shoes glide on the mirror-polished floor. She has lovely bright eyes and her tread is light at the start of a long shift. Her white, crisply laundered uniform used as a kind of armour to tackle a job I could never face. The career must have its rewards, but I would feel only despair, being so close to the maimed, the sick and the dying, seeing people only at their lowest ebb.

My father has said the nurses are great.

We have little else to talk about. And I have heard it said that people are often at their best on the wards, finding in themselves through illness, and the possibility of death, a calmness of mind they never knew they possessed.

They are treating my father with oxygen and Ventolin, plotting the hours for his medication, air and food on a chart. The oxygen cylinder is cradled on a trolley wheeled close to the bed. Colour-coded valves and pipes lead to the clear plastic mask that fits over his mouth and nose. There is a faint pressurised hiss. He lies there purple-lipped and still, his welted hands at rest on the clean, turned-down sheet.

With his illness deepening every day his movements have become minimal and cautious. The only sudden activity, the only dramas now, are the coughing fits. Terrible, lung-wracking bouts of coughing so harsh and so futile you want to clear his lungs for him, that coal-tar thick congestion. I would whisper any promise in God's stony ear if I could spare both of us from these coughing fits. A torture with no reward and no release.

I understand that cough. I know it from the inside. I was an asthmatic child. Still am asthmatic, because it is not a condition that ever really goes away, though it has been in abeyance for several years. I have an occasionally wheezy night, a tightening of the lungs as the airways narrow, and people notice my breathing's not right when I'm tired or stressed. But I don't think about it much. I've started to smoke again. Silkcut Purple. What is there to say? Pressure and weakness. His weakness and the pressure of seeing him die.

My mother will not forgive him for killing himself with cigarettes, and she'd go mad if she saw me smoking. Thirty-one
years of age and I hide that from her.

She is a strong-minded woman, and she has never understood the craving for a cigarette, or the unique comfort and
buzz of a drink. The addiction to all things sensual and stimu-
lating, to all that gratifies, whatever the price.

All my father's family had weak chests, the lungs always the
first thing to give trouble when a cold or a flu struck. They
were the kind of people who were a nuisance when they came
to stay, wheezing like demented accordions because of a
feather pillow or the wrong kind of mattress, damp mould, old
carpet, dust.

And my mother so proud of her clean house.

You know that old chestnut: cigarettes take ten years off your
life. Yes, but they're the last ten years. That was my father's
attitude. A bad chest, no resolve and a fatalistic outlook: 'We
all have to go sometime.' But his dying has not been a simple
business; it has dragged on, long after his last easy breath.

His sleep is light and troubled: low nuuuuhh... nuuuuhhh...
sounds escape from him. Terrors surfacing close to being said.

It would be a crime to bring him back to that fully
conscious battle for air, and it is a relief for me not to have to
face those needlessly open and bulging eyes of his. Eyes that
most surely plead to be released. 'Please,' they beseech the
attentive visitor, 'I want to die.'

I walk past other patients on the mend. Men grown bored at
the frail pace of recuperation, fed up with the newspapers and
the glossy magazines and the bumper books of crossword
puzzles from the hospital shop. Sallow and disconsolate scare-
crows in old pyjamas and dressing-gowns and absurd slippers
that should never have been allowed outside the tender privacy
of home bedrooms and firesides.

I drift towards the window to look out at the grounds. Institutional grounds. The same low-maintenance plants common to government and industrial buildings: dwarf conifers, untidy potentilla, evergreen hebe with a blush of red along the edge of the leaves. A much earlier and by now mature planting of weeping willows, silver birch and beechwood hedging, used to screen the perimeters of the hospital grounds. Rectangles of greensward right up to the paths between the labs, the out-patient clinics, and the mortuary.

The stark effect of the mortuary entrance is relieved by raised beds where lie the dormant bulbs of crocus, daffodil, narcissi, tulips, Siberian bluebells. I know the names because my father was a groundsman and gardener.

I was twelve years old. We were in the schoolteacher's garden. My father was pruning roses for beer money: pruning the stems back severely with a secateurs the teacher owned but did not know how to use.

'Do you like your teacher?' he asked.

'No.'

'What about school?'

'I hate it.'

'I wasn't much older than you when I had to quit,' he confided. 'There was no money at home, you see. The headmaster said it was a crying shame. It was a crying shame I couldn't go any further. That's how he put it.'

He believed in education, and so did my mother, and for their sake I plodded on through secondary school but dropped out of college to become a piss-tester in a veterinary laboratory. I have not married.

'Bud trouble.' That's what he called it, the things a man will do, the extraordinary lengths a man will travel, for sex.

He was popular with women, though not a ladies' man; there was never anything polished or affected about him. Instead of saying hello, he'd say: 'How is the cat jumping?'

Dressed up in his good suit for a photograph, you might mistake him for an office worker, dark strands of Brylcreem in his fair hair and skin that burned before it tanned. Heavy-rimmed glasses that were the fashion then, his eyes an in-between colour. But he was an outdoor man all his life: the way he'd cup a cigarette in the palm of his hand, safely out of the breeze, the neck button of his shirt undone, a rim of white vest inside a plaid shirt. I don't think he ever wore wellingtons in his life, always leather boots, with the tops of his socks outside his trousers. A man not meant for ties: the ties that fit around your neck, or the ties that hold a rambler in the one place.

He was in great shape back then from digging and wheel-barrowing clay. His lungs worked at full capacity, taking on ten- and twenty-mile cycles in the evenings after work, going to set-dances and hops and rambling houses. Recounting later for an audience in the pub the formalities of those times.

'Are you dancing?'

'Are you asking?'

'I'm asking.'

'I'm dancing.'

Courtships conducted in the moon-beam glimmer of a flashlamp hooked to the handlebars of a high black Raleigh bicycle, criss-crossing the back roads with tumescent teenage energy. Going further everytime.

And then my mother, a town girl with her head full of notions, but bringing both of them down to earth when she tells him: 'I'm pregnant.'

My sudden arrival before they were nine months married. The frustrations of a young family when another baby arrived soon after, then another. The money-trap of low-wage Ireland in those years, and later ill-health (the lungs, naturally, but also water on his knee joints after all that spade work) ending in welfare reliance. And along with these outward setbacks, a life veering steadily away from its centre. A man travelling further into the more remote parts of himself, away from family and duty, until that condition that was not callousness, but a defiant apartness, had become so absolute it was all that was left.

By the time I began to consider him as something more than the presence a child registers as Daddy – by the time I saw him as a living, breathing complicated adult – he was past intimacy or explanation. Is that the nub of my present distress? Is that the reason I keep coming back, night after night?

I have never been able to grasp his stony acceptance of the abuse my mother flung at him; his indifference to the tears and accusations after his break-outs and boozing sprees; his refusal to give up the cigarettes even when his health broke. Did he not recognise the seeds of humiliation and pain that were planted and allowed to grow every time I was sent to collect him from the pub? Every time he forced me to wait for him to finish his drink, part-bribed with a glass of lemonade and a bag of crisps, while fresh pints were ordered, and I had to remind him that Mammy was looking for him, that his dinner was ready, that we all wanted him to come home.

Why wouldn't I admit it? Before he passed away I wanted some impression of him other than the specimen I'd labelled and shelved as: The Man Who Kept our Home in a Hell.

On the road below, the emergency beacons of an ambulance spring on and the blue light splinters silently against the window as it lurches away into the falling dark.

Our house crackled with the friction of two people who just couldn't pull together. I was a bed-wetter, a listener at the plain wooden newel post at the top of the landing to the commotion down below. A child in the habit of wandering a long way off on my own and not telling anyone where I'd been. A child who sulked up trees. A child who took guilty pleasure hearing my mother's anxious voice calling out for me in the dusk.

'I'll teach them,' I used to think. 'They'll miss me and they'll be sorry.' And sometimes I went so far as to imagine them, holding hands at last, standing over my small white coffin.

Evidence of trauma? Perhaps. But I didn't torture animals –
well, not many, and I had a reasonable excuse. It started with
an educational toy bought for me one Christmas. A Thomas
Salter chemistry set that came with a tray full of test-tubes and
a spirit burner and sparked an interest in science and dissecting
frogs with a purpose. It finished with a dead-end job in a
veterinary laboratory.

But I do not blame my father for my present frustrations,
and I do not dwell on the impact of the rows that raged in our
house: always over his weakness of character, his spending too
much on drink, killing himself with cigarettes, not finishing
jobs started with great intentions and then abandoned for want
of – want of what? I don't know. Perhaps it was because he
decided that nothing in the end was finally worth doing. And
then again maybe it was for want of any reward. For want of
respect. The respect of his children, who openly called him a
bum. Or for want of approval – something with which my
mother was never forthcoming. There was approval for her
sons, yes. Christ, we could do no wrong. Even today we are her
flawless little darlings, bar the odd slip-up. But respect? No, he
never had that. She lacerated him with the only weapon she
had, her tongue. And we listened and believed. Children do.

The good-looking nurse returns. She hoops the screen curtain
around the next bed.

'Sorry, I have to take some more blood,' she says.

There is a faint murmur of consent.

It is not a deep and unconditional attachment that brings
me back to spend my evenings in this ward that allows no
privacy. I know that. But it is only this moment that my mind
allows the real dilemma, the reason I arrive in hope and leave
again after every visit feeling cheated. Not by his condition; he
is too far through for such an unlikely reversal. What the peculiar light this evening reveals is my true purpose. The knowledge
that I can't bring myself to say the one thing I really want to tell

him. The one thing I know I will never tell him. Know he'll die
before that happens.

Jesus, not tears. Not now.

He lies there taking himself off towards death, furtively as
always, despite the tender care of that lovely, clear-eyed nurse –
whom I should beg to meet me later if I had an ounce of
courage, but I know I won't. My father is dying, the bastard,
he is leaving me. And I will never get to tell him that I am sorry
that I always took my mother's side; the provider of the most
constant source of affection (an excuse more cloying than an
asthma attack, as I fight for one simple breath of truth).

Say it, say it for God's sake. That from a very young age I
totalled up my mother's one-sided account of you and decided
you were a liability. I absorbed and accepted her version of
you: a weak man who cared nothing for yourself, and thought
even less about your family.

Only tonight, staring red-eyed out this hospital window,
some evolving impulse has begun to question and reassess
what really took place, what the real causes were.

That last Saturday you rang. Wheezing over the phone in the
first awkward silence. But I knew it was you. I couldn't believe
you'd called. You never called.

'Have you anything on?'

'You need a lift,' I guessed, because you never learned how
to drive.

'Aye.'

You were shaved and wearing your good suit and a light
raincoat with the buttons open when I collected you at the
front door. We drove past the usual stops until we reached the
church. There was a vivid yellow county council van waiting in
the car-park. You got out and shook hands with the man from
the council. Together you walked as far as the graveyard, went
through the iron turnstile in single file and up the cement path
between the headstones. You took your time, stopping every

couple of minutes to get your breath back.

From the driver's seat I saw it all as a dumb-show. The white tape measure, and the man from the county council placing out the dimensions. You both paused to consider the view before signing a docket for the plot. A plot of ground other men would have to dig.

You came back down the path, your coat ruffled open in the breeze and the lining exposed.

'Well, that's done,' you said when you were settled back in the car.

We moved off.

I knew you needed a drink, and we were nearing your regular pub. The pub where my mother used to send me to beg you to come home. The one pub in the world I'd vowed never to set foot in again. I heard you say quietly: 'You'll take a drink.'

'No.'

I stopped directly opposite the pub door. The light that day was strong, and the corridor into the back lounge was deeply shadowed.

'I'll call for you later,' I said, and I allowed you to step into the dark passage alone.

I should go. Nothing will be said tonight. Communication between us dried up a long time ago. Yet, while I have always looked on my father as a heavy drinker and a home-wrecking alcoholic, I recognise that he did not drink any more than I do now. And where did that lead? That it is not just his asthma and a family plot I've inherited. That I have more of his traits than any image of myself had previously allowed. And, more importantly, that I have made no better job of coping.

'You can go for a cup of tea if you like. There is a restaurant on the ground floor.'

'Sorry?'

The nurse with the nice eyes is standing by a medical trolley near the window.

'Tea!' she says.

I nod but I do not move.

'He planted these grounds,' I tell her.

She doesn't understand.

'It was his first job.' I gesture at the view below.

She glances out the window. The branches of the trees are dark and the rain has brought down the last of the frost-damaged leaves.

She looks at my father and then back at me.

'Let him rest.'

Patrick McCabe

The Hands of Dingo Deery

STATEMENT OF Det. Insp. Norman Jenkins, Willesden Police Station.
April 15, '95: 9.05 a.m.

To All Staff

What follows is a truly tragic story. It was found in the pocket of Mr Dermot Mooney after he had been remanded in custody following the assault on PC Higgins on the Kilburn High Road last evening. Initially I had no sympathy for the accused, having witnessed the various bruises on Constable Higgins' face, not to mention the rips both in his tunic and trousers. To be quite frank, I became exasperated by his insistence that he was a 'poet', as he termed it, and a 'cartographer of the heart's secret landscapes'. It was only later, when secretly I observed him alone in his cell, in the full throes of his oratory, that I began to understand at last the motivation of a man who goes throwing himself through the roof of a public building, namely, The Willesden Cinema, not to mention chuckling and laughing like a man possessed. And, of course, when challenged, calling an officer of the law 'a shitehawk from Hades itself'!

It soon became clear to me that this man's journey through life has indeed been a 'Via Dolorosa'. It is my considered opinion that we ought to meet his request for an opera cape and two reams of writing paper with magnanimity. Furthermore, although I am not a literary

*man, I do not believe anyone can read what follows –
which is effectively the story of his life – without falling
about the place, their eyes welling up with tears. Which is
why I bring you this heart-rending, passionate tale of a
man's lone struggle with 'the capricious vagaries of fate'
(Dermot's own words). I defy all staff to read it and then
think, 'All this man is fit for is punching policemen and
drinking cans of McEwan's export.'*

Ladies and gentlemen: The Hands of Dingo Deery.

For many years now I have lived alone, within the four grey
walls of this narrow room, the tremulous silence intermittent-
ly broken as the tube trains cut through the tar-black night
with their cargo of ghostly, pallid faces, as if in relentless,
heartbroken pursuit of something lost a long time ago, just the
peaceful harmony which once pervaded my entire being has
been bitterly wrested from me. How many years now have I
paced these accursed floorboards, imploring any deity who
cares to listen to return to me the bountiful tranquillity which
once was mine and end forever this dread torment which greets
me like a rapacious shade each waking day!

And now, as I stand here by the window, watching with
leaden, emotion-drained eyes, directly below me in a single line
of mocking, waltzing calligraphy, at last they confront me, the
wicked jagged ciphers which, all this time, I have feared would
one day rise up from my blackest dreams like wicked flares
from the pit of hell: THE SECRETS OF LOUIS LESTRANGE
– CAN YOU SURVIVE THE 1,137 WHACKS?

My nightmare began some thirty years ago in a small town in
the Irish midlands. I had come to spend the summer with my
uncle, who was the headmaster in the local school. He had of
late acquired some measure of fame as an ornithologist, and it
gave me great pleasure indeed to accompany him on his regular
lectures in the various halls and venues throughout the country.

It is not my intention to imply that my duties were in any way onerous, for in truth, beyond the simple erection of the screen and the operation of the slide projector, there was little for me to do. I carried the briefcase containing my learned relative's notes, it is true, but such was his erudition that he made little use of what he termed 'needless paraphernalia', and it was of such insignificant weight that it could have been comfortably borne to The Temperance Hall (in which establishment it was his practice to deliver orations on the habits of our feathered friends) on the back of the average house fly. What a privilege it was for me to turn the metal disk yet another semicircle as, in basso profundo, he would declaim, 'Slide please!' while his neighbours and friends looked on admiringly.

As I look back on those days now, they always seem to me suffused with the colour of burnished copper and within them, time does not appear to move at all.

Afterwards, I would stroll casually through the cooling streets, making the acquaintance of the elderly gentlemen who whiled away their hours on the summer seat discussing the imminent ruin of the country and the putative prowess of assorted thoroughbreds in contests that had yet to be.

I would regularly share a lemonade with them, perhaps on occasion pass around a packet of Players. Laughter and an unbending faith in the goodness of our fellow man was a common bond amongst us all.

Little did I know then that already the peace and contentment which only recently had transformed my life would, within only a few short months, have slipped irretrievably from my grasp!

No, at the time, there was little doubt in my mind that where I had had the good fortune to find myself was indeed the most idyllic town on earth, and had you taken it upon yourself to share your intimations that darker times would soon be discerned on the horizon, I would have extrapolated from your spurious, clandestine philanthropy nothing more than a bitter, small-minded and wholly despicable envy. I would have scorned mirthfully and packed you off about your business. For, if ever a truth were spoken, it was that evidence of dissension in that sweet little hamlet there was none. Save, perhaps, the awesome figure of a well known layabout by the name of Dingo Deery, who, at odd intervals, would appear wild-eyed in the doorway of the hall and bellow at the top of his voice, 'Shut your mouth, Lestrange! What would you know about it! You wouldn't know a jackdaw if it walked up to you and pecked your auld whiskey nose off!' Whereupon he would spread his arms and assail the stunned, mute assembly: 'You think he knows about birds? He knows nothing! Except how to beat up poor unfortunate scholars for not knowing their algebra! Look at these hands! Look at them, damn youse!'

When he had spoken these words, he would break into a sort of strangled weeping and raise his palms aloft, and indeed there were few present who could deny on first viewing those bruised pieces of flesh that they undoubtedly had seen wear and tear beyond reasonable expectation, even for someone of his social standing. 'Cut to ribbons,' he would cry hoarsely. 'Cut to ribbons by Lestrange! Him and his sally rods! Oho, yes – you were handy with them alright, Lestrange! But mark my words – you'll pay for what you did to Dingo Deery, I can tell you that!' Then, with a maniacal cackle, his recalcitrant, cumbersome bulk would be forcefully ejected, the distasteful echo of his combative ululations lingering in the air for long afterwards.

But such incidents were indeed rare, and otherwise life proceeded serenely: Yuri Gagarin was in space, Players cost one and six, and John Fitzgerald Kennedy was undoubtedly the possessor of the cleanest teeth in the western hemisphere.

It was to be many years yet before the arrival of colour television and the first drug addicts.

But how deceptive is reality! For, even as I sat there, my face being gently stroked by the soft and dusty light of the midday sun, drawing deeply, exultantly on the Players, little did I know – indeed, how could I have known – that events were already proceeding apace which would ultimately result in the idyllic calm which I treasured not only being torn apart like a piece of cheap material in some Godforsaken huckster shop, but see to it that I would remain haunted – yes, for there can be no other word for it – for the rest of my mortal days!

The first day I met Mick Macardle, I knew instinctively all was not as it should have been. Deep within me, I heard a timorous voice cry, 'Withdraw! Withdraw while you still can!' The languid sunshine, however, and the soothing breeze of the early afternoon conspired in silence to usher away any such uncharitable and unnecessary suspicions.

But now, as I languish here in my one-bedroom prison, forgotten in a city which remembers no names, my heart has crusted over and no such beguiling veils remain to blur my vision, and with staggering clarity I see what ought to have met my eyes in those days of benevolence-blinded myopia, a sight which, had I not been poked in those organs by two large, metaphorical thumbs, should surely have swept through my soul like an arctic wind.

The thin cigar hung insolently out of the side of his mouth. A black raven's wing of Brylcreemed hair fell ominously down over his alabaster forehead. His lips were two ignominious pencil strokes, his moustache not unlike a crooked felt-tipped marker line as might be drawn by a small child. More than anything, however, what ought to have telegraphed to me the imponderable depth of the man's reptilian nature was the slow slither of his arm about my shoulder, the hiss of his silky sibilants as he crooned in my ear, 'Don't worry about a thing!' Then, out of nowhere, he would erupt into inexplicable torrents of laughter, the flat of his hand repeatedly falling on the broad of my back as he cried, 'You leave it to Mick! I'll take care of it!'

'No prob!' he would cry, sawing the noun in two like a cheapskate magician in a tawdry show.

How I should have loathed the man! But no – my innocence and desire to think the best of all fellows won the day, and even when he passed by my uncle's house in his new Ford Consul, waving through the open window like a visiting dignitary from a Lilliputian puppet state, I chose to ignore the unspoken counsel of my instinct, preferring instead to align myself with the views of those citizens of the town who ranged themselves about him – some, indeed, claiming kinship – as they declared 'One fine butt of a lad!' and insisting furthermore that there was 'No better man in this town!'

The abrupt nasal-spurt of his megaphone could be heard far and wide as his glittering Consul zig-zagged through the candy-striped streets of summer. 'Yes!' it would bark, with metallic brio, 'Yes, ladies and gentlemen! Mick Macardle for all your movie requirements! Why not drop along to Mac's Photography Shop at number 9 Main Street? Come along and see what we have to offer! If you want your sprocket spliced, then look no further – Mick's your man! Eight millimetre transfer a speciality! Weddings, christenings, confirmations! Never be negative with Mick Macardle! Mick Macardle's the movie man! No prob! Yes, siree!'

Thus, life proceeded. The church bells would ring out across the morning town, the womenfolk give themselves once more to the fastidious investigation of vegetables and assorted food-stuffs in the grocery halls, brightening each other's lives with picaresque travelogues of failing innards and the more recent natural disasters, delaying perhaps at the corner to engage in lengthy discourse with Father Dominic, their beloved pastor. 'That's not a bad day, now,' they would observe, the clergyman as a rule finding himself in fulsome agreement. 'Indeed and it is not,' he would respond enthusiastically, occasionally a dark cloud of uncertainty passing across his fresh, close-shaven features as he added, 'Although I think we might get a touch of rain later!'

Observations of similar perspicacity would provide a further ten minutes of eager debate before they would once more proceed on their way, past Grouse Armstrong snuggled up in the library doorway, the single American tourist snapping gypsies in the hotel foyer (Couldja throw a little more grit on your heads, guys?) and Sonny Leonard, the local minstrel, rehearsing 'I Wonder Who's Kissing Her Now' into the neck of the bottle which served as his microphone.

Sadly, even at that transcendent moment, as I gave my heartiest approval to the maestro's impromptu recital with rousing cheers of 'Good man, Sonny!' and 'More power to your elbow, young Leonard!' disturbing events were already proceeding as the sleek limousine bearing Mick Macardle cruised silently through the streets of Amsterdam, by the side of the ambitious long-fingered entrepreneur, a sinister man of foreign complexion who, within hours, would be outlining his proposition in an outwardly unremarkable lock-up garage, its dimly lit interior, however, festooned with tattered pictures of young ladies in abbreviated attire. Helpless females of tender years being pursued by villains of the wickedest mien sporting pork pie hats, their misfortunate quarries crying helplessly from the suspended cages in which they would ultimately find themselves. Forced to become slit-skirted temptresses leering through uncoiling cobras of smoke, captured for ever in calligraphic captivity as the houndstooth letters whorled all about them in a dizzying, soporific swirl! That same houndstooth lettering that would later choke my soul in bondage like so many miles of barbed wire: EVIL VIRGIN THRILLS! RUNAWAY GO-GO PSYCHOS! I MARRIED A NAKED MADMAN!

Despicable memories which course through me like a slow-acting poison; the very thought of my uncle and me adorning that Gallery of the Damned like an eerie step across my grave.

Mick Macardle tapped one eighth of an inch of ash from his thin cigar as The Dutchman ran his tongue along his upper teeth and fanned his fingers on the oil-stained tabletop. 'Very well, Mr Macardle,' he began. 'That arrangement suits me fine. For each copy you deliver on time, you will receive the sum of five hundred pounds sterling. However, I must emphasise that I can only accept eight millimetre, as the films are for private distribution. I cannot emphasise how keen my clients are for this type of product, and you may rest assured that demand will constantly outstrip supply. Do you feel you may be able to rise to meet the demands, Mr Macardle?'

To which the brown-suited businessman responded by paring the nail of his index finger with a marbled pocket knife, flashing his gold tooth, and grinning. 'No prob!'

With one wave of his Woolworth's wand began my Golgotha.

To the poor, glorious but innocent souls of the town, he had not been on an evil, self-seeking mission which was soon to shatter for ever the harmony that existed amongst us all, but merely, as he cheerfully volunteered, 'Visiting the mother in Dundalk! She has a bad dose of the shingles!'

As was their wont in times of difficulty, the commiserations of the local people knew no bounds. Their admiration of such forbearance as he displayed in his time of trial was deep and respectful. 'How do you manage to keep going at all?' they inquired of him. 'Ah,' he would reply, with a modest shake of his head, 'I have great faith in St Anthony!'

Apart from these unsettling events, my life continued as before – setting up the screen, making tea for the various societies who never failed to be impressed by my uncle's oratory, his statesmanlike imperturbability displaying any hint of fragility only on those occasions when the door would open and a familiar figure appear, crying, 'I'll give you Cicinurrius Regis! I'll give you Torquoise-Billed Yellow Jacket! I'll give you Long-Necked Hoppa Tail! Look at these hands, Lestrange! One day you'll pay for what you did to me! Make no mistake, you'll pay alright!'

As the door slammed and the retreating Dingo Deery undulated down the hallway, little did I realise just how prophetic were his words.

It was also my custom in those days to dine occasionally at an establishment known as The Pronto Grill, which was presided over by a gentleman of Italian extraction who busied himself singing selections from the various light operas and furiously polishing drinking glasses. Over a sumptuous repast magnificently prepared by the kitchen staff to whom I had become affectionately known as MORE TAY! because of my predilection for consuming inordinate quantities of the soothing, tan-coloured liquid with my meal, I would watch life proceed before me in the warm street outside, at times fearing that such was my ecstatic state that I might collapse in a faint on the formica table before me.

For, in truth it was not the exquisite quality of the comestibles alone that drew me to my quiet cove adjacent to the steaming chrome of the coffee machine, but the soft voices of the young convent ladies who would converge there in the afternoons, rapt in their sophistry and drawing elongated shapes in the spilt sugar.

Perhaps I had spent too long in the company of my beloved uncle – to this day I cannot pronounce upon that with any measure of certainty – but sitting there before me, I knew that beyond all shadow of doubt, I watched them as they became transformed, their splendour now so dazzling and variegated it was as if Gauguin, the master, were himself somehow present, bearing these wonders with him from his Tahitian Eden.

Marvels destined for my eyes alone. And how I gazed upon them, magically lit now by the angled shafts of clear sunlight that criss-crossed the mock terrazzo floor of the restaurant, squatting before me now in their rainbow-hued magnificence, what I can only describe as my Birds of Paradise.

Thenceforward, rarely a day passed but I winged with those exotic creatures across the Elysian Fields of my soul.

Sadly, like The Poet's, and indeed that of the Quattrecento of the South Seas, my Paradise too was soon to be taken from me.

I was swaying hypnotically in that netherworld of the imagination, partaking of a brimful cup of sugared Brooke Bond, when what seemed as nothing so much as the passing of an unseen spectre awoke me and I looked up in horror to see Dingo Deery huddled deep in conversation with my pulchritudinous fledglings, with their wings folded over as if in protection or a prelude to his spiriting away. How my dream was shattered by the sight of his monochromatic amplitude! Through the crevasse of my fingers, I could see his tiny eyes, phosphorescent with deceit, and in the instant, I watched with a growing sense of unease as he drew the sleeve of the painter's overall across his mouth in a manner that banished the Tahitian genius, perhaps, I considered, never to return.

I fled, despondent, and walked the desolate streets. I felt as if something precious had died on me. I gave myself to Bacchus and that night slept beneath the open skies.

It is hard to say, even to this day, when things began to go wrong between my beloved uncle and me. Perhaps it was the fact that after my hasty departure from the café, he was forced to hire a horse and cart in order to locate me whilst I hopelessly fell from tavern to tavern. His first words to me that fateful night as he came upon me in the open field where I lay beneath the stars were palpably void of the affectionate feeling to which I had come to expect in my dealings with him, and we made our journey homeward in silence. There can be no doubt that shortly after this incident, a certain note of sourness became detectable in our relations.

This, however, was just the beginning. Within days, events had taken an even more serious turn. Uncle began to disappear for long periods, without so much as a word of explanation. The only indication that he had returned at all would be the gentle closing of the drawing room door, the soft click to which my ears were to become accustomed as I lay there in the night waiting for the first light of dawn to touch the window. His absences grew increasingly more frequent until, at last, as I stood by my bedroom window watching the silver dawn rise up over the rooftops, I clenched my fist in the pocket of my purple, quilted dressing gown and at last confronted the fact that I could no longer deny: there was nothing for it but to investigate and discover once and for all the mysterious genesis of Uncle Louis's burgeoning eccentricities and the cause of his bewilderingly inexplicable nocturnal peregrinations. There was no longer any doubt in my mind that the animosity toward me was deepening by the day. Night after night I trawled my tormented conscience. Surely a single incident of boorish behaviour on my part could not have provoked such a bitter volte-face? Was there something else I had forgotten? Some vile act I had committed unknownst to myself while in the grip of the demon grape? A murder, perhaps?

I paled. I wrung my hands in desperation as the grey-coated inspector of my mind paced the floor once more, investigating himself with rigorous, indeed fevered application. But it was all to no avail. The entropy of the vocative served only to confuse me further and the nets of my interrogations were returned nightly, sadly empty once more.

However, as luck would have it, a certain pattern began to emerge. It gradually became clear that my relative's by now seething misanthropy was not directed solely at me. It had begun to extend to almost every citizen in the town.

It was after what I, for the purposes of narrative, shall call 'the telephone incident' that I realised I could no longer indulge in my procrastinations, and that any further dalliance on my part would undoubtedly be construed by future generations as moral cowardice. I had been standing for some time with my ear pressed to the oaken door of the library when, in odd, strangely muted tones, I heard him utter the words, 'So, you think I am at your beck and call, Mrs, do you?' followed by the ringing crash of the bakelite receiver as it was slammed into its cradle and I heard him bellow, 'No! I won't be available for ornithology lectures! Tonight or any other fecking night! So put that in your drum and bang it!'

The muffled, indecipherable mutterings which followed seemed to cloak the entire building in a Satanic bleakness.

It was clear that I could delay no longer, and I determined at once to unscramble as best I could this maddening conundrum, this ravelled web of perplexity that enshrouded my dear relative's life. That very night I began my vigil in the doorway of the tobacconist's which was situated directly across the road from the house. For three successive nights I remained at my post, and there were many occasions when I was tempted to swoon into the luxurious arms of hopelessness. At last, however, on the fourth night of my vigil, my patience was rewarded and I froze as the massive front door of the house slowly opened and out stepped my uncle into the first, hesitant light of dawn. Hesitantly, he scanned the empty street and then, pulling the collar of his sports coat up around his neck, began to stride briskly into the morning with his binocular case slung over his shoulder.

It was only when he turned left at the humpback bridge bridge that I realised he was making for the woods outside the town.

At once the scales fell from my eyes and I felt myself shrink to no more than five or six inches in height. Silently I upbraided myself. How could I have been so foolish! To think

ill of my dearest uncle! In those moments, it all became clear to
me and I understood perfectly, implicitly, the reasons for his
recent erratic behaviour. His late night pursuits of his ornitho-
logical obsessions had exhausted his body to the point where
he had become the victim of an almost Hydesian change in his
personality. And, like Hyde of course, he was completely
unaware of it. I determined at once to waste no more time. I
would be brutally frank and honest. Such a decision caused me
no concern whatsoever. I knew he would see reason. I knew
that within a matter of days he would be back to himself and
between us, all would be as blissful as before. In that moment
of realisation, I exulted.

I continued to follow Uncle Louis until he arrived at that
clearing in the woods which overlooks the valley, from whence,
he had on many occasions reminded me, it was possible at any
one time to command a view of over thirty indigenous species
of bird.

At first I thought that perhaps my nightly vigils had eroded
my resilience to the point where my own mental equilibrium
was already affected. Then, through a process of what might
be termed cerebral massage, I succeeded in persuading myself
that because of the all-pervasive heat which we in the town had
been experiencing of late, such hallucinations – for what else
could anyone call them – were unavoidable in such weather.

Between my dalliance and my delusions, my fate was sealed.

'Stay right where you are!' a raucous voice snapped. There was
no mistaking the lumbering rotundity.

The corner of Dingo Deery's mouth curled like a decadent
comma of flesh. I gasped and fell backwards on to a spiky
clump of bracken, my foot, without warning, sinking into the
marshmallow softness of a freshly manufactured cow pat.

The binoculars fell from my uncle's grasp as a swish of
leaves stifled his cry.

I tried to run, but it was already too late. I found my neck locked in a vicegrip as a megaphone-wielding Macardle appeared from the undergrowth, flanked by two of his burly henchmen. I watched helplessly as he stubbed his cigar on a bed of pine needles with the sole of his white Italian shoe, then slowly approached me, smiling faintly, squeezing the flesh of my cheek as if inspecting a fattened beast in a squalid market. He turned from me with disdain.

'Not bad!' he snapped. 'He'll do!' before abruptly losing interest in me and stalking off barking 'Action!' into his pathetic trumpet.

I had to avert my gaze, for I could no longer bear to look upon that gross pantomime of the perverse.

There, before my eyes, were my Birds of Paradise, divested of all but the most insignificant articles of clothing, howling with glee and mirth as they cavorted lasciviously on the flattened grass. The bunched, fleshy fingers of Dingo Deery, like so many pork sausages, caught me just below the spine as he bellowed, 'Go on then – look away, you hypocrite! Pretend you don't see it!' Saliva dripped from his tobacco-stained teeth as his mocking eyes bit into me. Then he turned to my cowed relative and snarled, 'Louis Lestrange the Peeping Tom! Maybe you could tell us a little bit about that, Master? How about a lesson on that, eh? Today, boys, we are doing peeping! Haw haw haw!'

His mirth was unbridled as he continued. 'Thought you could get away with it, didn't you? I've been watching you for weeks, spying on us with them binoculars of yours! Oh yes – I've been watching you, Master Peeping Tom Lestrange, and now, my friend, you are going to pay! You're going to pay for what you did to these – ' he paused as the colour drained from his face '– these hands.' He raised his two hands and displayed for all to see the lesions and contusions, which even after all these years had not healed, the legacy of so many miscalculations in a chalkdusty schoolroom of the long ago. His head seemed to swell to twice its normal size as all the blood in his body coursed towards it, his two extremities hovering menacingly in front of my uncle's face like two blotched table-tennis bats of flesh.

'I'm sorry,' croaked my uncle. 'If there's anything I can do to make it up, please tell me!'

But it was too late for any of that. It was clear that no one could help us now.

We found ourselves bound and gagged and imprisoned in the back of a foul-smelling vehicle which, it instantly became evident to us as we lay there back to back like a nightmarish set of ill-proportioned Siamese twins, had been used in the very recent past for the transportation of poultry.

'Keep them in there until they have manners knocked into them!' I heard Dingo snarl, and the fading jackboot stomp of his wellington boots was the last sound that came to my ears before I collapsed at last into a dead faint.

As the days passed, our only contact with the outside world was the thin sword of light which shone when the double doors would swing open, a foul smelling bowl of near-gruel shoved towards us, our only means of sustenance throughout our captivity. How long was it going to go on, that wretched cacaphony of sound that assaulted our eardrums daily, like so many aural poison darts, as we sweated in the darkness of our murky dungeon? 'Oh my God!' we would hear them shriek in orgiastic delight. 'That's great! Keep doing that!' as Macardle's coarse sibilants exhorted those poor, corrupted creatures to indulge themselves to the point of what I knew must be a certain destruction. 'Come on, girls!' he would cry. 'Get stuck in! Put your backs into it!'

In my ears, the sound of bodily fluids intermingling was the roar of some terrible Niagara.

How long we spent in our foul confinement I cannot say. When at last they came to their decision regarding our fate, we were bundled out into the harsh light of day to confront the despicable

Macardle, now wearing a white shirt emblazoned with the three lurid rubrics, MAC. A grin flexed itself as he flicked his cigar and stared into my eyes. 'Ever done any acting, boy?' he inquired. 'No,' I croaked, feeling the first faint blush coming to my cheeks, and it was then he raised his hand and slowly opened it to display the photograph of my Uncle Louis, in what has been described as *flagrante delicto*, helpless as he lay in their powdered arms, folded in the delicate wings of my beautiful Birds of Paradise.

'I wonder what the parish priest would make of this?' snickered Macardle, as he secreted the photograph in the inside pocket of his brown leather jacket.

'No, please!' I cried. 'Don't send it to the parish priest! Anything but that!'

Macardle coughed and pared the nail of his index finger with his marbled pocket knife.

'And just what's in it for me if I don't?' he quizzed me stonily, his bead-like eyes slowly rising to meet mine.

'I'll do anything you say,' I said then, resigning myself at last to my fate.

After that, everything is a dream. The nightly agonies of conscience which I suffered, I cannot even begin to chronicle here, for it would be too painful. All I can remember are the sad, hurt eyes of my dear Uncle Louis as the oaken arms of Dingo Deery gripped him once more and hurled him forward with a snort of derision, and the schoolmaster sank once again beneath a flutter of wings and the flying feathers of what once were Gauguin's masterpieces. But etched most of all on my mind is the twisted, salacious expression on the face of Mick Macardle as he distributed a variety of crook-handled canes which he had purchased for a pittance in a London East End market, and with which, through the medium of his barking metal trumpet, he instructed the cast, with unmistakable, lip-trembling glee, to 'Bate him harder! Hit him again there, girls!

Give him all you've got!'

I hid my eyes as the blows rained down on the reddening flesh of my beloved uncle, his elderly moons thrust skyward as they continued to yelp excitedly: 'This will teach you! You won't be spying on us again in a hurry, you filthy-minded old rascal! Take that!'

The days passed in a black delirium as we were subjected to indignity after indignity; each day another can of eight millimetre film sealed and labelled, just as surely as our fate. Tears come into my eyes as those words return once more, thumbed that day by Deery on to a glinting can: THE SECRETS OF LOUIS LESTRANGE.

I cannot continue. Sometimes I think perhaps it was all a dream, for that was how it appeared when it was over: the cameras spirited away, the convent reopened, the single tourist gone from the hotel – nothing remaining but the flattened yellow grass and the soft, contented chirp of the chaffinches. I began to think, maybe there had never been a Dingo Deery, a Mick Macardle, a thin moustache?

Would that it were true! I shall never forget the sight of that narrow, mean mouth, the unmistakable smell of cigar smoke that enshrouded me as I felt his hand upon my shoulder: 'If you ever breath a word of this,' he hissed into my ear, 'the bateing Lestrange got will be nothing to what's coming to him!'

I thought of my uncle, his spirit now broken beyond repair, his white-swaddled hands for all the world the blunt stumps of a war veteran as he picked his way sheepishly through the cooling streets.

Oh, yes, Mick Macardle and Dingo Deery existed alright, for in the few days that remained to me in the town, they missed no opportunity to humiliate me, whispering discreetly as they passed close by, 'I believe you're a powerful actor, young man!' and 'Did you ever try the stage?'

I began to dread these forced intimacies to such a degree that I became a virtual recluse.

The long, hot summer came to an end. Grouse Armstrong met his death in an accident with a Volkswagen Beetle and the only sound to be heard now in The Pronto Grill was that of the proprietor whistling his lonely tune, dreaming of Palermo. Not long after, Mick Macardle opened a supermarket, the very first of its kind in the country, and ever since is to be seen cruising around brashly in his open-topped convertible in streets that are now littered with drug addicts and disco bars. I understand he has entered politics and resides in a magnificent, converted castle on the outskirts of the town, with Dingo Deery resplendent in his blue security uniform by the electronically surveyed gates, his embroidered extremities now encased in gloves of the softest calf leather.

What bitter injustice there is in this world!

And now in this great city, as beneath my window the cinema doors open and the hunted, clandestine penumbrae emerge from the subterranean flesh-palace to shuffle homeward like so many tortured specters, I realise at last there is little for me to do now but accept the hand that fate has dealt me. For, having hastily terminated my academic studies and fled the country all those years ago, who am I to complain of a lowly position with Brent County Council? For in truth, they have treated me most fairly, and my supervisor has informed me that the section of Kilburn park for which I am responsible is considered impeccable and utterly leaf-free, and has been singled out for special mention by the visiting inspectors on more than three occasions.

Yes, the old men have long since passed away now, the summer seat taken away and broken up for firewood. To smoke a Players cigarette now is to put oneself in great mortal danger and they say that since Yuri Gagarin returned from space he has become a complete vegetable. But I shall not rest.

Deep inside, my quest shall go on, my relentless search for refuge from those terrible memories and the wanton destruction of what was once a beautiful dream.

Which, of course, they shall never know. How would they, those sad, anonymous creatures who shuffle homeward to their waiting, unsuspecting wives, their base desire sated? How are they ever to know that what they have just witnessed on that oblong obscenity they call a screen is the vilest of lies, a distortion, a cruel, ugly trick played by a cheap magician? Would they listen to me if I were to cry out from the very pit of my soul, 'THE SECRETS OF LOUIS LESTRANGE! It is lies, my friends! Lies! This is all lies! A pack of despicable, unwarranted lies! Don't believe a word of it!'

No, in my heart I know they would not. So, I have no choice but to go on, with the memory of those days which were once suffused with the colour of burnished copper receding within me, nothing more now than a bit player from the last reel of the deserted cinema of life, where a silent, would-be ornithologist, once honoured and revered beyond all rustic pedagogues, sits alone in the back row, chuckling to himself without reason as he tries to focus on the past and the way it might have been before a thin moustache, a cruel twist of fate and 1,137 whacks of a crook-handled cane brought an old man and a poor young adolescent boy to within eight lonely millimetres of hell.

Vincent McDonnell

The Milking Bucket

THERE WAS black frost on the day Tom and Nora Mallee died; and that other who'd borne my name for the few minutes of his short life. It was Nora's wish, and as she lay dying she insisted that the name Jimmy be added to the baptismal rite performed by the midwife. This I learned later, for my mother thought then that it wasn't suitable knowledge for a ten-year-old boy.

What my mother didn't know – what no one has ever known – was that I held myself responsible for the events of that March day. Though a grown man now and aware that I played no part in what occurred, I still sometimes feel the burden of those far-off events. Why else was it that I recently returned from England for the first time in thirty years, determined to right wrongs? Or was it that I was really seeking revenge?

I returned to find my birthplace utterly changed. The house still stood, but with windows and doors open to the elements, slates missing from the roof and the fireplaces overflowing with the debris of rooks' nests. But I could still sit, if I so wished, on the stone steps, where as a boy I sat with the other village lads, and dreamed of the future.

But no trace remained of the Mallee place and grass grew where the house had been. I tried to figure out where exactly in the yard the giant sycamore had stood, but childhood is an imperfect recorder, and time had so distorted my memories it was as if I'd viewed them through water.

But nothing can distort my memories of the March day the Mallees died; as I hurried from school I was anticipating an evening of play when dinner was wolfed down and my chores completed. But tragedy had come like Jack Frost to touch everyone: there was no play, and surely for the first time in living memory no children's shouts rang through the bohreens or over the freshly 'top dressed' fields.

Instead we stood by the sycamore in Mallee's yard, our minds numbed by what had happened. Now and again a child attempted to play, but was stilled by our collective disapproval. Eventually they all dribbled home, driven by the dusk and by stories of a man with a tail and cloven hooves; or else responding to repeated calls from silhouettes framed in lighted doorways – Pateen, Mikeen, Maureen – the names ringing on the frost-tight air.

I lingered after they'd gone, unable to accept that Tom and Nora were dead, and that I had helped to kill them. For hadn't I been their friend and known their kindness? Hadn't I known, as my mother had often repeated, that they were better living persons than those who mocked them? Hadn't the milking buckets endorsed my mother's words? Hadn't they taught me to see what ignorance and superstition and prejudice is, and how a man might love a woman?

On the day they bought the buckets I was there with the other children, hidden behind the privet hedge which surrounded Mallee's house. It was a place from which we often observed and made fun of them.

'You'll have to be buying a milking bucket today from the travelling shop,' we heard Nora say at the end of what had been a long argument. 'And that's that. Else what'll you milk the young heifer into when she calves?'

'By go', woman!' Tom shouted in exasperation. 'I'll milk her into the piss-pot.'

Laughter betrayed us and we scattered as Tom charged across the yard, his hobnailed boots ringing on the flags. Nora's screeches followed us, her voice embittered by twenty barren years of marriage. 'They're cursed,' I'd often heard people say.

'It's no wonder God never gave them childer and him not darkening the church door since the day he got married.'

To me a curse meant a certainty of hell, and my child's imagination gave a horrifying reality to the idea of burning flesh. In vivid nightmares I saw Tom Mallee burn because God had cursed him for learning the ways of evil during his time in America. And as part of this curse, God had allowed no gooseberry bush to grow in Mallee's yard under which they might have found a baby.

In revenge Tom stole other people's babies which Nora boiled alive in the big black pot which stood outside the front door. Afterwards she fed them to the dog which slunk about the yard, its face composed entirely of teeth.

Those fears were for the dark and the aftermath of ghost stories. And for the Saturday visit to confession, when in the examination of conscience the abomination of such sins as telling lies and missing your prayers loomed large; and hell was the eternal scald of boiling porridge accidentally poured into my child's wellington, skin peeling off with the boot.

But on the day of the argument over the milking buckets, I had no fear and was looking forward to my usual treat when the travelling shop came. I gathered with the other children around the large van, taste buds expectant at the thought of gob-stoppers and bulls'-eyes. So I was there when Nora Mallee came and bought tea and sugar and bread soda; and Sunlight soap and a wick for the oil lamp; and finally a galvanised bucket. And I was still there when Tom came for his half ounce of Walnut Plug and another bucket.

'Sure, amn't I just after selling one to Nora,' Mike Moran said.

'Her, is it? Tom said. 'What would I be doing with her bucket.'

'Well, I've only the one bucket left,' Mike said. 'With a bit of a dent in it. Would that be doing you now?'

'It'll have to do,' Tom said. 'But you'll have to be knocking a bit off. And let ye be off with ye,' he shouted, turning on our sniggers. We scrambled to a safe distance, and as Tom walked away we chanted: 'Two buckets... two buckets...'

My world and that of the Mallees might never have touched if their dog hadn't bit me. My initial memory of fear and the trickle of warm blood down my leg is overshadowed by what followed. Nora, responding to my terrified screams, came rushing from the house and before I knew it had bundled me into the kitchen, past the pot which, close up, seemed large enough to accommodate myself.

Tom was eating his dinner and rose from the table without a word. He took down the shotgun from the wall and a single cartridge from a box on the mantelpiece, its case as red as my flowing blood. He went outside and I heard the thud of the gun closing and a shrill whistle. At the sound of the shot I felt the first stab of pain, and began to sob. Nora smothered me to her, and in the blackness of her skirts and shower-of-hail apron I smelled turf smoke and ashes. I sensed her anguish and her desperate need for fulfilment, a boy too young to be laid open to such naked, human yearning.

From that day on I never taunted the Mallees again. Nora seemed to take a liking to me for she always came out when I passed. She would have a slice of currant bread for me, spread with homemade jam. Or a baked potato, split open. I would juggle it from hand to hand until it was cool enough to eat, licking the yellow butter that dribbled from the ends of the split. And on days when the travelling shop came, she would give me a penn'orth of bulls'-eyes.

Sometimes she took me into the kitchen and I would stare in awe at the shotgun, next to God because it too could take life. I drank mugs of bitter-sweet buttermilk, still warm after churning. And as the passing summer left hay fields bare and cattle with the promise of aftergrass, I ate huge chunks of apple pie washed down with glasses of red lemonade. But there were no more displays of desperate emotion.

By autumn my fear of Tom had gone, and sometimes I caught a twinkle in his dark eyes as I helped him about the yard. Together we fed the pig he would kill before Christmas, but I no longer believed that he ripped its throat with his teeth. I helped shoo the last few hens to roost and sometimes I fed the suck calf while Tom finished milking, both of us silent as deaf mutes.

All this time something puzzled me. It was the fact that Tom always used Nora's milking bucket. Yet he had said that he would never use hers. And hadn't he bought a bucket of his own so that he wouldn't have to?

It seemed natural to ask why, and one day in the kitchen I did ask. Nora laughed and I saw her exchange a look with Tom from which I was excluded. 'Sure hasn't his bucket got a dent in it,' she said, still laughing. She reached out a hand to ruffle Tom's hair, and as she passed his chair he slapped her hard on the backside. To my surprise they both laughed, and I found our two worlds spinning apart as if they were no longer subject to the laws of gravity. After that I never mentioned the buckets again.

It's said that childhood is an idyll. But in reality it's the furnace where the future is forged, where the everyday events of life can sometimes take on terrible proportions. For me the horrors began with the rumour that Nora was going to have a baby. At first I disbelieved it, but it was easier to disbelieve than to accept that what Nedser Gannon told me was true. His analogy of what the bull did to the cow was too brutal for my child's mind. After all I still believed in the miraculous properties of gooseberry bushes.

My mother eventually yielded to my persistent questions, confirming that Nora was pregnant. And unknowingly confirming what Nedser had told me was true. 'Nora's expecting a baby,' my mother said, 'and after all those years. You must have brought her good luck,' she added, and in an unexpected burst of spontaneous affection and need, she held out her arms to me. But now the mother image was contaminated by the goings-on of farm animals and I shrank from her and ran, and she laughed at what she must have supposed to be a growing boy's shyness.

From now on I avoided the Mallees. But sometimes from the shelter of the privet hedge, I spied on them. Nora's stomach slowly swelled, but I couldn't accept that there was a child in there. But there was something there and it threatened my whole existence. And as the bitterness left Nora's face, I took it for my own.

One day the Mallee's new dog betrayed my presence to Tom. 'Come out of there,' he shouted, and frightened by his rage I obeyed. 'Here,' he commanded as he might command the dog, and I entered the yard to stand before him.

His shouts brought Nora from the house and she came over to join us. 'It's Jimmy,' she said, sensing Tom's anger. 'Sure, he wouldn't do nothing.'

'I caught the bugger red-handed,' Tom said. He turned to look at her, his eyes softening. And with that single gesture I feared him no longer. Once I'd been terrified of him, had imagined being boiled alive in the pot. But now I knew that he slept in the bed with Nora, and did unspeakable things to her. He was human now, a man who put his arms around a woman and told her that he loved her. 'He had to,' Nedser had said. 'Otherwise it wouldn't have worked. That's what was wrong all the time. He couldn't tell her he loved her. But my mother says you changed all that.'

'Sure, Jimmy wouldn't do anything, Tom,' Nora repeated now. 'Doesn't the dog even like him.' The mongrel was about my legs, licking frantically at my scratched, brown skin. 'Come on in, Jimmy,' Nora went on, 'and I'll see what I've got for you.'

I went with her reluctantly, past the pot which was a simple cooking pot now, nothing more. Even the shotgun seemed insignificant, and I was no longer in awe of it. Nora gave me a slice of currant bread layered with butter and blackberry jam, but I refused it. I saw the hurt on her face and was glad. I was the embryo torturer seeing the first sign of weakness in my victim.

'Take it,' she said, but I shook my head like a donkey. 'What's the matter, *a ghrá?*' she asked, and child though I was I knew I'd hurt her. But to inflict pain on another is power, and to the impotent power is precious.

'That,' I said, pointing at her distended stomach. 'I hate you,' I shouted. 'You're cursed... cursed... I hope you die. I hope you all die.' I struck the bread from her hand and ran blindly from the house. Tom shouted in surprise as I charged past him, and I thought I heard Nora cry out. But I paid no heed. I ran along the boreen leading to the common, the dead briars scratching my bare legs. But the physical pain was bearable. I reached the common and threw myself face-down on the heather and sobbed bitterly, sensing for the first time a foreshadowing of the future and of my own mortality.

I never spoke again with the Mallees, and a few weeks later I returned from school to learn that they were dead. 'Nora borned a monster with two heads, and died of fright,' Nedser told me. 'They say it was the devil himself, and that it laughed with one mouth and cursed with the other.' He strung the expletives together, and I shrunk from their power. 'Tom had to hold the monster down while Annie Doyle baptised it,' Nedser went on. 'And it must've been the devil because the water boiled. After the baptism Tom choked it and it took him a whole hour to kill it. Someone must have cursed them,' Nedser added, 'for something terrible like that to happen.'

Distraught with the horrors of what my curse had brought about, I never thought to question Nedser's story. Had I done so, would he have known which head had been baptised? Or if both had been and the water had boiled twice? Had I asked I might have exposed the fact that Nedser was as much a child as I was. But I never doubted his story and if I wanted proof didn't I have that too. For hadn't Tom taken the shotgun after he'd killed the monster, and shot the cow and the calf; and then put the barrel in his mouth and splattered his brains all over the whitewashed cow byre walls.

But for me it was only beginning. Almost overnight my mother and I were ostracised and found ourselves taking the place of the Mallees. Even Nedser deserted me and said I was the son of a devil-lover. I blamed my curses for this, and every night I prayed to God to forgive me. But He never answered my prayers.

'We're going to leave here, Jimmy,' my mother told me one day. 'We're going to go to Manchester to be with your father.' She held out her hands to me like she'd done before, and this time I gave myself up to her.

We emigrated one wet June day, and not a single person came to say goodbye. My mother's face was set as if in plaster, and as the hackney car turned at the end of the road, she never looked back. Through the thirty years I was with her in Manchester, I never forgot that moment, though I did come to realise that my curse on the Mallees had not brought about those terrible events, nor was it the reason for our having to leave.

My mother never gave me a reason as to why we'd been ostracised, and only spoke of injustice and prejudice and super-stition. The truth I learned after her death when I was sorting out her affairs. I found it in small cardboard box containing her most precious possessions.

Among her things I found a scrap of a newspaper cutting and a few letters from her relatives in Ireland. The word tragedy cropped up in the cutting, but it was the small headline that held my attention: 'Suicide Denied Catholic Rites or Burial.'

As I read the piece and the letters, I learned that Nora and her son Jimmy had been buried together in the local cemetery, while Tom had been buried beside the famine grave in the

grounds of what once had been the workhouse. Neither neighbour nor priest had attended Tom's burial, but my mother had
been there and had said the rosary.

So it was I returned with some vague idea in my mind of
righting the wrongs. I would have Tom's bones exhumed and
buried with his wife and son and a headstone erected on the
grave.

But when I stood by Tom Mallee's grave, all I felt was
peace. The area was lawned, and grass and a few intruding
daisies grew there. I bowed my head in silence over what was
now but a pile of bones in earth; stood like people from the
beginning of time have stood, when confronted by the greatest
mystery of all.

The workhouse was now a school for handicapped children, and from an open window their high-pitched voices
drifted out. The sun was warm on my face, and branches of the
nearby trees cast moving shadows on the ground. I could imagine the children coming to this spot to pick the daisies, their
feet pattering on the fertile earth.

In that moment I realised that the past cannot be changed,
and that prejudice is but a reaction to what we do not understand. Here in this place Tom Mallee was at peace and only a
fool would think of disrupting it. Maybe this was what he
would have wanted. How could we ever know? I turned away,
and as I went out the gate I heard the joyful shouts of children
let out to play.

Lucille Redmond

Our Fenian Dead

AFTER THE rebellion I went to America. Everyone was dead or scattered; there was no reason to stay.

I trekked around for a while doing factory or bar work. I had never served my time to any trade, being a farmer's son. In a Louisiana town they needed seasonal pickers; when that was over I heard I might get something in a bar. They'd like the way I sang Irish songs. They wanted blues, though, so sometimes I sang blues, and American songs with their simple structure.

Under the gaslight the men and women looked blue: blue-black or blue-white. Tonight, I thought, I will sing a song from my home place. I sang in my own language the words that meant:

Going west by the sandy shore, put the flags on the masts
Ah, do not bury me in Leitir Calaidh, that is not my
  people's place
No, bring me west to Muighinis, the place where they will
  cry loudly for me
Lights on the hills... I will feel no loneliness there.

I met Joe O'Grady in Canal Street and he brought me home to the room where he was staying. He pumped up the lamp; it roared as the paraffin sprayed out at pressure and lighted. He put on a cigarette and smoked at it for a while, warming his hands at the globe. The kettle was sitting on the cold hearth. O'Grady cleaned and kindled the fire and filled the kettle. The man he shared with would soon come in and need to use the bed, and O'Grady would go on night shift. He told me the news from home. He had a weapon for me to hide and to hold against the day.

'I'm not getting involved again,' I said to O'Grady, and he looked at me and said, 'Of course. Of course.'

I looked at O'Grady, twenty years old now, his fair hair clogged with dust, his lungs troubled by a habitual cough, his face lined already. He'd been working in the copper mines, and the metal was in his skin so that his skin and face were darkened, giving his eyes a pale, eerie look, but when he opened a button of his shirt, I saw his throat as white and innocent as it was in Liscullane.

He sat there, shirtsleeves rolled back over his arms, muscles playing under the skin which looked so young and tender, untouched by the raw wind; his hands, though, were roughened by the callouses of work.

'Is there plenty of work?' I asked him, to keep the conversation going. 'Is there work to be had?'

'Ah, there's work alright,' he said, soaking up the gravy with his bread and looking up at me from under his lashes; 'there's work for those who want it.'

'What are the crowd like that run the unions?' I asked, knowing from talk I'd heard that he was one of the men involved. There had been something, an informer...

'Oh, we look after our own,' he said and again he gave me that look from under his lashes.

'I'll hold it for you, but that's all I'll do,' I said, taking the gun wrapped in its waxed paper. That's how it starts.

'There was an informer...' he started to say, but I stopped him with my hand. A piece of information, that's what it takes. Soon you're inside again, part of it all, talking about some man's death in a mundane room, a sour taste on every awakening.

I was sick for a while, but I'd saved wages, so I could lie in bed watching pictures on the walls. If I walked all day for ten months I'd be home, but for the sea. On the feast of St Brigid I went to a ceilidhe. It was in a big room, steaming from body heat. The people there knew all the steps. I leaned against the wall and watched. They all had the American tan, all-over single-coloured faces.

A man and a woman had a row. He made to strike her. A man told him to step outside and fight. An old copy of the *Irish Independent* lay folded on the shelf that ran round the wall. I picked it up and smelled the print. A stain of water lay on one word. I left the paper there and walked out. The night air was hot as a factory's breath. I followed a family who walked ahead. They went into a house and kindled a lamp in the kitchen. I could see them sit from where I stood in the lane looking in. They laid out a supper and ate it; two children washed and dried the delft.

'You live too much in the past,' said a voice in my head, a voice from the past. 'You like it, you know.' The slim rim of light thrown by the lamp reflected as I moved into the dark-ness, darkness lit only by a narrow slice of moon. The sound of the ceilidhe was fading behind me, until only the fiddle could be heard, and the cries of the dancers.

In Canal Street I walked by the water, listening to hear if a fish would break the surface. There was an apple tree there, its fruit powdered with soot. Memories.

A Castle man told me he was once walking through the Bridewell and he heard a fellow crying. He stopped and looked into the cell and Brian Robinson was sitting there. He knew him, of course. He was surprised when he heard the crying, because that was the place they kept the real hard men. He said he was unrecognisable from the beating the Specials had given him when they interrogated him. He said: 'Is that you, Brian?' Robinson looked up at him with hatred and said something like 'You know it is.'

Now, Canal Street was empty for a while, and then a man came down from the end. He leaned against a post, coughing, then spat and walked on.

Streets aren't places to stop in; they're passages for movement. People go from one place to another. In the main street many people were going by, their eyes dreaming. In the side roads there was no one, except sometimes a dog moving as fast as a dancer, touching its nose to a wall or a post. My foot kicked a marble left from a child's daylight game, and I was in Liscullane.

Then: walking from the hills, holding the empty feed bag, apologising to the frost-stiff grass blades that broke under my feet, hearing the sleep-deepened croaks of the first magpies, seeing, as I came to the cottage in the hollow at the shelter of the hill, the grandmother, the child and the cat running to the gate to greet me.

'Am I late?'

'The day is young,' she said, her hand on the gate.

That very day Myles Farrell had broken his arm; his mother called for the doctor but the doctor was drunk; the grand-mother sent me across the mountain with Robinson to bring the boy in the trap to the visiting doctor staying there.

When we got to the doctor's lodging the landlord said to leave the boy there and he'd call the man to treat him. Outside, Brian was wiping down the horse with thraneens of grass; he turned and looked.

'There's no lights kindled in the house,' he said.

I looked and he was correct. The house was dark.

The gun was under the axle housing. We had been on some business the night before. I took it and went back into the house. The boy was lying where I'd left him. He was crying from the pain. I told the landlord to fetch the doctor, and he said: 'The man needs his sleep.' He said: 'I'll call him in the morning. Time enough.' Then I showed him the gun and he went and got the doctor. He set Myles Farrell's arm then, and I put the boy back in the trap and brought him home to his mother.

It was when I got home I heard the news, found O'Grady at the wall, waiting for my instructions. Word had filtered in, somehow, in the way word comes; some hungry boys meeting in the empty walls of a ruined home, watching as a man rows across a lake, a quick word spoken without thought. Sweet is the mouth which keeps silence.

I remembered, standing there, far over the sea, listening to the water of the canal stirred by the thick air. 'You've blinded me,' the man had said quietly to me, his voice conversational, as I stood blank of thought, holding the knife. Standing with the trickle running up the gully of the knife and across my hand under my sleeve, I was cast back, then, as I watched a rabbit torn by dogs, the memory of my mother's breast, of her blue eyes looking out beyond me.

'Did you bring the gun?' Robinson said that day. 'You were to bring it.'

'I was not,' said O'Grady.

The prisoner stood between us, looking from one to another. He knew our faces. All we had was the three spades we'd brought. The burial was fixed in all our minds.

'I told you to bring the gun.'

'You did not. You said you'd bring it.'

'But it's on the trap.'

'It is not, it's in the roof.'

'Go back and get it.'

'I will not.'

'He can't, we have to be fast.' The man we were waiting to turn into meat stood looking at the stone wall. Lichen was growing there, very pretty. Was he listening? I had a knife, too, the folding knife my mother had bought me when I planted her apple trees, with its rosewood handle and its gullied blade.

The prisoner didn't say anything, looking from one to another. I knew the back of his head better than his face: he sat in front of me in school. He was a good student. He was slapped in front of the class once, with the intention of breaking his spirit. He had spikes of uncut hair; I remember one hair was grey. I thought: he's greying young.

The four of us stood together in the middle of the field, three holding spades, a short digging spade and two long-handled slanes, and I also had my gullied pruning knife. A big rock was beside us, where my cousin and Robinson's had buried the cow.

'Kneel down and say a prayer,' said O'Grady, and the prisoner dropped to his knees suddenly.

'We all have to strike,' said O'Grady. The prisoner had joined his hands but they fell away from each other now.

'I can't,' said Robinson, but he dug the spade into the ground, and went away a short distance, holding his fists to the side of his face. The four of us stayed there, patiently waiting to accomplish this.

'We'll have to do it with the spades,' said O'Grady.

'I have the knife,' I said. The prisoner looked at me.

O'Grady hit him with the spade and Robinson ran at him and beat him with the edge of the short digging spade. His eyes were grey, as you could see through a flow of blood; it was in the whites of his eyes. The spade gave an ugly crunch. His head fell limp but rose again briefly.

Walking home, slapping the road dust from bloody canvas trousers as we laughed:

'Are you coming for the wake?'

'He was pissed altogether!'

'Go and shite!'

I fell against a wall, laughing, and grazed my wrist, and blood left a mark by the rust-red lichen. I felt very light-hearted.

It was a sharp day. I remembered that day, standing there with the rosewood-handled knife in my hand, a day I went with my father to the quarry and and hit a rock with a lump-hammer. The shape of a snail was nesting in the stone. 'It'll rot now, if it's exposed to the air, unless you treat the rock,' my father had said.

A fiddlehead fern was growing out of the wall by my face. Its coiled green tendril stirred.

On the sea I forgot. I was there with the boat, the smell of salt, the sailors calling, the sound of the sails. It was a fishing boat, one of the loose fleet that works between Maine and Galway, all the Atlantic ports. I kept travelling. I'll start again.

Six thousand miles away, five thousand hours away from that day. Now, a heron flew through the air; if not a heron, some American bird. The water sounded, freshening the dark. Somewhere there was the sound of a quarrel: angry words, a blow, tears with a heartbroken edge to them. A door closed, footsteps sounded, a dog cried out, the broken row of houses stood against the unlightened dark, I walked to the water's edge.

As I walk in the city, above my head the leaves of the slim, foreign tree they call oak here speak softly one to another: they have things to say. The wind calls out: Where are you?

A brougham passes on a parallel street: I recognise the sound, the grinding of iron-shod wheels throws me back to the two-wheeled cart and the trap with my rakish Vulcan tearing up the furlongs.

I am an echo-chamber for memories. The future was beginning to echo in me now, though, the future as well as the past.

Here in the southern states of this great group of nations, I hear slow speech, an echo of home. Passing on the streets I hear phrases brush my cheek; a child runs by, stops, turns and calls; a father opens his palm in a gesture.

In the morning I rise fresh from my bed to watch the day. The houses here are wooden, they are separated from the earth on which they stand; the house where I grew up was a room of clay. My brothers are gone from there now. The house will sink into the earth when it is untenanted. These wood houses, slatted and windowed, have many rooms but lack substance.

Soon enough I found out who was the informer O'Grady talked about: he was staying in the same house as myself.

A love affair was going on in my house. A seamstress in her fifties – an age comparable to the seventies in Europe – and a sprig of a platemaker in his late forties were carrying on a cautious and gradual embroilment. It was my opinion each would be well advised to settle with the other: they would get no better offer now, and might secure some happiness, or at least content.

One morning as I came home from the bar I passed his room. I was walking quietly, holding my boots in my hand. I could hear him talking in his room; it sounded as if he was having a conversation, but only one voice was speaking. I walked on and into my room, and there I washed and got into the bed.

The next night I woke again, and went down for the land-lady's dinner, which served me for a breakfast. When I passed his room again, he was talking still, in the same hurried voice. I went on again, but when I went into the kitchen to eat, the seamstress was not there, and the landlady drew me aside and told me that she had left the town. He was brokenhearted, the landlady said, with her breast throbbing and her eyes full of tears.

I went to wash myself at the pump, and soon he came down to stand behind me, to wait. His face was white, his eyes red, he was holding a letter; unusual for people here to read. I was curious.

As I washed he leaned back against the pillar holding the roof and began to sing to himself, a song that was going the rounds at the time, 'The Streets of Laredo'. But the tune was a little different, and he put in a grace-note here and there, he made it sharper, thrusting it out from the sentimental sound of this country.

'*An Éireannach thú?*' I said quietly without turning: are you an Irishman? But he just kept on humming and reading the letter he held in his hand. As I turned from the pump and ran my hands back through my wet hair, he put the letter back in its envelope and laid it down on the square hitching post beside the cloth I had left there to dry myself.

I went to take up the towel. He was pumping the pump-handle behind me, the water was gushing out. The letter had come a long way, and its journey was registered by postal carriers in a dozen places. Faintly, under the writing that covered the paper, the name of my home place came out to me: Liscullane. The name on the letter: Myles Farrell. I felt my blood run slow.

I walked in and through the kitchen, and nodded my thanks to the landlady, who was clearing up the plates from another shift of men who had eaten her food.

'Oh, Mr Byrne,' she called, 'there was a man looking for you earlier. I didn't know you were still here. He's gone up to the bar, I think.'

He wasn't in the bar when I got there, though, and I sat and thought, waiting for the place to fill up so that I could begin to hand them out their drink, talking to the women who sat by the mirror putting paint on their faces in the hopes of some custom for the night. I was sharing the work with a man from the Mississippi, an African, and this was his turn to sing, while I took the main part of the bar work.

He sang:

Honey, your hair grows too long
        Lord, Lord, Lord, Lord
I don't know where I'm bound
I'm going where nobody knows my name
        Lord, Lord, Lord, Lord
I don't know where I'm bound

I remember my young sister asking me what it was made a boy want to be with a girl, and I answered: it's a way of standing in a room, a look, a laugh; but here in the bar it was all settled, this way, what they were here for, there was no mystery.

The man finished his song and I sat at the piano and sang my songs, watching the women, and the men with their assessing looks, their wallets and their pocketbooks.

Brian Robinson and Michael O'Grady moved into my mind

without being asked and walked around in the bath-smelling dark. In the bar, one of the girls was going through the room with a glass puffer of lily scent, French she said, though I doubted it. I could smell the pleasant scent, now, at the side of the field, in the world of my past in my mind.

Irish towns with their riverine rhythms are flushed with people and horses at intervals: shops open or close, small manufactories shriek sirens to call their workers in, school-children rush home for dinner and back again, then the light goes and everything is silent. Here the streets are busy all the time, except for those back streets which see no one.

In my mind O'Grady said again: 'Stand up now,' but the prisoner could not stand. His legs failed him. He stared up, his mouth open with shame, and Robinson ran at him and lifted him, and tied him under his arms to the spade. He kept sliding down, and I struck him with the knife.

'You've blinded me,' he said. I think I struck him in the head; I can't remember. Sometimes I spring awake and I've just done it, but as soon as I look my memory fails. I struck him in the temple or in the tongue; under the tongue, up into the head, I conjecture.

The bar here is full of people travelling here and there; a depot, a roundhouse. Bills hang on the walls advertising of events here and elsewhere; singers and acrobats, magicians, despera-does, eccentric dancers, freaks, festivities, farces, harlequins.

I moved around it from table to table, stepping over the legs of men spending their pay, smelling the hot woman's smell of thick perfume as the girls tucked bills of cash between their breasts or under their skirts. It was then that I saw O'Grady, sitting in the corner, drawing a square filled with parallel lines on the table.

I moved over towards him, pardoning myself to the diners as I wiped their tables. They did not see me, shouting and laughing at the dancers, throwing back the whiskey, their faces shining as they spent the money they had earned.

O'Grady sat back in silence. As I came to his table he looked past me, keeping his eyes on the dancers who hopped and dragged their hips to the beat of the piano pounded by the sweating African. O'Grady's eyes were still, but his hands kept moving, drawing the square and the bars in it, the square and the bars.

'Are you in or are you out,' he said to me, as I mopped the table, erasing the picture he had drawn, smoothing the wood again to its sweep of grain. Our eyes met as I moved on to the next table.

At five o'clock in the morning on October fourteenth I stand with a cloth in my hand and listen. The bar is cleared, the ware washed, the chairs stacked, the windows open.

The clock is ticking; its chime is unwound; the hour hand is between IIII and V. Footsteps cross the floor above.

Outside a boat of a moon holds still in the tide of the sky. A sweaty dew lies on the stones. It is as soundless as a nightmare.

As I turn down the wick the light is sucked away and dark rushes into its vacuum. Tables and papers pulse as the light empties away.

I remember now a lissom-breezed autumn evening that we sat in the hollow of a hill, some three thousand people or more, to hear one man speak, and as he said each phrase the murmur went back through the crowd, repeating it, his words passing back in a whisper.

'In my years in English jails I had time to think, and time to dream, and the dream I dreamed was of Ireland.

'Ireland free, Ireland standing strong among nations, even though her ground must be watered by the blood of a thousand or a hundred thousand of her sons before this glorious day can come to pass.

'Destiny calls the sons of Erin to sacrifice. Destiny calls for the strong requirement that they pledge their blood to free an ancient nation ravished by an eternal wrong. Destiny calls, if it may be, for the ultimate sacrifice, for that pledge most sacred to Irish manhood, more sacred than life itself...'

Now I shut the piano. I shut the till. I close over the windows. I walk outside into the night sounding with crickets, the American night, the night full of light, with its air like breath that smells the same outside as in the tepid bar. The moon sails on, a ragged crescent, the mordant glow of Venus coming up now to join it.

There is the sound of liquid flowing. As my boot-heels lift from the dew, my footprints follow me. Here I walk on the stones, not on the sinking mossy grass of fields and paths.

Tom Phelan

In the Vatican Museum

IT WAS my first year in England. I was young, young and as full of piss and wind as a barn bullock in winter. The woman I knew from the church. She was always at the nine o'clock Mass on Sundays with her five brats. Regular little whore's melts they were, screeching and climbing all over the place and she kneeling there like she was deaf.

This one was a martyr, a holy-looking one that went on mouthing her prayers and staring at some private hallucination while her children tore the pews apart with their teeth. I'd be up there spouting my words of holy wisdom and no one hearing me and I longing to vault out of the pulpit and wring their necks. Imagine the headlines in the *Mirror... Massacre of the Innocents! Raging priest kicks the shite out of five babies.*

I approached this saint after Mass one Sunday and broached the subject of her bastards' behaviour. She jumped on me like I was a cockroach, right there on the steps of the church with everyone passing by. It was in March and there was an east wind blowing that would raise blisters on the bollicks of a bat. I was still in the vestments and they flapping around me like sheets on a clothesline. She screamed at me and her frightened babies gripping her skirts and looking at me like I was Jack the Ripper. I was so embarrassed I could have throttled the bitch there and then.

Murder on the Church Steps! With the wind howling at his vestments, his red hair like a flaming halo, the victim's children beating on his head and shoulders with their little fists, the Reverend Daniel Joseph Fitzpatrick knelt with one knee on the

*church steps, the other on the young woman's sternum, and
slowly pushed his thumbs down onto her screaming windpipe,
while the horrified witnesses stood paralysed, watching as the
foam dripped off the cleric's mouth like huge globs of suds.
The coroner said the victim died of drowning caused by the
large quantity of soapy water found in her lungs.*

In a matter of seconds everyone else had disappeared and
we were all alone on the steps. She stopped yelling to draw a
breath and when she heard the Sunday morning silence, she
looked around like she didn't know where she was. Then she
started to bawl. The water flowed down her face, down along
her neck and inside the collar of her shirt or blouse or whatever
it was she had on. Then she started talking. Oh, Father this and
Father that and her husband wouldn't get up for Mass, and he
coming from a good Irish Catholic family, Father, and he lying
there sulking and so cross he wouldn't talk and he like that for
weeks now, Father, because we can't afford another one and
we can't take any chances, Father, and I told him the curses of
God would hang around the rafters if he brought them things
into the house but he bought them, Father, and locked them in
the cupboard in their blue box but I can't let him do it, Father,
and all day long I think of them things in the cupboard and I
worry about what will happen on account of them, Father, and
he saying terrible things about the Pope and how would the
Pope feel if someone told him he could never eat again, Father.

Maybe the keen wind whistling up her skirts blunted the
keenness of her offensive or else she ran out of words. One way
or the other, she asked me to go to see her in her flat.

It was on a Friday I went – it was the day before the Grand
National and she gave me the name of the horse her husband
was betting on and I won fifteen quid. When I walked into her
place I nearly broke out. The flat was as greasy as a frying pan
on a Sunday morning. The floor was greasy. The walls were
greasy. The place stank. Karist! The baby was crawling around
on his hands and knees through the hairy scum on the floor.

The sink was so full of dishes you couldn't turn on the tap. The cleanest thing in the place was the cat licking the grease off its paws.

'Before we talk,' I said to her, 'we're going to clean. We'll start with the sink. I'll wash, you dry.' Don't ask me why I said it. It had nothing to do with God or divine inspiration or the Holy Ghost. None of that shite. It was just that the place was so fucking filthy that I had to clean it like you have to scratch an itch. We talked as we cleaned and all the time I was afraid the husband would walk in and me at the sink with my sleeves rolled up. We emptied the cupboards, scoured them out, squashed roaches with our shoes. We washed down the walls and scraped the floor before we washed that. I did most of it. She had to take breaks to succour her whelps who turned out to be far better behaved at home than they were in church.

When I finally got around to the subject of birth control, I asked her to get me the box of condoms from her husband's cupboard. She told me the cupboard was locked and she didn't know where the key was. 'Bullshite, woman,' says I, 'there's no wife in this world who doesn't know how to get past her husband's locks.' The whole thing was, she was mortified to even hear the word condom.

I bullied her till she brought them to me, and she holding them like you would a mouse that has been dead for a long time, by the tail. I sat there at the kitchen table with my hands resting on the box and I read her the riot act. I started off with the thing of keeping a clean house, a place where her husband would want to come home to, etcetera, etcetera. But she knew all that. He was angry at her because he wasn't getting his dues, as she called them. She was depressed because he was pissed off at her and she knew she had let the place go to hell.

Then I gave her a lecture about sex and marriage, sex and children, responsible sex, all kinds of sex, and she blushing like a nun. But I loosened up her chastity belt. Her mother was the one who put it on her and then Mother Church had welded it in place.

When I finished, I put the condoms in the middle of the table and I stood up and blessed them. I made up a new blessing as I went along: 'We thank you, Lord, for giving us the gift to create life and the intelligence to limit our creation to a few healthy and beautiful flowers instead of a patch of weeds. We call upon you to assist us in our wise decisions, by guiding the hands of the workers who make these condoms and by guiding the hands of the wives who lovingly fit them onto their husbands. May the Lord bless these condoms to defend and protect all mothers who use them.' She gasped out loud when she realised what I was doing. Then I said, 'I'm still alive and no lightning has struck me. These are good for you, woman. They are a blessing and it is your obligation and Christian duty to encourage your husband to use them.'

I was dying to take one out of the box because I'd never seen a condom. But now I wish I had taken one. I would have sent it to the Vatican Museum; after all, it was the first blessed condom.

That's how I did it. Washed the floor and blessed the condoms and after that there wasn't a sound out of her five little bastards in the church.

Desmond Hogan

Afternoon

S HE LAY in the hospital, which she hated, with nuns
running about and nurses slipping with trays of soup.

The soup was awful, simply awful. 'Package soup,' she
complained to Mary. Not the strong emerald and potato soup
of the bog-roads. 'I'll die if I stay here much longer.' Mary
looked at her. Her mother was ninety-one and the doctors had
stated there was little hope for her. The tribe of the Wards was
expecting death as their children would watch for the awakening of stars at night on beaches in Connemara.

Two Madges came and two more Marys came to see her
later that night. They stood like bereaved angels gazing at the
old woman who had mothered fifteen children, ten living, one
a doctor in London, one a building contractor in California.
The one who was a doctor had been taken by English tourists
before the civil war. He'd been a blond two-year-old, her
youngest at the time. They'd driven up in a Ford coupé to the
camp, admired the child, asked if he could spend the summer
with them. They never gave him back. Jimmy Joe was a building contractor in California. He'd gone to the golden state in
1925, seeking gold. He now owned a big house in San
Francisco and Tim, her great-grandson, had only that summer
gone to him and installed himself in the house, 'jumping into a
swimming-pool' it was whispered.

Eileen lay dying. As the news spread Wards and even
McDonaghs came to see her. They came with cloaks and blan-
kets and children. They came with caps and with fine hats from
London. They smoked pipes. They looked on with glazed eyes

telling themselves about history of which she had seen so much.

Mary recalled the wake for her husband twenty years before in the fair green in Ballinasloe, loud mourning and the smell of extinguished fires. In the fair green of Ballinasloe now bumpers bashed and lights flashed to the sound of music and the rising whine of voices and machines.

Tinkers from all over Ireland had come to Ballinasloe fair green as they had for hundreds of years, bringing horses, donkeys, mules. Romanies even came from England and gypsies from the South of France.

Eileen in her hospital bed often thought she heard the voice of the carnival. She'd first gone to the fair at the age of ten in 1895 when Parnell was still being mourned, as this area was the place of his infamous adultery, adultery among the wet roses and the big houses of Loughrea. You could smell his sin then and the wetness of his sex. Her parents made love in their small caravan. In Ballinasloe there'd been the smell of horse manure rising balefully and the rough scent of limestone. A young man had asked her age and said she'd make a fine widow some day.

She'd married at fifteen and her husband went to sea. He sailed to South America and to South Africa and the last that was heard of him was that he'd married a black woman on an island.

Eileen had had one child by him. The child died in the winter of 1902 on a bog-road outside Ballinasloe. It had been buried in a field under the mocking voices of jackdaws, and she swore she'd become a nun like the Sisters of Mercy in their shaded gardens in Ballinasloe.

But Joe Ward took her fancy – he'd become a tinker king in a fight in Aughrim – beating the previous king of the tinkers, who was twenty-five years older than him, in a fist-fight. He'd been handsome and swarthy and had a moustache like British army officers, well-designed and falling like a fountain.

They'd wedded in Saint Michael's Church on Saint Stephen's Day, 1906. Her father had told the bishop in Loughrea her previous husband had been eaten by sharks and the marriage had taken place without bother. She'd worn a Victorian dress, long and white, which the lady of the local manor had given her, a woman who'd performed on the London stage once with bouquets of paper roses about her breasts.

The priest had proclaimed them man and wife as celebrations followed on the Aughrim road, whiskey and poteen downed where a month before two children had died from the winter chill.

There had been dancing through the night and more than one young girl lay down with an older heftier man, and Eileen slept with a warm-legged man, forgetting about the odd clinging piece of snow and the geese fretting in the fields.

She became pregnant that cold, cold winter, holding her tummy as March winds howled and their caravans went west, trundling along Connemara roads to the gaps where the sea waited like a table. They camped near Leenane Head. Fires blazed on June nights as wails rose, dancing ensuing and wood blazing and crackling with a fury of bacon. They were good days. They'd sold a troop of white horses to the gypsies of France and many men went to bed with their women, stout in their mouths and on their whiskers.

They saw ships sail up the fjord at dawn and they bought crabs and lobster from local fishing men. When her belly had pushed out like a pram, she found Joe on the lithe body of a young cousin.

Her child perished at birth. She had thirteen children by Joe. They grew up as guns sounded and tinker caravans were caught in ambushes in East Galway. Joe was in Dublin for 1916. He saw the city blaze and he was bitterly disappointed as he'd come to Dublin to sell a mare and eat a peach melba in an illustrious ice cream house in Sackville Street. He returned to Galway without having eaten his ice cream.

Michael Pat, her oldest, found a dead parish priest lying in the bushes like a crow in 1921; the Tans had smitten him on the head. The tinkers had covered his body and fallen on their knees in prayer. The police came and a long stalwart ambulance.

The body was borne away, and Eileen and her children attended his funeral, bringing bouquets of daffodils stolen from the garden of a solicitor and banners of furze which were breaking to gold.

He was the last victim Eileen knew of, for Britain gave the men with their long moustaches and grey lichen-like hair their demands, and as they arrived in Ballinasloe for the fair there was more anger, more shots, and buildings in flame in Dublin.

Irishmen were fighting Irishmen. A young man was led blindfolded to a hill above the Suck and shot at dawn and the fair ceased for a day because of him and then went on with a girl who had a fruity Cork accent bellowing 'I'm forever blowing bubbles' across the fair green where lank and dark-haired gypsies from France smoked long pipes like Indians.

Eileen opened her eyes.

Her daughter Mary, sixty-two, looked like Our Lady of the Sorrows.

'O Mother dear, you're leaving me alone with a pack of ungrateful children and their unfortunate and ill-behaved children.'

Mary was referring to her drunken sons and daughters who hugged large bottles of Jameson in Dublin with money supplied by social security or American tourists.

'Sure they have picnics of whiskey outside the Shelbourne,' Mary had once told her mother.

As for their children, they were teddyboys and thieves and drunkards and swindlers or successful merchants of material stolen from bomb sites in Belfast. There was a group who went North in vans and waited like Apaches, swooping upon bomb sites after the IRA had blown a store or a factory.

It was whispered that the IRA and the Irish tinkers were in league, blowing the Unionist kingdom to pieces for the betterment of the travelling people and for the ultimate ruinous joy of a dishevelled and broken province. Middle-aged men sat in parlours in Belfast thanking God for each exquisite joy of destruction, a bomb, a bullet, while they drank to the day there'd be a picture of Patrick Pearse in Stormont and a shoal of shamrocks on the head of Queen Victoria's statue. 'It's a bad picture of the travelling people folk have,' Mary had told her. And yet more and more were becoming peaceable and settling in council houses in Swinford or Castlerea. These were the ones you didn't hear of. These children who attended school and were educated and those parents who worked and who tidied a new house of slate grey. 'They say Tommy Joe is in the IRA,' Mary had said. Tommy Joe was Eileen's fifth great-grandson. Apparently he wore roses in his lapel and turned up in distant places, meeting agents or big-breasted young women, negotiating deals of arms. He ran off to Libya at the age of seventeen with an Irish melodeon player who was a secret agent for a Belfast regiment.

That started him. 'It's been gin and tonic and sub-machine-guns since,' Mary had complained to Eileen before illness had confined her to Portiuncula Hospital, Ballinasloe.

As Eileen lay in bed surrounded by bustling seagull-like sisters from South America, news filtered through of violence in the fair green.

It was the first year there'd been trouble at the fair other than brawls and fights and lusts. Men had been beaten with bottles. A caravan had been set alight and an old man in the country had been tied in his bed and robbed by two seventeen-year-old tinkers.

Eileen grabbed her beads.

It was the North, the North of Ireland was finally sending its seeds of ill-content among the travelling people. Young men who'd been to Belfast had caught a disease. This disease had shaped greed, had shaped violence like a way of grabbing, a way of distrusting, a way of relinquishing all Eileen had borne with her through her life.

Talking to Mary now, she said, 'England brought me great luck.'

She and Joe had travelled the length and breadth of Ireland as mares grew thin and men looked like mummers. They'd settled outside Belfast, dwelling on a site beside a graveyard while Joe, being a man of intelligence and strength, found work in the shipping yard. She'd had eleven grandchildren then, and they hung their clothes like decorations on the bushes as her sons sauntered about Antrim on white horses repairing tin objects. One of her granddaughters fell in love with a minister's son. Eileen like her grandmother. She followed him about and when he ignored her she tore off her blouse, laying her breasts naked and her nipples like wounds, and threatened to throw herself into the Lagan.

Peader her grandson led her away. The girl cracked up, became babbling and mad and even after that went off with an old tinker called Finnerty, telling fortunes from palms, staring into people's eyes in Ballinasloe or Loughrea, foretelling people of death or scaldings or bankruptcy.

In the winter of 1935 Joe was beaten up and a young child seized by an Antrim lady who wouldn't let him go for two days, saying he was a heathen.

The sky dropped snow like penance and the Wards moved off, wandering through Donegal, past the mass rocks and the hungry bays and the small cottages closed to them and the hills teeming with the shadow of snow. There was no work for them and Brigid her youngest died of tuberculosis and four grandchildren died and Peadar and Liam took boats to America and were not heard of till they got to Boston and were not heard of again until 1955 when both were dead.

'It's like the famine again,' said Eileen, recalling days close to her birth when the banshee howled and young men and old men crawled to the poorhouse in Ballinasloe like cripples, seeking goat's milk.

Wireless blared jazz music as doors closed on them and Eileen cursed the living and the dead as she passed bishops' residences and crucified Christs hanging like bunting outside towns.

Her mother and father had survived the famine but they lived to report the dead bodies lying over the length and breadth of Ireland like rotten turnips. They'd reported how men had hanged their children in order to save them and how at the Giant's Causeway Furies had eaten a McDonagh as though he was a chicken. 'We'll leave this land,' she said to Joe. They tried to sell their mangy mares, succeeded in Athenry in selling them to an Englishman as thin as the mares, and they took off.

'Our people have been travelling people since the time of St Patrick,' said Joe. 'We should have been treated better than this.'

Sister woke her.

'Wake up, Mrs McDonagh. It's time for breakfast.' She was not Mrs McDonagh but the nun presumed all tinkers were McDonaghs.

Breakfast was porridge, thin and chill as the statue of Mary standing somewhere near.

Eileen ate as a young nurse came and assisted her as though shovelling earth into a grave.

'The tea is putrid,' complained Eileen.

'Whist,' said the nurse. 'You're only imagining it.'

Outside mists clung like a momentary hush. Winter was stealing in, but first there was this October imminence, standing above sweetshops and council houses.

She took one more sup of the tea.

'This is not good enough.' She called the nurse. A country girl made off to get her stronger tea as Eileen bemoaned the passing of tea thick and black as bog-water.

They'd set up camp in Croydon in 1937, and from that spot moved across England, repairing tin, selling horses, rambling north along ill-chosen seaside paths, paths too narrow for jaunty caravans. They surmounted this island, rearing right to its northmost edge, the Kyle of Lochalsh, John o' Groat's.

They camped in winter in mild spots where men shook herring from their nets as Eileen's daughters shook daughters and sons from their bodies, as the Wards germinated and begot and filled England with tinkers.

During the war they craved their little spot in Croydon, venturing north but once, shoeing horses in Northumberland, taking coast roads, watched by ancient island monasteries. They settled in Edinburgh winter of '42, but Eileen got lonesome for talk of Hitler and the air-raid shelters squeezing with people and she left a city of black fronts and blue doors and went south with Joe and her daughter Mary, widowed by a man who jumped into the sea to save a bullock from drowning.

They camped in Croydon. Mary married a cockney tramp and they broke Guinness into an old bath and feasted on it. Mary had three children and more people of their clan joined them.

At Christmas they had the previous year's trees fished from rubbish dumps and they sang of the roads of Ireland and ancient days, bombs falling as they caroused without milk or honey.

He didn't come back one day and she searched London three days and three nights, passing rubble and mothers bemoaning their dead children until his body was found in a mortuary. She didn't curse Hitler or his land. She fell on her knees and splayed prayers and lamentation over his dead body as further sirens warned of bombs, and, as her body shaking with grief became young and hallucinatory, imagining itself to be that of a girl in Connaught without problems.

They buried him in London. The McDonaghs and the Wards and the McLoughlins came and as it was winter there

were only weeds to leave on his grave but the women shook
with crying and the men pounded their breasts.

Above Eileen saw geese fly north.

She woke with tears in her eyes and she wiped them with
hospital linen. 'Joe, Joe. My darling lover. Joe, Joe, where did
you go, times when bombs were falling like bricks and little
girls were lying in the rubble like china dolls.'

She was leading woman of her tribe then. Her family gathering, hanging their washings like decorations.

At Christmas 1944 a duchess drove up with presents for the
children. She had on a big hat of ermine grey and Eileen
refused her gifts, knowing her kinsmen to have fought this aris-
tocracy for nine hundred years and realising she was being
made a charity of. Once in Ballinasloe she'd known a lady
who'd been a music hall artiste in London and who married
the local lord. That lady had addressed her as her equal.

Eileen had had hair of purple and red then and she'd had no
wish of charity. The lady of the house had found companion-
ship in a girl living in a tent on the edge of her estate.

'We'll go back to Ireland,' her son Seamus said at the end of
the war.

Eileen hesitated. She was not sure. The last memories had
been mangy. She and her family were English-dwelling now
and they received sustenance for work done and they abided
with the contrasts of this country.

She led her family north before deciding. Up by Northumberland and seeing a fleet of British planes flying over, she
decided on embarking.

The customs man glared at her as though she was an Indian.

'Are you Irish, ma'm?' he said.

'Irish like yourself,' she said.

He looked at her retinue.

'Where were ye?' he said. 'In a concentration camp?'

They travelled straight to Galway. Its meadows still were
sweet, but on the way men had looked crossly at them and

women suspiciously. This was the land her parents had travelled. It had not even a hint of the country beset by famine.
Cars were roaming like hefty bullocks, and in Athenry as they
moved off from Ballinasloe, little Josephine Shields was killed.

A guard came to look at the crash.

'I'm sorry,' he told Eileen. 'But you can't be hogging these
roads. Something like this has been bound to happen.'

They buried the little girl in Galway. There was a field of
daisies near by and Eileen's eyes rose from the ceremony to the
sea spray and a hill where small men with banana bellies were
playing golf.

'I'm leaving this land,' she told herself.

They journeyed back to Liverpool, erupting again on the face
of England, germinating children like gulls. They moved north,
they moved south and in Croydon, standing still, Eileen met
Joseph Finnerty, half-Irish tinker, half-French gypsy by his
mother's origin. They married within two months. He was
thirty-nine. She was sixty-two. She was good-looking still and
welcomed his loins. Their marriage was celebrated by a priest
from Swaziland and performed in Croydon. Tinkers came from
Ireland, more to 'gawp' said Eileen, and gypsies, wild and
lovely from France.

'My family has broken from me like a bough,' said Eileen.
'Now it's my turn for the crack.'

Men of ninety found themselves drunk as hogs in hedges
about Croydon. A black priest ran among the crowd like a
haunted hare and a young girl from Galway sang songs in Irish
about deaths and snakes and nuns who fell in love with sailors.

Eileen looked at the London suburb as though at the sea.

'I can return to Ireland now,' she said.

She brought him back and they travelled widely, just the
two of them for a while.

She brought him back to old spots, Galway and the
Georgian house where the gentry lived and the girl from the
London music hall of the last century. They went to the sea and

marvelled at the wayside contrasts of furze and rhododendrons in May.

Joseph played a tin whistle and there was dancing along the way and singing and nights by high flames when a girl stepped out of Eileen like a ballerina.

'The years have slipped off your face,' people told her. They went to a dance one night in Athenry where there was jazz music and they danced like the couples with the big bellies and the bouncing hair.

'I'll take you to my mother's country now,' said Joseph, so off they went in a van that wheezed like a dying octogenarian through France.

They passed houses where they heard music the like Eileen could not understand, thrilling music, music of youth, music of a cosmos that had changed.

They passed war ruins and posters showing brazen women. They weaved through towns where summer lingered in February and rode hills where spring came like an onlooker, gazing at them with eyes of cherry blossom. They lingered on a mound of earth as they caught sight of a blue, blue sea.

They got out.

'This is my real home,' Joseph said. 'The Camargue. My mother's people came from here. This is the heart of the tinkers' world. I was born here, of a father from Kerry and a mother from Saintes Maries de la Mer. I was gifted with second sight and feet that moved, so I spent my first days in Ireland and saw the fighting and the flags and the falling houses, and then I came back here and danced the wild dances and loved the strong women. From Marseilles I went south.' He pointed. 'Over there is Egypt. I arrived there when I was twenty-six and from there my life flows. I recall the palm trees and the camels as though it was yesterday. I went there and understood, understood our people the world over, the travelling people, men who moved before gods were spoken of, men who – who understood.'

'We are of an ancient stock, my father used to say,' said Eileen. 'We were here before St Patrick and will be when he's forgotten.'

'Our secrets are the secrets of the universe,' said Joseph, 'a child, a woman with child, a casual donkey. We are the sort that Joseph was when he fled with Mary.'

Sand blew into Eileen's eyes as she drank wine for the first time. In March she watched young men with long legs from Hungary ride into the sea with red flags. It was the feast of St Sarah, patron saint of gypsies.

They carried her statue like a bride betrothed to the sea and praised her with lecherous and lusty tongues.

The summer was already taking the shape of summer, a blue, blue sea.

'In October they come again to celebrate,' Joseph explained. 'They are faithful to their saints.'

She sat on sands where she drunk bottles of wine and bottles of Coca-Cola and walked by the sea which asked of her, 'Is this folly?'

She wanted to go home. She wished like a child fatigued of fun to see Ireland again.

'I'd like to take off soon,' she said to Joseph, but she saw coming across his face a villainous look. He was drunk with red wine and wandering by the sea like an old man in Leenane. 'I want to go,' she told herself. 'I want to go.'

Summer edged in. She plucked wild flowers and wondered about her children and her children's children and asked herself if this her cup had not brimmed too high. 'Was it all folly?' she demanded of herself. Was it a madness that drove people littler than herself into Ballinasloe mental hospital to enquire daily if they were saints or sinners. She began to wonder at her own sanity and placed wine bottles full of wild roses on the sands of Camargue before crying out, 'Am I going mad? Am I going mad?' They brought her first to a priest, then to a doctor in Marseilles. They left her alone in a white room for two days.

'Joseph Finnerty, I curse you,' she said. Then he came and took her and placed her on a horse and rode towards their caravans in Camargue. 'We're going back to Ireland,' he said.

They arrived on a June morning and they set tracks to Connaught. The day was fine and on the way they heard that O'Rourke, king of the tinkers, was dead. 'You'll be the next king of the tinkers,' Eileen said.

She arranged he fight Crowley, his opponent, in Mountshannon. Women stood by with Guinness and cider and children paddled among the fresh roses and geraniums. She saw her lover strip to the waist and combat a man his senior and she recalled her father's words,

'Lucky is the man who wins ye.'

This man over the others had won her.

She wrapped a shawl about her as they fought and fell to the ground. In the middle of combat her gaze veered from fight to lake where birds dropped like shadows.

'I have travelled at last,' she said. 'There's a hunger and a lightness returned to my body. A grandmother and mother I'm not no more, but a woman.'

After Joseph fought and won they drove off to a pub pushing out from a clump of rhododendrons and celebrated.

'Jesus, Mother,' said Mary. 'Have you no sense?'

'Sense I haven't but I have a true man and a true friend,' she said.

She was held in high esteem now and where she went she was welcomed. Age was creeping up on her but there were ways of sidling away from it.

She'd jump on a horse and race with Joseph. He was a proud man and faithful to her.

Also he was a learned man and conversed with school teachers.

In Cairo he'd had tuition from French Jesuits. He spoke in French and English and Romany and could recite French poets or Latin poets.

When it came to his turn at a feast he'd not play the whistle but sing a song in the French language.

Finally he grew younger before her eyes as she grew older. In France she'd fled because it was a bad match. Here there was nowhere to go.

It was lovely, yes, but her eyes were becoming crisscrossed like potato patches.

'I have reached an age that leads towards the grave,' she wept to herself one evening. 'I am an old banshee.' Joseph comforted her, not hearing, but maybe knowing.

She watched him bathe in the Shannon and knew he should be with a woman younger than her but that yet she loved him and would cut her throat for him. She saw in his eyes as he looked from the water the stranger that he was and the stranger that he was going to be.

In 1957 he fell from a horse in the fair green in Ballinasloe and was killed.

She remembered the curse on him in the South of France and knew it to have come true.

She watched the flames burning and coaxing at the wake and recalled his words in France. 'Our secrets are the secrets of the universe, a child, a woman with child, a casual donkey. We are the sort that Joseph was when he fled with Mary.' He was educated by French Jesuits and held corners in his tongue and twists in his utterances. He was a poet and a tinker and a child of the earth.

She recalled the lady in the manor long ago who'd befriended her, to whom she'd go with bushels of heather on summer evenings.

Why was it that woman had been haunting and troubling her mind recently?

It had been so long since she'd known her, yet she bothered her. Had it been warning of Joseph's death? All her life, despite the fact she was just a tinker, she'd met strange people.

From the woman in the manor who'd asked her to tea one

day, to the French gypsy who'd become her lover as old age
dawned upon her. He'd been the strangest of all, brown face,
eyes that twinkled like chestnuts in open pods. Yes, he'd been a
poet as well as a lover. He'd been of the earth, he'd gone back
to it now. He'd possessed the qualities of the unique like the
cockney music-hall girl who'd attracted the attention of an
Irish peer and came to live in a manor, finding a friend in a
tinker from a hovel of tents and caravans.

She watched the flames dance and saw again the white
horses of Camargue, flurrying in uncertain unison, and would
have walked into the fire ablaze had someone not held her and
comforted her and satiated her as her moans grew to the sound
and shape of seals in bays west of Ballinasloe.

'Eileen, wake up. Do you know what's happened? They've
killed an old man.'

Eileen looked at her daughter. 'Who?'

'Tinker lads.'

Eileen stared. So death had come at last. They'd killed an old
man. 'May they be cursed,' she said, 'for bringing bad tidings
on our people. May they be forsaken for leaving an old way of
life, for doing what no travelling people have ever done before.'

As it happened the old man was not dead. Just badly beaten
up.

Some tinkers had gone to rob him, took all and hit him with
a delft hot-water jar.

'The travellers have already gone from the green.'

'Ballinasloe fair week without the tinkers,' Eileen said.
'What a terrible sight the green must be.'

She saw more tinkers than she'd ever seen before.

They came like apostles as a priest rummaged with broken
words.

'Is it dying you think I am? Well, it's not dying I am,' said
Eileen.

She saw five children like the seven dwarfs. 'These too will
grow to drink cider outside the Gresham in Dublin,' she

thought, as candles were lit and the priest talked about the devil.

Her great-grandson Owen was living with a rich American woman in an empty hotel in Oughterard. 'What next?'

Her head sunk back.

She saw Joseph again and the flames and wanted again to enter but knew she couldn't. She woke.

'If it's dying I am, I want to die in peace. Bring me to the crossroad in Aughrim.' A Pakistani doctor nearly had concussion, but the solemn occasion speeded up as a nun intervened. Young nurses watched Eileen being carted off.

They laid her on the ground and a Galway woman keened her. The voice was like sharp pincers in her ears.

Now that they were saying she was on the verge of death, ancient memories were budging and a woman, the lady of the manor, was moving again, a woman in white, standing by the french windows, gazing into summer.

She'd had fuzzy blonde hair and maybe that was why she'd looked at Joseph more closely the first time she saw him. She had the same eyes, twinkling brazen eyes.

She heard again the lady's voice. 'No, I won't go in,' answering her husband. 'It's not evening. It's just the afternoon.'

Eileen woke.

The stars shone above like silver dishes. The bushes were tipped with first frost.

She stirred a bit. 'Is it better I'm getting?' she wondered. She moved again and laughed.

Her bones felt more free. She lifted her head. 'They might be killing old men but they won't kill me.'

She stirred. A girl heard her.

Women shook free from tents and gazed as though at Count Dracula.

In the morning she was hobbling on a stick.

She hobbled down the lane and gazed on the Galway road.

'I'll have duck for dinner,' she said. 'Ye can well afford it with all the shillings you're getting from the government.'

At Christmas she was able to hobble, albeit with the help of a stick, into the church, crossing herself first with holy water.

Marina Carr

Grow a Mermaid

THE CHILD leaned across the blue formica table and read the advertisement, her grubby little fingers leaving snail tracks under the words – GROW YOUR OWN MERMAID.

The child looked at the words in amazement, read it again, slowly, more carefully this time. The same. Underneath the caption was an ink drawing of a tiny mermaid in a fish bowl, waving and smiling up from the page. Behind her was a sea-horse. He too was smiling. The child, bewitched by the mermaid's smile, smiled back and waved shyly to the tiny beautiful fish woman. Send 25 cents, the advertisement said, and we will send you mermaid and sea-horse seeds. You put them into water and they grow and can even talk to you. The child imagined waking up at night and going to the fishbowl for a chat with the mermaid. What would mermaids talk about, the child wondered.

*   *   *

The child's mother stirred beans in a pot over the cooker, her black corseted behind moving in one controlled sway with the spooning motion. Over by the range Grandma Blaize was fossicking for some long forgotten thing. She was pulling it out of the air above her head with her fingertips. The child looked at her and then the child's mother turned to look as well, still stirring the beans, sideways now. Both mother and child watched as Grandma Blaize pulled some invisible treasure to earth. She saw them looking at her and gave them a quick smile, a dart of old gums and leathery tongue, before her face took up that careful concentration of fossicking and pulling again.

'Ara stop it, Grandma Blaize!' the child's mother snapped.

Grandma Blaize ignored her. Tonight or tomorrow she'll have stepped into the other world. Once the fossicking started she was on the descent. The child liked her best at this point, the moment before going down. The child imagined that Grandma Blaize was pulling open a door with a magic thread, a door on somewhere else, anywhere, but away from here.

'Mom, look,' the child said, holding up the picture of the mermaid. The mother left off stirring the beans and came over to the child.

'Oh that,' she said, glancing at the magazine the child was reading.

'Grow your own mermaid,' the mother read. 'Did you ever...'

Her voice trailed off as she too was bewitched by the little mermaid smiling and waving from her fishbowl.

'Well I never heard the likes a' that,' the mother said, sort of dismayed, but still looking at the mermaid.

'Can we, Mom?' the child asked.

'Can we what?'

'Can we send away for a mermaid?'

'We'll see.' Her mother sighed and returned to the burning beans.

*   *   *

The child's mother was building a house on the lake of the palaces. From the end of the field of their own house they could look across and see the new house. It was halfway there now. The child's mother said it was a secret. The child wasn't to tell any of the Connemara clique because they'd wonder where the money came from. The money was borrowed from four banks, the child's mother whispered, and when your daddy sees this house he'll fall in love with it, especially the music room, and he'll come back, for good this time. Some nights, they'd talk for hours about how they'd decorate the house. 'Windows, windows everywhere,' the child's mother whispered in the dark. They slept together a lot since the child's father had gone. 'And your room,' the child's mother whispered, 'will be all in yellow, with a yellow sink and yellow curtains, yellow presses and a yellow carpet.' The child didn't like yellow but said nothing. She wanted her room blue and green, like a mermaid's room. It didn't matter; she'd pull the blue and green from an invisible string, the way Grandma Blaize did, and then the mermaid would arrive. Some nights the child's mother held the child so tight she couldn't breathe. The child grew sticky and hot as her mother whispered into the quilt about 'that bastard!' and 'all I've done for him' and 'this is how he repays me'. The child would try to put her hand outside the covers to get a bit of cool air on it and the child's mother would grab it and pull it back into the slick heat of the bed. 'My little darling,' the child's mother would croon as the child lay there soaked in sweat, with her mother's damp face on her neck. The child fought back a scream. Down the hall Grandma Blaize sang 'The Connemara Lullaby'; she was in the other world now and would speak to no one but herself until the end of spring. The child lay there in the dark, growing a mermaid.

First the water from the lake of the palaces, then a Tupperware box, then pour in the mermaid seeds and stir it all gently, and the next day a mermaid would be floating on her back, smiling at the child. And the child would say, 'Hello, little mermaid.' And the mermaid would sing a song for the child about the sea, about castles and whales and turtles and whole cities and families who lived under the sea. And the child would tell the mermaid all about school and her friend Martina, who played with her sometimes, and about the time they saw a balloon in the sky and chased it for hours. The child would tell her about Pollonio, the fairy she never saw, but knew lived down Mohia Lane. To make it more interesting for the mermaid, the child would pretend that she often met Pollonio. The child slept as the mermaid grew away out in the dark at the edge of the child's dream.

*   *   *

Grandma Blaize lay in bed fighting with the ghost of Syracuse. Propped by pillows, pulling on an opium pipe, she snarled at the ghost of Syracuse. 'Gorgin' ya'ar gut was all y'ever done, ya *stroinseach* ya!' She takes another puff to calm herself down after this exertion. The ghost of Syracuse was the husband who stepped out the door one day 'to get a breath of fresh air' and never came back. That was thirty years ago. The child watched through the keyhole. He'd sent her a postcard from Syracuse, 'Weather lovely, skies purple most every night, try it sometime.' Grandma Blaize had it covered in plastic and punched it at regular intervals. The child rocked with laughter and banged her nose on the door knob

*   *   *

The child ate sweets belonging to her sick brother and the child's mother ordered the child into the black and red parlour. The child waited. After what seemed for ever the child's mother appeared in the doorway with a wooden hanger.

'Now strip,' the child's mother said and watched while the child took off everything. Afterwards, lying on the sofa with welts as big as carrots on her legs, the child slept and dreamt of a man with a pitchfork who lived under the sea. 'How long?' the child whispered.

'Soon, soon,' the man with the pitchfork answered. The child woke to find her mother standing over her. 'Have you anythin' to say to me?'

'Sorry, Mom.' It was an ancient ritual between them.

'And you'll never do it again?'

The child wavered, looked away, treasuring the small rebellion.

'Will you?' the mother said, a whiff of anger coming off her that would reignite given the least excuse.

'No,' the child half-yielded, but it wasn't enough to appease, the child could sense. Her mother was insurmountable in this mood and the child valued the unwelted slivers of her chubby torso. The child surrendered. 'No, never again.'

The child's mother gathered her up in her fat, still young arms. The child counted her breaths, slowly, carefully. They matched her mother's footsteps on the stairs. A mermaid would die in this house, the child thought.

*   *   *

The child's father returned and magicked nuts out of their ears and made pennies hop. One evening he came in, wearing his big blue crombie and sat the child's brother on the blue formica table.

'I can make you disappear,' the child's father said.

The child's brother puffed out his little chest, delighted to be the chosen one. The child watched, wishing it was her.

'The only problem is,' the child's father said, 'you can never come back.'

The child's brother's face crumpled up as he began to cry.

'It's alright,' the child's father said. 'I won't make you disappear.'

The child's brother still cried, ashamed he was crying in front of his father and his sister.

'It's alright,' the father said,' 'I won't do it.'

The child stepped forward.

'Make me disappear,' the child said.

'You can't come back.'

'I don't want to,' the child said.

The child's father shook. 'You're too young for this trick.'

The child's father left the room. The child took her brother's hand.

'Come on around the back and play where Mom and Dad's not looking.'

The child's brother allowed himself to be led from the house, tears forgotten, childish dignity returning. They played in the ash pit and drank water from the kitchen drain. It tasted of turnip and tea leaves. They weren't caught that time.

* * *

The child got up on Sam Morrison's tractor one day with her brother and her mother and Grandma Blaize who was fighting with herself on top of the dresser. The child's father lifted her up on to the trailer and put her on the black sofa. The child's mother laughed. She wore a new dress and a new hair clasp for her thick dark hair. They drove down the lane and stopped outside the new house at the lake of the palaces. A swan glided by, a pike leaped, the mermaid sang.

The child's father went away again, in the middle of the night this time. The child's mother knocked the child's brother's head through the glass door. The child counted her breaths, sharp and shallow. Her brother looked at her as the child's mother held him while the doctor cleaned the wound.

'It's so hard to watch them,' she whispers to the doctor. The doctor nods. Later the child's mother took them into the Oasis for knickerbocker glories. The jelly was gold and green, the colour of the mermaid's tail.

* * *

At night the child dreamt her mother was cooking her on the range and serving her up to the tinkers with homemade bread.

The child woke screaming, her mother's boiling hand slobbering over her. The child preferred the nightmare.

*   *   *

Down in the room Grandma Blaize tears a map of Syracuse into a thousand pieces and smokes them in her opium pipe. She throws in the Sea of Galilee for good measure.

The child's mother sits by the window nightly, looking out on the lake of the palaces. The music room is empty. She drinks Paddy and red and kisses her children. The child heaves at her mother's whiskey breath. 'Any day now,' the child's mother whispers. 'Any day now.'

*   *   *

The child's mother walked into the lake of the palaces one calm night with the moon missing. The child's father returned, for good this time. He skulks along the lake shore with his weak old whingy eyes. 'He pisses tears,' the child whispers to the mermaid and they both laugh in the silent house. The child's brother rarely speaks now and never to the child. They exchange glances over banana sandwiches and their father's runaway eyes. They haven't drunk from drains in years, not together anyhow.

*   *   *

When they dragged the lake of the palaces for her mother's body, the child sat in the reeds strumming her tiny guitar. She only knew 'My Darling Clementine'. C. G seventh. C again. 'Oh my darling, oh my darling, oh my darling Clementine, dwelt a miner, forty-niner, and his daughter Clementine. Light she was and like a fairy and her shoes were number nine, now she's gone and lost for ever, oh my darling Clementine.' The child sang, strumming her small guitar as a pulley raised her mother in the air, then they lowered her till she skimmed along the surface towards the child in the reeds. They didn't stop until her head was resting on a clump of rushes, a few feet from the child. 'Oh my darling...,' the child sang.

From the child's vantage point, her mother was not unlike the mermaid, bar the pike teeth-marks on her left arm. They'd tasted her and left her to the eels, the dirtiest eaters of all. But the eels hadn't touched her. Maybe they hadn't time or maybe eels too had their standards, the child thought. She strummed her guitar and looked away from her mother's cold heron stare.

'That's enough, child,' a man in the boat said.

The child sang louder. This was the real funeral. The coffin on tick, the procession, the sanctimonious hymns, the concelebrated Mass would all come soon enough. The Connemara click there, grabbing on to her with their battered claws and defeated lumpy old backs. The child coughed away a titter of amusement at their mouth of the grave *mhuire strua* antics. She insisted on wearing her blue jeans instead of the black velvet gibble they'd bought her. They never forgave her for that. It wasn't real, none of it. Strumming her tiny guitar in the reeds was, with her mother skimmin' towards her stinkin' of goose scream and the bullin' moon.

*   *   *

The child's father took the child and the child's brother into the dining room.

'In memory of your dear mother...,' he said, the whinge gaining strength at the back of his craw. The child looked at him in disgust.

'In memory of your dear mother I'm going to remain celibate for six months.'

The child blushed.

'What's that?' the child's brother asked.

The child knew.

'I won't sleep with anyone for six months.'

The child ran from the room. Later the child found a box of magazines in her father's cupboard. All lurid fat women's gees. The child put them under her bed. The next time she looked they were gone. The child knew who had them. That night she tore one of his eyes out in a dream. The next night she sewed it back in.

One by one Grandma Blaize pulls out her teeth. She lays them on her dressing table. They're soft as toffee. The child sucks one. It tastes like old knickers. The child crunches down on it with her own strong white horse's teeth. The tooth slivers like a soft mint. The child spits it in the lake of palaces and eats a fistful of grass. It tastes of swan's wing.

*   *   *

The child sleeps for twenty years. The mermaid who never came is long forgotten. Walking down the street one day, the child takes off her mother's wedding ring and hurls it in a dustbin.

It disappears among old chips, cigarette butts, an ice cream cone half-eaten. The child goes home and sleeps.

*   *   *

The child is in a swimming pool. It seems she will never reach the bottom, then she does. A fortress door creaks open, a flash of golden fin, the mermaid appears.

'At last, you've come at last,' the child says.

The mermaid smiles, that smile of years ago at the blue formica table. The child braces herself for the watery descent. The mermaid's tail lights the way.

Mike McCormack

The Terms

O N T H E very evening I burned down the left wing of our
house, my father told me that he hated me. He just stood
there in the shadow of the gutted roof thumbing a shell into the
rifle, making no bones about it nor putting a tooth in it in any
way, just telling me quietly and for the last time that everything
about me made him sick, everything: the massive dome of my
head with its lank fringe, my useless legs and piping voice –
most of all the lack of shame and outrage in my heart. He told
me again that all the cruelty and misshapen ugliness of the world
was summed up in my body and that he could not suffer it a
moment longer. Then he told me that he was going to kill me.
Frankly this wasn't news to either of us. Somehow we seemed
to have always known that our relationship would come to
this; it had been fated from the beginning to end in some swift
settlement of accounts, some bloody reckoning. Putting it
another way, neither our house nor our world was big enough
for two people such as us.

Lately however, and for some reason I could not fathom, I
had begun to dream of something else. My sleeping hours had
been filled of late with shapeless images of truce and acceptance, compromises, it is true, which fell a long way short of
love and redemption but nevertheless something to be getting
on with. However, when I saw my father thumbing home that
shell I realised that he knew nothing of my dreams.

'I'm going to shoot you stone dead,' he said evenly. 'And
what's more I'm going to shoot you in the back.'

'It's not going to be a fair fight then. I don't have any

weapons to hand.'

'I'm going to give you a fighting chance,' he said. 'You're going to get a fifty-yard start over open ground and I have only one shot. If you make it, don't come back. Here's two hundred and fifty pounds to help you make a start in the world just in case. Invest it wisely. I'd recommend government bonds.'

He handed me a wad of notes and I made some quick calculations. Normally my father was an excellent shot. In clear light I had seen him drop fleeing rabbits at one hundred yards. Now, however, there were other factors to consider. It was late evening and the autumn sun was well in decline. Shadows crawled everywhere and gave shapes and profiles an enormity they did not truly possess. Also I could see that my father's temper had begun to smoulder; little things gave him away. A tremor had entered into his white-knuckled hand as he gripped the rifle and a bead of sweat had broken out under his nose. Already I was beginning to fancy my chances, but I still wanted further adjustments to be on the safe side.

'How about a head shot?' I said. 'You're always telling me that my head is too big for my shoulders.'

'Only at forty yards, beyond that whitethorn.'

'OK.'

'Plus ninety quid.'

'That's down to four pound a yard. It started out at five.'

'That's the law of diminishing returns. Take it or leave it.'

I thumbed the notes of the wad and handed them over.

'How do I know you'll only take the one shot?'

'One is all I'll need. Besides, I've only got one shell in the breech and if I have to reload you'll have gained another twenty-five yards. At that distance you'll be well in the clear.'

'What happens if I only get wounded? Suppose I take it in the lung and lie there bleeding to death?'

'Then I will leave you there and the crows will make short work of you. I'll walk out every day for as long as it takes and see how your death is progressing. On the day of your death

I'll dump a bag of lime over you and within two weeks there won't be a trace of you except for a small, damp pile of chalk in the middle of that field.'

'A bag of lime isn't much of a memorial.'

'You're not much of a son.'

'Suppose I make a miraculous recovery and wake up to find that you have come and stolen my fortune? What then?'

'That won't happen. Whatever else I am, I'm not a thief.'

'You won't try and profit from my death? A young, smooth body like mine would fetch a fair penny from research institutes or on the organ donor market. It would have considerable freak value. You might take off to Latin America with a mistress.'

'No, there will be no profiteering. This is a matter of principle not profit. Besides, there's not much of you in it and I'd prefer you to go to hell all in one piece.'

'I'm glad. I don't fancy the idea of some clueless medical student with a hangover poking around in my guts. The thought of it alone would put me off my stride. Nevertheless, you'll have a lot of explaining to do.'

'I'll tell everyone that you set fire to the house and took off in shame and fright. I'll dissuade any search party by telling them that you know every one of these hills and forests and that you will probably return in your own good time. I'll tell them that you were depressed lately on account of your condition.'

'That's a dirty lie. I've never once been depressed by what I am.'

'*You* haven't but *I* have. Every time I look at you I sink deeper into misery and despair. Right now I'm so low that if I sank any lower I'd disappear into the ground.'

By now the sun was a heavy rind over the hills and the earth glowered in shadow. The terms had been set out and I could think of nothing else I wanted to add to them. I was very calm and confident. I believed that at that moment I possessed every piece of worthwhile wisdom and knowledge in the entire world, every axiom and formula and instruction that was going to enable me to live longer. Nevertheless I wondered, did my father have any parting words to send me on my way?

'You're not going to wish me good luck or anything?'

'There's no point in wasting fortune on a dead man.'

'Then I guess I'll be on my way.'

'We seem to have covered everything.'

I jogged out to the starting post, moving at a steady lope, conserving energy. The ground was even and the going firm, a wide stretch of pasture sloping away from the gable of our house to a downhill finish running into the conifer plantation at its furthest edge, about one hundred yards distant. I had no worries that my father would cheat and shoot me in the back within the agreed range. This was his game and he had defined the terms and he would honour them with that vain integrity that only the truly wretched possess.

Ten yards from the whitethorn I burst into a sprint, running in a sharp zigzag from left to right and rolling my head. I passed the bush and veered wildly into its shadow, putting it between my father and myself. Ten yards beyond the bush and I was making good ground, breathing evenly and almost in the safety zone. Then there was a massive explosion in my head, a sunburst of white light, and I was cast up into the air as if by a giant hand, hurtling forward almost on the verge of flight. I pitched through the gloom like a missile, and then all was darkness.

Jesus, I had to hand it to the little runt, he wasn't going to make it easy for me. There he was, running faster than I would have thought possible on those useless little legs of his and jogging that massive head from side to side as if it were some sort of beach ball.

I knew the moment I lifted the gun to my shoulder that I'd been hoodwinked. The little bastard had kept me talking just long enough for the sun to disappear beyond the hills. His head was nothing more than a blur between the ridged walls of the gunsights and he was darting from side to side, shortening and lengthening each burst at random. He was now abreast of the bush and he suddenly veered behind it and disappeared from sight. The canny bastard had put the bush between us and, with the field dropping away behind it, he would now never emerge into the open. I would have to shoot through the tree. I saw a gap in the foliage and sighted through it, waiting for his head to bop into the open space. When it did, filling the bottom of the space, I waited a split instant before the rifle boomed and recoiled heavily in my shoulder. I saw his small body come hurtling sideways out of the silhouette, swimming through the air before crashing to the ground and tumbling head over heels in an untidy mess of arms and legs. And I knew then that it was all over; I knew that my son and only child, Edward Coon the second, was dead.

Edward was neither dead nor seriously wounded; he was just out cold with barely a scratch on him. The bullet had grazed the top of his head, parting his thick hair with a terrific red lesion which cut through to the bone of his skull. He just lay there on his back breathing lightly as if he had lain down for a nap.

I saw straight away that his condition placed him outside the terms of our agreement. He was neither dead nor seriously wounded, but the danger now was that he might wake in a matter of hours and wander off into the world as an imbecile with neither wit nor memory, easy prey for thieves and male-factors. This was not what we had settled on. I wanted him either dead or alive, not queering up creation further as an idiot.

I picked him up and turned to the house. His head lolled heavily off my elbow and a thin rivulet of blood seeped through his hair. His tongue lolled thickly from his mouth. As I gazed upon him I saw for the umpteenth time how everything rank and misshapen in the world was summed up in this small bundle of flesh and bone. This child of mine seemed the very distillate of all the world's cruelty and malice. But beneath my disgust there welled also a deeper, more unspeakable feeling. It rose through my heart and leaked into my throat, swelling it and threatening to choke me. It had the same intractable presence as the rifle which lay across my son's chest.

For the first time in my life I recognised clearly that everything in my son which repulsed me was nothing more than my own mirror image.

I woke with a brutal headache; some implacable demon was working in my skull with a lump hammer. My room, a horrid prospect, smelled of charred timber and petrol. Shafts of light spilled through the shattered roof, settling in the room like converged lances. I walked through the ruined hallway and into the kitchen, clutching my head in my hands. My father sat at the table cleaning the rifle, yanking a pull through from the barrel.

'You don't look like God and you're not forking stiffs into a furnace. What happened?'

'I creased your skull and you fell unconscious.'

'And you took pity on me?'

'No. I just honoured the terms of our agreement. Have a drink, welcome home so to speak.' He pushed a bottle of whiskey across the table to me.

'No thanks, you know well I'm only a minor.'

'Suit yourself. I would have thought that any man who had come within a hair's breadth of hell would want to celebrate his deliverance.'

'I'm not in the mood for festivities. I just want to get my head together.'

I pulled up a chair and watched him cleaning the gun. No matter how many times I had seen him do this simple task, the way he worked those stubby fingers of his still enchanted me. The guile and seamless grace of his movements. I had often reflected that somewhere in him there was a craftsman howling to get out, someone with patience and poor eyesight who worked with precious materials and terrifying degrees of accuracy. He laid down the rifle suddenly and stared into space for a long moment.

'We can't go on like this,' he said finally. 'It's nothing personal but this has got to end. People like you and me have no place any more in the world, Edward. We'd be better off dead.'

'Speak for yourself.'

'That's what I'm doing. I am so lost, so lost. It's a matter of scale, I think. We're told every day that the world is getting smaller and smaller and that distances are narrowing down, bringing the peoples of the world together in harmony. But for people like you and me it just gets bigger and bigger until we've dropped right through the meshes of it and into this pit. We have no life any more.'

'Was it ever any other way?'

'Yes,' he said vehemently. 'Yes, it was. There was a time when we had status and valuable skills. It's hard to believe that people like us were passed down from kings to princes as part of inheritance and that we were privy to their inmost thoughts. And it's harder to believe that some of us were real artisans and craftsmen, shoemakers and fullers and spinners of gold thread, diamond prospectors even. Did you know our forebears trafficked in foundlings for depleted bloodlines and that we made ends meet with a bit of cradle-snatching? All honourable trades in their own worlds. But not any more, that's all gone now. Now we're not even good circus material. History has passed us by, Edward, and we're dead men, dead men both of us.'

'That's not unusual. The world is full of people who have been passed over by history – gypsies, tinkers and so on.'

'Yes, but none have fallen so low. We are the lowest of the low; right now we are neither men nor beasts, we're just nightmare creatures stalking a no man's land between myth and history.'

'You're just full of self-pity.'

'Don't patronise me, Edward. I've lived long enough to be able to distinguish pity from disgust. I cried for six months when your mother died and I couldn't eat for two after the first time I held you in my arms. I'm not likely to confuse the two. At this moment I'm so sickened by myself I couldn't summon up the energy to puke. And while we're on the subject of disgust, tell me, why did you burn down the left wing?'

'That was an incomplete job. If you hadn't come along I'd have burned down the whole house. I was hoping that when you came back the whole thing would be destroyed and we could go off together and make our own way in the world. I wanted a new start. There was a time when I thought this house was our sanctuary and refuge. And it was too for many years – our own little scooped-out space in the world where we were safe and without enemies. But over the years this sanctuary has turned into our prison; there's no house around here for miles and we have no friends or function any more. Now I think it is time to up roots and move on. Somewhere out there, in the vastness of the world, I know there is a small place where we can find our niche.'

'Doing what?'

'I don't know. I was thinking in terms of adventure and destiny, taking every day as it comes, you and me facing fortune head on.'

He closed his eyes as if experiencing some vast weariness.

'That's a young man's game, Edward. I'm too old for that kind of optimism.'

He was right. I saw for the first time how all his years of rancour and bitterness had eaten away the fabric of his soul. He had about him now an air of utter defeat. It ran in every line of his body, coursing through his arms and legs and chest and into the curve of his blunt spine. Some terrible weight seemed to have settled upon him and it came as an immense shock to see that he was now almost shorter than myself.

By this time the gun was cleaned and he was tidying away the oil and the lint. I hadn't seen the hacksaw on the table and I noticed also that a piece of the barrel was lying loose beside it. He had sawn another inch off the stock, customising the gun yet further. He handed it to me.

'Take it,' he said. 'It should handle lighter – I've shifted the balance nearer the stock. Today it's your turn. The same terms and no arguments.'

I felt my eyes start in their sockets.

'I can't do that,' I whispered in disbelief. 'I can't. It's just crazy.' I retreated a few steps from the gun he was holding at arm's length. 'I can't.'

'Take the gun, Edward,' he insisted. 'Take it.' He thrust it suddenly on to my chest.

'No,' I yelled, 'no!' I fended the gun off wildly with my hands.

'This isn't an order, Edward, it's a request.' He had me pinned against the wall now, laying the rifle across my chest. He took his hands away suddenly and I found myself holding it. A calm, solemn note entered his voice.

'I've hated you from the moment you entered the world and I've hated you all the more because you are my son. I didn't think the world could commit the same atrocity twice in the same place. But I was wrong. And worst of all I've felt neither shame nor remorse for my hatred. Now, not once in all these years have I ever asked you for anything, not once because what did a wretch like you have to offer, you who had less grace than I did? But now I'm asking you for this one thing. Take the gun and be my son, just this once and final time.'

The gun burned in my hand but I could not let it go.

'Is it what you really want?' I blurted.

'Yes, it's what I really want. I cannot suffer this any more.'

He turned and made his way quickly through the back door and outside he stood facing towards the field. The day was cruelly lit; a high, unseasonable sun flared in the sky like magnesium, casting neither shadow nor illusion. My father turned into the field and I could see by the way he moved, the slouched gait and the hopeless slope of his shoulders, that he wasn't going to make it. I was filled with sudden panic.

'Dad,' I cried.

'Yes.'

'Run hard.'

He turned without a word and continued on his way, and when he got to the starting post he just kept on walking.

Biographical Notes

SARA BERKELEY was born in Dublin in 1967 and produced her first 'novel' at the age of eight. During her teens she came to the attention of Dermot Bolger, publisher of Raven Arts Press, who encouraged her writing and published her early work in *Introductions 3* in 1984. Her first collection of poetry, *Penn*, was published in 1986 to critical acclaim, and was short-listed for the Irish Book Awards and the *Sunday Tribune* Arts Awards. In 1989, her second collection *Home Movie Nights* was published. Her most recent collection is *Facts About Water* (Bloodaxe/New Island, 1994). *The Swimmer in the Deep Blue Dream*, her first collection of short stories, was published in 1991. Since graduating from Trinity College, Dublin, she has lived and worked in London and the United States.

DERMOT BOLGER was born in Dublin in 1959. Poet, editor and publisher, his novels include *The Journey Home*, *The Woman's Daughter*, *Emily's Shoes* and *A Second Life*, and his plays include *The Lament for Arthur Cleary* and *One Last White Horse*. "Father's Music" is the prologue of his novel by the same name, which was published by Picador in April 1997.

MARINA CARR was born in Tullaghmore, Co. Offally in 1964 and now lives in Dublin. Her plays include *Low in the Dark* (1989), *The Deer's Surrender* (1991), *This Love Thing* (1990), *Ulaloo* (1991), *The Mai* (1994) and *Portia Coughlan* (1996). A new play, *By the Bog of Cats* is due to be staged at the Abbey in 1998, and she is also working on a piece for the Druid at the Project. Awarded the Hennessy short story award in 1996, she was writer-in-residence at the Abbey in 1996–7, and she won the Susan Smith Blackburn Prize in 1997.

EVELYN CONLON was born in County Monaghan. She has published two collections of short stories – *My Head is Opening* (Attic) and *Taking Scarlet as a Real Colour* (Blackstaff) – and a novel, *Stars in the Daytime* (Attic/Women's Press. Her second novel, *A Glassful of Letters*, will be published in 1998.

JENNIFER C CORNELL was born in the United States and spent much of the 1980s in Northern Ireland, working with the Cornerstone cross-community project in Belfast and completing an MA in Peace and Conflict Studies at the University of Ulster in Derry. She is currently an assistant professor in the English Department at Oregon State University. Her short stories have been published in literary magazines such as the *New England Review*, *Tri-Quarterly*, and the *Chicago Review*, and have been included in the *Best American Short Stories 1995* and the *1996 Pushcart Prize* anthologies, and in *The Faber Book of Contemporary Stories about Childhood*, edited by Lorrie Moore. In 1994 she won the Drue Heinz Prize for Literature for her first collection of stories, *Departures*, which was published in Ireland and Britain under the title *All there is* in 1995. She is currently completing a non-fiction book on the representation of Northern Ireland in British television drama.

PHILIP DAVISON is author of four novels: *The Book-Thief's Heartbeat* (Co-op Books), *Twist And Shout* (Brandon), *The Illustrator* (Wolfhound), and *The Crooked Man*, which was published by Jonathan Cape in January 1997. He has co-written two television dramas – *Exposure* and *Criminal Conversation*. His first play, *The Invisible Mending Company*, was performed on the Abbey Theatre's Peacock stage in February 1996. Short stories have appeared in *Cyphers*, *Cimarron Review* and Bloomsbury's *Soho Square*. He lectures at Dun Laoghaire College of Art and Design.

URSULA DE BRÚN was born in Dublin in 1952 and was edu-
cated in Dublin and New York. Her work has been included in
Francis McManus Radio Stories (Mercier) and *Phoenix Irish
Short Stories 1996*. She recently completed a three-act play for
stage, and previous plays have been produced at Andrews Lane
Theatre and Andrews Lane Studio and also on RTE (Radio).
She won the P. J. O'Connor award in 1994. As a student of the
BA Modular Degree at UCD she read philosophy for three
years and began reading Greek and Roman Civilization in
September 1997.

RODDY DOYLE was born in Dublin in 1958 and was for
several years a teacher. His books published to date and currently available are *The Commitments* (1987), *The Snapper*
(1990), *The Van* (1991), *Paddy Clarke Ha Ha Ha* (1993), and
The Woman who Walked into Doors (1996). His plays include
Brown Bread and *War*.

CIARÁN FOLAN was born in Newtown, Cashel, Co. Long-
ford and later moved to An Spidéal, Co. Galway. He now lives
in Dublin where he teaches. His stories have been widely published in Ireland and England, and have appeared in several
anthologies. He won the RTE Francis McManus Short Story
Award in 1987. His first collection, *Freak Nights*, was published by New Island Books in 1996.

DESMOND HOGAN was born in Galway in 1951 and helped
found the Irish Writers Co-op. His novels include *The Ikon
Maker*, *The Leaves on Grey* and *A Curious Street*, and he is the
author of several collections of short stories. He has travelled
extensively and is based in London, where – after a long silence
– he recently published *The Edge of the City*, a collection of
travel writing.

BRIAN LEYDEN lives in Dromahair, Co. Leitrim. He is the author of the short story collection *Departures* (Brandon, 1992). His work was the subject of the Jacobs Award winning radio documentary *No Meadows in Manhattan*. He is a regular contributor to radio, including *Sunday Miscellany* and a past winner of the Francis McManus Short Story Award. He has been a guest performer at the Rural Development School, the Merriman Summer School, the Green Ink Festival in London and the Ireland and its Diaspora Writers and Musicians Tour of Germany (1996). He was the Irish author chosen for *The Alphabet Garden*, an anthology of European short stories. He has edited issue seven and issue eight of the acclaimed literary journal *Force 10*. He received an Arts Council Bursary in Literature in 1994. *Death and Plenty*, a novel, was published in 1996 by Brandon.

AIDAN MATHEWS was born in Dublin in 1956. His work includes two books of poetry, *Windfalls* and *Minding Ruth*, and several plays, among them *The Diamond Body*, *The Antigone*, *Exit-Entrance*, and a translation of Lorca's *The House of Bernarda Alba*, as well as two collections of stories, *Adventures in a Bathyscope* and *Lipstick on the Host*, and a novel, *Muesli at Midnight*. He has won many prizes, most recently Italy's Cavour Prize for Foreign Fiction (1995) and the Literature Award of the Irish Arts Council (1996).

PATRICK McCABE was born in Clones, Co. Monaghan in 1955. He worked as a national teacher in several Irish towns before moving to London. He is the author of three novels, *Music on Clinton Street*, *Carn* and *Butcher Boy*, which was short-listed for The Booker Prize. His stage adaption of *Butcher Boy*, *Frank Pig Says Hello*, was a major success in the 1992 Dublin Theatre Festival and has since toured extensively. Neil Jordan's film of *Butcher Boy* was released in 1998.

PHILIP MacCANN was born in England in 1966, but came to Ireland at an early age. A graduate of Trinity College Dublin, his short story collection, *The Miracle Shed*, (Faber and Faber) was highly praised on publication in 1994.

MOLLY McCLOSKEY was born in 1964 in Philadelphia. She was raised in Portland, Oregon. Since 1989 she has been living in County Sligo. She has won several short story awards, including the RTE/Francis McManus Award and the Fish Publishing Award (Cork). Her first collection, *Solomon's Seal* was published in April 1997 by Phoenix House.

MIKE McCORMACK was born in 1965 and now lives in the west of Ireland. In 1995 he was awarded the Rooney Prize, and in 1996 his first collection of short stories, *Getting it in the Head* was published by Jonathan Cape.

VINCENT McDONNELL was born in Mayo in 1951. For many years he lived in London where he worked as a service engineer. His first radio story was broadcast on LBC in 1984 and he won the *Ireland's Own* Short Story competition in 1987. Since then his short stories have won several other prizes and have been published in a wide selection of magazines. They have also been anthologised in: *New Writings from the West*, edited by Val Mulkerns; *The Mayo Anthology*, edited by Richard Murphy; *The Applegarth Review*, edited by Gabriel Fitzmaurice; *A Page Falls Open*, various editors; *Writings One*, edited by Dennis Collins. His first novel, *The Broken Commandment*, was published in 1988 and won the Guinness Peat Aviation First Fiction Award in 1989. His second novel, *Imagination Of The Heart*, was published by Brandon in 1995. He has also written for children and Poolbeg have published three of his books: *The Boy Who Saved Christmas*, 1992; *The Knock Airport Mystery*, 1993; *Children of Stone*, 1994. His latest children's book, *Can Timmy Save Toyland*, was published by Relay Books in 1996. Vincent McDonnell now lives near Newmarket, Co. Cork with his wife, Joan, and their son.

BERNARD MacLAVERTY was born in Belfast in 1942 and has lived for many years in Scotland. He has successfully adapted his own novels, *Lamb* and *Cal* for the screen and published several volumes of stories, including *A Time to Dance*, *The Great Profundo* and *Walking the Dog*. His latest novel, *Grace Notes*, was published in July 1997 by Jonathan Cape and was shortlisted for the Booker Prize.

MARY O'DONNELL, who was born in Monaghan, is a poet, fiction-writer, critic and translator. Her publications include the acclaimed novel *The Light-Makers* (Poolbeg), nominated by the *Sunday Tribune* critics as the best new Irish novel of 1992. Her fiction also includes the more recent *Virgin and the Boy* (Poolbeg, 1996), a vivid behind-the-scenes story of the Irish rock scene, and *Strong Pagans* (1991), a collection of stories. Her stories are also available in anthologies, including *The Irish Eros* (Gill & Macmillan), *Award-Winning Short Stories* (Marino) and *Home* (Gill & Macmillan). Her poetry collections include *Spiderwoman's Third Avenue Rhapsody* (Salmon, 1993) and *Reading the Sunflowers in September* (Salmon, 1990). A third collection, *Unlegendary Heroes*, is due shortly. A former drama critic, she has a special interest in arts criticism and combines writing with the teaching of creative writing, as well as some general lecturing. She is an associate editor of the arts broadsheet *WP Bi-Monthly*.

GLENN PATTERSON was born in Belfast in 1961. He is the author of three novels: *Black Night At Big Thunder Mountain*, *Fat Lad* and *Burning Your Own*, which won the Rooney Prize and a Betty Trask Award. His latest novel, *The International*, will be published this year. He has been writer-in-residence at University College, Cork (1993-4) and recently completed

three years as a writer-in-residence at Queen's University
Belfast. He was also Creative Writing Fellow for a term at the
University of East Anglia.

TOM PHELAN was born on a farm in Mountmellick, County
Laois in the Irish midlands. He attended St Patrick's Seminary,
Carlow, was ordained and worked in England for several
years. In 1970 he emigrated to the United States, where he
earned a master's degree from the University of Seattle and
eventually left the priesthood. He now lives in Freeport, New
York, with his wife and two sons. He has published two highly praised novels, *In the Season of the Daisies* (Lilliput 1993)
and *Iscariot* (Brandon 1995).

PATRICK QUIGLEY grew up in Monaghan where he worked
on a farm, in a mental hospital, and a chicken factory until he
moved to Dublin in 1972. He was politically active in the
1970s ('A Marxist without really knowing what that implied'),
involved in trade unions, community organisations, etc. He
now works for Dublin County Council and also runs a literary
group in his area. His short stories and poems have been published in *The Irish Times*, *Raven Introductions*, *Stet* and
Ireland's Own. His first novel, *Borderland*, – 'A debut of
remarkable assurance, polish and control' (*The Times*) – was
published in 1994 and won an award on publication in
German.

LUCILLE REDMOND is a writer and critic whose articles
appear in *The Irish Times*, *Business & Finance*, *Sunday
Tribune*, *Interactive Tribune*, *Web Ireland* and *Technology
Ireland*. Her short stories have appeared, among other places,
in *The Irish Times*, the *Irish Press* (she won a Hennessy Award
for her first story, 'The Shaking Trees', and was awarded an
Allied Irish Banks New Irish Writers Award for her first collection), and the collections *Krino 1986-1996*, *Modern Irish
Stories*, *Paddy No More* and *Silent Heroines*.

Acknowledgements

Sara Berkeley's "To Prevent Rust, Weeping and Bleeding" copyright © Sara Berkeley 1997.

Dermot Bolger's "Prologue" to *Father's Music* (Picador 1997) is reprinted by permission of the author and Harper-Collins; copyright © Dermot Bolger 1997.

Marina Carr's "Grow a Mermaid" first appeared in the *Sunday Tribune* and *The Hennessy Book of Irish Fiction* (New Island Books 1995); copyright © Marina Carr 1994.

Jennifer C Cornell's "Wax" copyright © Jennifer C Cornell 1997.

Philip Davison's "Bag of Jewellery" copyright © Philip Davison 1997.

Ursula De Brún's "Signs" copyright © Ursula De Brún 1997.

Roddy Doyle's "The Lip" first appeared in *The Big Issue* and is reprinted by permission of the author; copyright © Roddy Doyle 1994.

Ciarán Folan's "Start of a Great Adventure", from *Freak Nights* (New Island Books 1996) is reprinted by permission of the author; copyright © Ciarán Folan 1996.

Desmond Hogan's "Afternoon", from *A Link with the River* (Farrar Straus 1989), is reproduced by permission of the author, c/o Rogers, Coleridge & White Ltd; copyright © Desmond Hogan 1980.

Brian Leyden's "The Family Plot" copyright © Brian Leyden 1997.

Patrick McCabe's "The Hands of Dingo Deery" first appeared in *Here's Me Bus!*, and is reprinted by permission of the author; copyright © Patrick McCabe 1995.

Philip MacCann's "A Drive" copyright © Philip MacCann 1997.

Molly McCloskey's "Losing Claire", from *Solomon's Seal*

(Phoenix House 1997) is reprinted by permission of the author; copyright © Molly McCloskey 1997.

Mike McCormack's "The Terms", from *Getting it in the Head* (Jonathan Cape 1996) is reprinted by permission of the author; copyright © Mike McCormack 1996.

Vincent McDonnell's "The Milking Bucket" copyright © Vincent McDonnell 1997.

Bernard MacLaverty's "A Legacy and Some Gunks" is reproduced by permission of the author c/o Rogers, Coleridge & White Ltd; copyright © Bernard MacLaverty 1995.

Aidan Mathews' "Charlie Chaplin's Wishbone" is reproduced by commission of the author, care of A. P. Watt Ltd; copyright © Aidan Mathews 1997

Mary O'Donnell's "Twentynine Palms" copyright © Mary O'Donnell 1997.

Glenn Patterson's "Roaches" copyright © Glenn Patterson 1997.

Tom Phelan's "In the Vatican Museum" copyright © Glanvill Enterprises Ltd 1997.

Patrick Quigley's "The Girl in the Yellow Dress" copyright © Patrick Quigley 1997.

Lucille Redmond's "Our Fenian Dead" copyright © Lucille Redmond 1997.

Some other fiction from Brandon

The Alphabet Garden
European Short Stories
A unique collection of short stories from twelve European countries, including fiction by Michèle Roberts, Brian Leyden, Javier Marías, Nuno Júdice, Ib Michael, Annie Saumont, Paola Capriolo, Atte Jongstra, Ana Valdés and Henning Boëtius.
ISBN 0 86322 189 0; 224pp; paperback £7.95

Jennifer Cornell
All there is
Winner of the Drue Heinz Literature Prize
"Ms Cornell writes with a burnished melancholy and a soft wit, rolling out an undulating series of elegant images [in stories which are] lucid, inventive and teeming with overlapping memories, like creamier versions of William Trevor's wry fables." *New York Times*
ISBN 0 86322 209 9; 160pp; paperback; £6.95

Brian Leyden
Departures
"Brian Leyden speaks very directly to a culture in transition from pre-modern to post-modern. With tremendous economy he is able to articulate a whole culture. He has a real grasp of the form of the short story and he is stylistically superb."
Prof. Thomas Doherty, *Booklines*
ISBN 0 86322 154 8; 190pp; paperback £6.99

Brian Leyden
Death & Plenty
"Brian Leyden is a skillful craftsman and, most importantly, he knows what he is writing about... The writer has an acute sense of how the old insular rural Ireland has changed... A very solid first novel. A little gem." *Sunday Tribune*
ISBN 0 86322 218 8; 256pp; paperback £5.99

Patrick Quigley
Borderland
"A debut of remarkable assurance, polish and control." *The Times*
"A memorable tour-de-force... a stunning and quite beautifully imagined novel." Joe O'Connor
ISBN 0 86322 179 3; 254pp; paperback £6.95

Vincent McDonnell
Imagination of the Heart
"*Imagination of the Heart* holds up a mirror to the bleak side of Irish life. The result is a riveting and disturbing read and so starkly drawn are the characters that they will stay with you long after his book is put down." Alice Taylor, *Sunday Tribune*
ISBN 0 86322 215 3; 256 pp; paperback £7.95

Tom Phelan
Iscariot
"Tom Phelan's second novel leaves us in no doubt about his talents as a keen, indeed harsh, observer of humanity... By weaving a litany of characters rendered in a composite of opposites he mirrors the balancing of argument that is his peculiar horn of a dilemma. One on which sex predominantly features. But ultimately one on which Tom Phelan's world view is tempered with a warm, forgiving, humanity with the exception, that is, of the Catholic Church." *Sunday Tribune*
ISBN 0 86322 212 9; 288 pp; hardback £14.99

Chet Raymo
In the Falcon's Claw
A novel of the year 1000
"Raymo's gift is to bring to life that distant time, vividly but without straining the reader's credulity... There are many strands in this fine novel – love, religion, the stars and the nature of time, church politics, Latin and Irish verse – and they are skilfully put together in a vigorous language that invokes a fresh, unexplored Europe of 1,000 years ago." *Sunday Tribune*
ISBN 0 86322 204 8; 224pp; paperback £6.95

Gerry Adams
The Street and other stories
"About all the stories there is a certain elegiac quality: a sense that something important is slipping away, being lost... The warmth of Adams's writing comes from the affection of a man for the remembered things of his past... *The Street* demonstrates that Adams can write well." *Times Literary Supplement*
ISBN 0 86322 147 5; 160pp; demy 8vo; paperback £6.99

John B. Keane
The Bodhrán Makers
"This powerful and poignant novel provides John B. Keane with a passport to the highest levels of Irish literature." Irish Press
"A thorough, pained loving account of a lost world – with the novel itself an act of cultural survival." *Kirkus Review*
ISBN 0 86322 085 1; 353pp; paperback £5.95

Books by Walter Macken

City of the Tribes
These "dreams on paper", as he described them, have as their principal focus the city and people of Galway.
ISBN 0 86322 228 5; 256 pages; hardback £12.99

Brown Lord of the Mountain
"Macken knows his people and his places and his love of them shines through." *Examiner*
ISBN 0 86322 201 3; 284pp; paperback £5.95

God Made Sunday
"Macken's scene is a western Eden, moments after the Fall."
The Scotsman
ISBN 0 86322 217 X; 222 pp; paperback £5.95

Green Hills
"More valuable than sociological studies, [these stories] show the skill of the dramatist." *Books Ireland*
ISBN 0 86322 216 1; 220 pp; paperback £5.95

Quench the Moon
"Where the writer knows and loves his country as Walter Macken does, there is warmth and life." *Times Literary Supplement*
ISBN 0 86322 202 1; 413pp; paperback £5.95

Rain on the Wind
"It is the story of romantic passion, a constant struggle with the sea, [and] with poverty." *Irish Independent*
ISBN 0 86322 185 8; 320pp; paperback £5.95